The jungle was unnaturally silent

The whir of the ever-present insects was missing, as was the sound of the birds. Mark felt his fear grow and he tried to label it irrational. Celeste was safe. She was having a cool drink, waiting for him to come and find her.

The image dissolved and he was left with the harsh reality that Celeste was in danger. He knew it. It was a certainty in his mind that made his body rush forward at a reckless speed.

A dozen yards ahead, the glint of moonlight against something metallic caught his eye. He slowed his pace, curious and yet also apprehensive. As he came upon the shiny object at the side of the road, he saw what he'd dreaded. Celeste's necklace lay in the sand of the road. Beside it was the perfect print of an enormous jaguar.

ABOUT THE AUTHOR

On a trip to Mexico several years ago, Caroline Burnes was captivated by the Maya ruins at Chichén Itzá. She enjoys traveling and finds Central America and Mexico of particular interest. She's hoping her next vacation will be in Ireland, a country she has long wanted to visit. Currently, she lives in Mobile, Alabama.

Books by Caroline Burnes

HARLEQUIN INTRIGUE

86–A DEADLY BREED
100–MEASURE OF DECEIT
115–PHANTOM FILLY
134–FEAR FAMILIAR

Don't miss any of our special offers. Write to us at the following address for information on our newest releases.

Harlequin Reader Service
901 Fuhrmann Blvd., P.O. Box 1397, Buffalo, NY 14240
Canadian address: P.O. Box 603,
Fort Erie, Ont. L2A 5X3

The Jaguar's Eye

Caroline Burnes

Harlequin Books

TORONTO • NEW YORK • LONDON
AMSTERDAM • PARIS • SYDNEY • HAMBURG
STOCKHOLM • ATHENS • TOKYO • MILAN

To David and Gail Haines, with much love

Harlequin Intrigue edition published January 1991

ISBN 0-373-22154-1

THE JAGUAR'S EYE

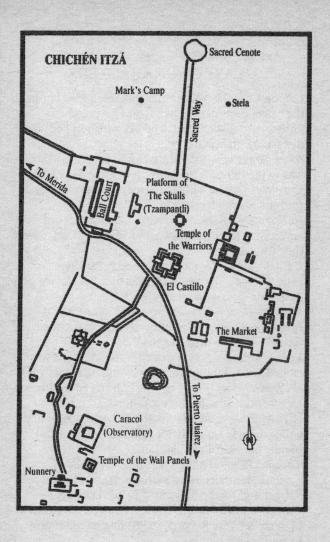

CHICHÉN ITZÁ

Sacred Cenote

Mark's Camp

Stela

To Merida

Sacred Way

Ball Court

Platform of
The Skulls
(Tzampantli)

Temple of
the Warriors

El Castillo

The Market

To Puerto Juárez

Caracol
(Observatory)

Temple of the Wall Panels

Nunnery

CAST OF CHARACTERS

Celeste Coolridge—An SEC scandal landed her in the Maya ruins of Chichén Itzá. Her presence awakened a distant past, and her vacation became a disturbing nightmare.

Mark Grayson—A dedicated archaeologist, Mark was in pursuit of a legendary jewel, the Jaguar's Eye. Was Celeste's life the price he'd have to pay to find the Mayan treasure?

Roberto De Solarno—Educated, charming and ambitious, Roberto knew all of Mark's secrets. Were they for sale?

Daniel Ortiz—He put up the money for the expedition at Chichén Itzá. Was he a benefactor or a desperate man with no scruples?

Carlotta Bopp—Maya history was her past and future. A woman of great power, she befriended Celeste. But for what purpose?

Barry Undine—A man driven by jealousy, he was capable of anything. How far would he actually go?

Wilfredo Nome—Paid by Mark, he owed his life to Celeste. But who held his loyalties?

Alec Mason—Celeste's uncle had been mentor and colleague. He was only too willing to step in and handle her SEC investigation.

Thomas Ibba—Thomas was the best guide in Cancún. His friendship with Celeste put him in danger and forced him into a painful choice.

Charles and Rebecca Tretorn—The Tretorns lived a high style. Were Rebecca's spending habits simply excessive—or criminal?

Prologue

From the prophecy of the Priest Abbam Xupan

In the katuns to come, the rule of the Maya will be swept off the edge of the earth. White men with golden beards will storm the land of the Yucca on the backs of flying beasts with snorting nostrils. Thunder will be heard in the south and deadly epidemics will come to our land. Destruction will come from all directions. A time of evil will destroy our people.

Legend of the Jaguar's Eye

These things will come to pass. The tiger and the eagle will be cut down by the powerful white man. The sun will strike the metal hair and never penetrate the metal face of the white man. Only the dying will know his savage voice and bloody fingernails. He will not come alone, but with many forms of pestilence.

Many of these events come not from the white man, but from the Maya. The clouds that contain all living things watch our people and see our mistakes. The forest has suffered. The hot wind blows over us and we see our crops begin to wither and die. We have opened the door to our destruction. Our time is passing, even as I write.

The count of days will continue for many katuns. Beneath the fiery face of the sun, the Maya sleep among the stones, waiting. We are like the corn, hungering for the blessing of the water to sprout forth. At this time the air will burn. Across the land the earth will tear. Our people will scatter from water to water, blown by the winds. Stripped of our power and heritage, we will fade away.

Only a few will remain to tend the graves of the mighty Maya. Those who believe in the power and the word of Quetzalcoatl will wait for the new age, the new dawn. They will dance at the altar of the god and sing praises.

Armies of ants will traverse the sacred altar. The orange blossom of rebirth will appear at the base of the wall of the skulls. A jaguar, cunning and angry, will stalk the sacred grounds of Chichén Itzá to remind all that the ways of the gods cannot be ignored any longer. He will speak with a human voice. Sacrifices must be made. Small children will speak the name of Quetzalcoatl and it will be a warning to the white man.

Quetzalcoatl's messenger, the serpent, will arrive and multiply in great numbers. The small serpent will begin to bite. The face of the sun will never falter, and the fields will begin to burn.

At this time, Quetzalcoatl will return to save his chosen people. On the altar of El Castillo he will show himself. But before that day, the sun will send his mate.

You will know her by her flaming hair, a gift of the sun. Her arrival will please the gods. This is the time when the white man and the Maya will blend their bloods to create a new people. She is the chosen mate of Quetzalcoatl, and she must be prepared for him.

Because she is of the white man, she will resist. Follow the ways of our people. Prepare her with much gentleness, remembering the deer who hides in the forest. Favor her with blue, the color of sacrifice.

On the day of Lamat, when the sun quarters the horizon, remove her to the silent home of those who rest to meet the God Quetzalcoatl. In the blue smoke of the pipe, leave her. In the whir of the small creatures the approach of the god will be heard. Be joyful and celebrate.

Chapter One

March 1. It is the day of Muluc on the Maya calendar. Deep within the earth there is thunder and moans. The legend is awakened. The count has begun.

"Am I being fired?" Celeste Coolridge walked to the street-side window of her private office in the prestigious brokerage firm of Stuart McCarty and scanned the Tampa street so far below. The blood rushed through her veins, almost drowning out the sound of Victor Rosen's well-modulated voice.

"Until we have some answers, the firm's position is that it would be better for you to leave. Consider it a vacation." The office, like most others, was half glass with a view into the central bull pen. Rosen glanced into the main office out of the corner of his eye. Everyone's attention was focused on him, knowing that he was confronting his top salesperson for the year. It was clear that he still found it hard to believe that by-the-book Celeste Coolridge was accused of insider trading, but he had to stand tough. Everyone knew that was the image Stuart McCarty expected him to convey.

Celeste turned to face her boss. She'd never liked him, but business relationships didn't require liking. Until this moment, though, she'd never thought him a spineless fool.

"Is this a paid vacation?" she asked, her jaw clenched.

"Be reasonable, Celeste. I can't pay you while you're being investigated. The home office would be on me so fast..."

"Do you think I'm guilty, Vic? You know that if you suspend me it's as good as saying you think I did it." She stepped right up to his face, close enough so she could watch the way his eyes looked at her and then his gaze slid away. That was all she needed to see.

"It isn't my place to decide your innocence or guilt. As I said, the SEC is investigating." He held up both hands in a placating gesture. "You're not the only one under suspicion, you know."

"I'm the only one at Stuart McCarty, am I not?" she fired back. She didn't wait for him to answer. "I expected you to stand up for me, Vic. I always thought you'd do at least that much."

Feeling some thirty pairs of eyes riveting into his back through the glassed wall, Victor Rosen squared his shoulders. "You might as well clear out your desk. I'm not certain how long the investigation will take, and Stuart McCarty considers you suspended until your name is cleared."

He turned on his heel and walked out, leaving the office door open.

Celeste went straight to her phone and buzzed her assistant. "Marcy, bring in a box, please."

"Yes, Ms. Coolridge."

Celeste could tell by the young woman's tone that she knew what had happened. She looked out at the bull pen. As she met each pair of eyes, their owners turned away. Not a single person came to offer her a word of encouragement. She was a virtual leper in the financial community. She still had her license—for the moment. Big deal. Until her name was cleared, she was finished as a broker.

Marcy brought in the box, biting her lip the whole time to staunch her tears. Celeste dismissed her with a wave. She pulled open each drawer, dumping the contents into the box. Taking several files of personal papers from the cabinet, she folded the lid of the box together and picked it up. She'd send someone for the rest.

She didn't want to, but she couldn't stop herself from turning at the doorway and surveying her office one last time. For the past three years she'd been a rising star at Stuart McCarty. She'd spiraled from the ranks of the bull pen to a private office. She was following in her Uncle Alec Mason's considerable footsteps, and doing a damn good job of it. Until this ridiculous accusation.

She swiveled abruptly and faced the bull-pen area. In a quick sequences of faces she read sorrow, fear, worry, anxiety and—glee. She stopped at Barry Undine and smiled.

"It isn't over, yet," she said loud enough for everyone, but especially Barry, to hear. "I'm innocent and I'll prove it."

"Maybe your uncle can help you out of this, too," Barry said, hooking a thumb under a pair of red suspenders. "But then, I thought he'd be here by now. Isn't he usually around to give his little princess everything she wants?" He looked significantly at the closed door of Alec Mason's private suite. As one of the most revered brokers in the firm for the past twenty years, Alec Mason was accorded luxury office space with solid oak walls and impenetrable privacy. He was in the upper echelon of a very stratified business.

Celeste sorely missed her uncle's presence, but she knew this was a moment she had to face alone. Uncle Alec was her mentor and her friend, but he wasn't her guardian angel. He'd warned her about this the night before, when he'd first caught wind of the rumors floating through Stuart McCarty. He'd known Vic was going to suspend her, but he couldn't intercede.

She shifted the weight of the box and walked out, back as erect as a West Point graduate.

A SHUDDER OF doubt rippled gently down Celeste's back as she parked at the restaurant. Bern's was busy, as usual, and there was no sign of Alec's sleek black Mercedes. He was never late. It was one of his characteristics. Punctual to a fault, her aunt Eloise had often said with grim humor. The memory of her dead aunt only deepened her feelings of depression. This wasn't a time to remind herself that with the exception of her uncle, she was on her own. Instead, she had to remember that she'd worked hard, that she was innocent, and that justice would prove that. She might have been suspended, but she wasn't convicted.

It had been two days since a *Wall Street Journal* reporter had linked her name with a trading scam and she'd been forced out of her job. So far, the only evidence that had turned up in the case seemed to implicate her more. She couldn't work and she couldn't relax. She felt as if she'd been tied in a knot and left to twist in the sun. The only hope she had was Uncle Alec. She clung to the memory of his voice, so calm and reasonable and self-assured.

"An accusation isn't a conviction. Don't panic, we'll clear your name. Just get out of town and let me handle it. Really, my dear, the best thing you can do is vacate."

And that was what she was doing at Bern's—meeting her uncle to discuss vacation plans. He had some wild scheme for a treasure-hunt vacation that he'd rigged up to take her mind off her troubles, as if that were possible.

She parked the car eyeing the silky black Tampa sky, which glistened with stars. A strong northerly wind and thunder had warned earlier of a storm, but that threat had blown over. It was safe to leave the top down on the '57 T-Bird. The real question on her mind was whether or not to leave town, as her uncle insisted. She knew he was trying to spare her any further humiliation by getting her away, but the idea of tucking tail and running didn't appeal to her. She was innocent and she had no reason to leave. Convincing Uncle Alec of that fact was going to be a hard sell. He was a tough man once he made up his mind to something.

She entered the dark interior of the posh restaurant and gave her name. She followed the maître d' down a long, brick-lined hallway and up a flight of stairs to a series of private rooms. Small, almost circular, each room included closed-circuit television sets, stereo systems and lots of privacy.

"Will someone be joining me? If Alec Mason is here, I'd really like to speak with him."

"He isn't here. Your waiter has received instructions, I believe." He bowed and left.

Celeste looked around. The room was the perfect place for a secret meeting, a little intrigue, just as her uncle had promised when he'd gone on and on about the trip he'd planned for her. She couldn't actually remember a single detail. She should have listened more attentively, but her mind was absorbed with horrid newspaper stories and ugly rumors.

The flash of the closed-circuit televison signaled the set had been turned on. She expected to see some local entertainer, instead she saw two hands holding up a newspaper. She recognized the *Tampa Herald* and leaned forward. "Broker sells more than bonds." The headline was black and ugly. The picture beneath it was hers. She was at a private dining table with Branden Olsen, one of her oldest clients. He was patting her hand on the table.

She remembered the occasion. Olsen had taken her to lunch. She'd told him about a certificate series he liked. He'd patted her hand in appreciation, a gesture of elderly approval from a sixty-eight-year-old man. Looking at it splashed across the page with such a lurid headline, though, Celeste felt dirty.

"This is the way it is going to play out," Uncle Alec's voice said softly. "It's ugly and brutal and damaging. The best thing you can do is get out of town. Remove yourself from the scene. If you're gone, the story will die down. Once the titillating factors are quelled, I'll have a chance to get to the bottom of these things." The camera pulled back to reveal Uncle Alex's worried face. He offered a smile. "You have to go, Celeste. For me as well as you."

She felt a shock at the idea that her trouble might affect his business standing. If that was true, then she would have to get out of town for a few days. Besides, she wasn't doing anything except hiding out from reporters, anyway. Maybe Uncle Alec's vacation idea was the best plan. The screen went blank.

She sighed. Uncle Alec was right—she had to get out of town just so things would cool off. The videotape at Bern's had been an effective approach, she had to give him that. She'd never felt so exposed in a public place.

"Excuse me, miss." A waiter placed a magnificent slice of strawberry cheesecake and a steaming cup of coffee down in front of her. So, Uncle Alec had delivered the hard facts, and now he was trying to cheer her up with her favorite dessert. She didn't have the heart to eat a bite.

She was on her second cup of coffee, waiting for her uncle to put in an appearance, when the waiter slipped a small box onto the table.

"For you," he said, moving rapidly away.

It was a flat box and she opened it. Inside was a new leather folder for carrying traveler's checks and a gift certificate for a very generous amount. A note was enclosed that read; "Locate your passport, you'll need it." She picked it up in awe. Europe? Africa? Where was he sending her? In the bottom of the box was another folded note. She opened it and began to read. "The Tampa night is clear. Aren't you glad?" It took her a moment to gather the meaning and connect the cryptic note with her convertible. Uncle Alec had left something in her car. She took a last sip of coffee and then she hurried out of the restaurant.

As soon as she got in her car, she began to search. Her fingers found a large manila envelope on the seat beside her, and she resisted the urge to tear into it before she got home. The night was warm and the open top of the car might scatter the contents all over the town.

Drinking in the crisp Gulf tang, she crossed the bridge that divided her home on Davis Island from the main body of Tampa and then whipped the T-Bird down the palm-fringed road. The early March air was delicious, filled with the promise of cool nights and wonderful afternoons. She'd have many days without having to go to the office. She silently gritted her teeth and pushed that thought away.

With her jaw still clenched, she pulled into the garage of her home. She picked up the manila envelope and unlocked her door. When she was inside, she snapped on the light and flipped the envelope over and ripped it open. Color pictures of beaches from around the world cascaded about her feet. There was a handwritten note:

Take plenty of sunscreen for your pretty, fair skin.

"Where is he sending me?" she whispered aloud into the empty kitchen. It was twelve-thirty, but she had no desire for sleep. After all, there was no deadline to get to work in the morning. She was without responsibilities for the first time since she'd started college and had afterwards gone straight into the stockbrokerage business ten years ago. She could indulge her curiosity a little.

She started a fresh pot of coffee and rifled through the papers. There was no ticket, but there was a note from Delta Airlines. She was scheduled on a flight out of Tampa International in one day. There were no other details, just the flight number and time. She had plenty of time to pack. She shook her head. Uncle Alec was impossible. He'd decided to make the whole trip a game, a real vacation. She could probably call the airlines and fuss enough to find out more details, but she didn't want to do that. She'd play along with her uncle. It gave him pleasure to plan for her. The least she could do was cooperate.

When the coffee was made she took a cup into the small study. The library was well stocked with expensive editions of the classics she loved. She rummaged through her books until she unearthed the world atlas. Beaches were what she was looking for. Her long, sculpted nail traced imaginary lines to every possible beach. There were plenty in the Caribbean, as well as Mexico and along the Pacific Coast. Australia was a possibility. There were Gulf Coast beaches, too, along Mississippi and Alabama. That might be a place

for a few days of rest. The red tip of her nail moved across
the page as she sipped the coffee and tried to second-guess
her uncle. At last she closed the atlas and settled her empty
cup on the desk. She took a small notecard and scribbled a
hasty message, hoping Uncle Alec would never know she'd
been unable to eat a bite.

> Cheesecake was more delicious than I remembered.
> Bern's was a real trip. Thanks. I'm on my way to ad-
> venture.
>
>   Love, Celeste

She'd post the card at the airport when she left town. That
way Uncle Alec would be able to keep up with her progress.
She rose with a sigh, realizing that her uncle's plan was already working, just a little. After her severe depression
about her career, she was actually looking forward to
something.

She turned off the lights and walked down the thickly
carpeted hall to the large, cool bedroom she'd so carefully
decorated.

THE PLANE TOUCHED down and Celeste pressed back
against the seat to absorb the shock. In a matter of moments they were disembarking in Cancún, Mexico. The
laughter of several groups of tourists mingled together to
create a happy and expectant sound.

The flight had been perfect. It had been hard work, but
Celeste had spent the entire trip convincing herself that she
was eager to vacation, to swim in the crystal blue waters.
She'd always wanted to learn to dive. Now was her chance.
There was wind-surfing, dancing, waterskiing, shopping—
all of the pleasures she'd denied herself for years. Her ticket
was open-ended. She could stay as long, or as short a time,
as she wished. She had only to relax, to allow herself a few
days to rest after the trauma of Tampa.

The check at customs was perfunctory, and Celeste was
quickly waved through. The airport was open and filled with

a bustling noise that made clear thinking next to impossible. She was suddenly aware that she had no idea where to go or what to do. She found her luggage and moved it to a corner so that she could better examine the packet that contained her ticket. There was no hotel name. Nothing.

She felt someone's eyes staring at her and she casually shifted her position. The man who watched her was leaning against a support. Tall, bronzed, with dark blue eyes, he assessed her in a manner that was neither friendly nor unfriendly. He looked at her almost as if she were another species. She met his stare until he turned away.

"Señorita Coolridge?" The small Mexican voice drifted up to her from behind a large stone pillar.

Celeste whirled around, but there was no one.

"I've been waiting for you, *señorita*." The voice came again. This time she saw a crop of dark hair barely taller than the stack of luggage that stood beside her.

"Yes, I'm Celeste Coolridge."

"*Sí*. You are as beautiful as I was told you would be. A goddess with hair from the sun." A young boy stepped around the baggage and stuck out his hand. "I am Thomas, your guide for the entire time you will visit our city."

"Thomas," she repeated, taken with the child's grown-up manner and bright, dancing eyes.

"I am a first-rate guide and my English is impeccable. I know this city from top to bottom. The best bargains, the best restaurants, the best connections. I even know the best musicians." He grinned at her, displaying white, perfect teeth. "We will get along fabulously, Miss Celeste. You will be glad that Thomas is the guide for your vacation."

"I see," she said. "And where are we going, Thomas?" She cast a glance over her shoulder. The man was staring at her again.

"I have your room waiting at the hotel. Once you are refreshed, I will escort you to dinner," Thomas continued.

"You've made all the arrangements?" Celeste asked, amusement rippling through her throaty voice. The boy was hardly twelve, but he conducted himself with all the confidence of an adult. She couldn't help but wonder where Uncle Alec had found him. With Thomas leading the way, she could instantly see that her stay in Cancún would be unusual, and very busy.

With complete authority, Thomas picked up her bags and strode from the airport to the busy street that ran beside it. With a gesture of authority, he hailed a taxi and threw open the door for her.

"We will go to the hotel, and you can refresh yourself. Then we'll go to dinner. Whatever you wish, you must ask me and I will get it for you. *Sí?*"

"*Sí,* Thomas," Celeste replied as she slipped into the taxi. Their conversation in the airport had been punctuated by a strange, cadenced whistling that she'd at first taken to be the sounds of the porters as they moved the luggage around. Once outside she discovered that the area was covered with large black birds, a type of crow that made the noise. They clucked and whistled to each other, oblivious of the humans that hurried among them.

The trees were incredibly green, a lushness that hid the rocky, barren ground beneath their branches. The vivid blue sky was the backdrop for a perfect afternoon.

"Tomorrow we should explore the shops and perhaps take a boat out to an island for some diving. Do you dive?" Thomas was seated beside her, his brown eyes watching with a vivid curiosity.

"I haven't ever tried," she said slowly.

"Good. I am an excellent teacher. In a matter of a few hours, you will be as good as Señor Bond. I watch all of his movies. He is wonderful," Thomas said.

"James Bond?" Celeste asked in astonishment.

"Yes, you know him?" Thomas asked, his face lighting up with expectancy.

"Not personally," Celeste replied quickly. "But I know who you're talking about."

"One day, when I am grown, I'm going to be a spy like Mr. Bond. Fast cars, danger, adventure. That's the life for me." Thomas leaned back in the seat and looked out the window. "Until then, I am your guide."

He broke into a tirade of Spanish with the driver and the cab picked up speed.

"What did you tell him?" Celeste asked. She hadn't been able to follow a word of the rapid-fire conversation.

"I said you had to go to the bathroom and to hurry up."

"But that isn't true. I'm in no hurry."

"Americans are always in a hurry," Thomas countered. "That way, you will get to see more of Cancún. Besides, there is a man who seems to be following you. We should leave him behind."

Chapter Two

The god sitting among the stars is lonely. Much time has passed since the rumble of iron forced him to leave his home and choose a different path.

Mark Grayson's gaze drifted back to the tall redhead as she stood by a mountain of luggage—all matched and all leather. There was not a doubt in his mind that she would somehow show up to dig at the ruins of Chichén Itzá. She bore the stamp of the idle rich. He looked away, then found himself staring at her again. One thing about women with money, they certainly knew how to dress. The buff slacks and green silk blouse were arresting, especially with her tumbled auburn hair.

Suddenly aware of him, she matched him stare for stare, and he turned away. She wasn't his concern. At the moment he was waiting for his partner, Roberto de Solarno, to come in with some equipment they desperately needed at the dig. After months of searching, they had finally located a large pillar of stone. The find had created a small stir of excitement among the dedicated archaeologists at Chichén Itzá.

"I was hoping you'd forget and leave me stranded in Cancún for the night." Roberto, silent as a fox, was at Mark's side. He patted Mark's shoulder in a friendly greeting, as his gaze followed Mark's to the slender redhead.

"And I thought you were too involved in your dig to notice the beauties of the female form."

Mark smiled. "My grandfather used to tell me that it never hurts to look. Did you get the motor we needed?"

"Absolutely." Roberto's smile was radiant. "I also spoke with Señor Ortiz about halting the tourist aspect of the dig, but he refused to consider the idea. He thinks you are greedy and don't want to share the wonderful sensation of unlocking the mysteries of the past." His gaze drifted back to the woman and he lifted an eyebrow in appreciation. Interestingly enough, she'd been taken in charge by a local boy.

"Ortiz is a moron! If the glyphs are on the underside of the stela, as I suspect, we could be much closer to the secret of the Jaguar's Eye." Excitement put an edge on Mark's voice.

"I'm not certain Ortiz has a shred of faith in your legend, Mark. And you have to remember that he is our benefactor." Roberto lifted one shoulder in a shrug. "It is best if he doesn't take the legend too seriously. Can you imagine the hype he could put on that! He'd be hosting champagne brunches for every pottery fragment we unearthed."

Mark sighed. "You're right. We'd have no peace at all if he were aware of the tremendous archaeological value of such a discovery. If we can find it."

"If it exists." Roberto laughed at the expression on Mark's face. "The equipment is safe here at the airport. Why don't we go into Cancún for a nice leisurely lunch, maybe an evening of fun. We've been at the ruins for the past month—without a break."

Mark started to reply, then shook his head. "Wilfredo is in town, too. Why don't you both take an evening off and enjoy the beach and the ample supply of beautiful tourists. I'll take the motor, take care of some business and head back."

"One night won't make a difference, Mark. You, most of all, need to relax a little. Perhaps a few tender caresses under the Mayan moon?"

Mark shook his head. "To me, every moment makes a difference."

"A candle that burns so intensely melts far too fast." Roberto eyed his partner with a hint of disapproval.

"Better to burn fast than not at all," Mark said, forcing a smile. "It's what I want, Roberto. Really. But I don't begrudge the rest of you taking some time for fun. In fact, I agree with it."

"I'll see you tomorrow, then."

"Tomorrow." Mark waved goodbye and strode out of the passenger terminal to his battered Land Rover.

"ROSES! UNCLE ALEC is really putting on the polish." Celeste tipped the porter who brought in the flowers. As soon as he closed the door, she found the note in the bouquet and opened it.

Wear white tonight. Be prepared for the unexpected.

What was her uncle up to now? She put the note aside, with an amused smile, and began to unpack. He intended to jam every moment with surprises and twists. That way she wouldn't have time to worry about what was happening in Tampa.

When she opened the closet, there were several dresses already hanging there, one made of layers of cool white gauze. With a murmur of appreciation she withdrew it and held it to her. It was a work of art, a perfect dress for the hot climate.

She chuckled to herself. There was even a pair of white sandals in her size. Uncle Alec was a thorough man.

She heard Thomas's knock and let him in. "So, what are the plans for tonight?" she asked him. It was peculiar, asking someone else what she was to do with her time—especially a twelve-year-old—but she was glad for the boy's company. With his alert presence, she didn't have time to dwell on career problems.

"Let me see," he rolled his eyes up as if calculating. "You have reservations for dinner at nine and then there will be a surprise."

"What kind of surprise?" She rumpled his hair. "I pay very well for information. Can the young Señor Bond be tempted?"

"No amount of money could make me break my word." Thomas's face was solemn. "I have much...reputation. No matter how much I wanted to tell you, I promised that I would keep all the secrets."

"I like a man of his word," Celeste said, aware of how seriously Thomas took his responsbilities. "Anyway, I guess it would spoil the fun if I knew too much."

"Refresh yourself after the journey. I will escort you to the restaurant at nine and make the arrangements. Until then," he smiled and left the room.

Celeste finished unpacking and then toured the grounds of the hotel. The stucco building was surrounded by a riot of color. Flowers in red, pink and yellow contrasted vividly with the white plaster walls and red tile roof of the hotel. It was one of the older structures, with more atmosphere than the contemporary hotels.

The gulf was a crystal blue that blended with the sky on the horizon. The white sand of the beaches dazzled her, beckoning with the promise of lazy warmth. She found her swimsuit and a book and settled in a lounge chair for a read. If it wasn't heaven, it was pretty darn close.

She was ready at nine when Thomas knocked on her door. He rode in the taxi with her to a restaurant that featured a mariachi band and fresh fish grilled over a mesquite fire. He was explaining the merits of traditional Mexican music when the taxi halted. "See you tomorrow," he said unexpectedly.

"What? You aren't going to eat with me?"

"No, *señorita*." His grin was devilish. "Those are not my instructions."

"But I will meet a tall, dark stranger..." She laughed at Thomas's startled expression. So, Uncle Alec was up to another of his tricks. She would just have to wait.

"Good night, Señorita Celeste." Thomas waved as the cab pulled away.

The restaurant was filled with laughter and the music of the band. She dined alone, determined to keep her mind off the events transpiring in Tampa. She focused her interest on the other diners and the Spanish words she recognized in the songs. Her high-school Spanish classes were coming back to her, and she was surprised and pleased.

"Miss Coolridge?"

She turned to confront a short man in a severe black suit. "Yes?"

He placed a slender box on her table. "My compliments. It will protect you against your enemies. Once you put it on, do not remove it." He bowed and left as silently as he'd arrived.

Celeste opened the box with a twinge of nervousness. What enemies? The extraordinary jade figure was of a serpent. From the open mouth of the serpent, a woman emerged. The work was primitive but incredibly beautiful. It dangled from a substantial gold chain.

"Uncle Alex strikes again," she said, excited as she took it from the box. Jewelry had never been one of her passions, but the jade figure was compelling. There was something about the serpent and the Mayan legends. Some god, perhaps, but she couldn't remember exactly.

The stone had been recently polished, but it looked very old, maybe very valuable. Well, Uncle Alec was known for his extravagances. Once when there had been a rift between Aunt Eloise and her mother, Uncle Alec had sent carpenters to build a real tree house for Celeste for Christmas. Knowing that her mother could not refuse such a wonderful present for her daughter, Uncle Alec had selected the perfect gift to settle the rift between the sisters.

She worked the clasp behind her neck and felt the jade figure settle in the small hollow above her breasts. There was the comfortable feel that it belonged there. Protection against her enemies! Who were they? She started to run down a list of the brokers in her office and forced herself to stop. She was on vacation! Her fingers, unbidden, curled around the figure. She signaled the waiter for the check.

"It has been arranged," he told her, smiling. "And I believe there is someone to see you." He nodded to a tall, dark stranger who stood watching her with speculation.

"Yes?" she said when he arrived at her table.

"My name is Phillip. I've been instructed to teach you the Latin dances," he said, smiling. He held out his hand. "Dance with me."

Three hours later, exhausted but a far more experienced dancer, she hailed a taxi and went back to the hotel.

Against her better judgment, she placed a call to Tampa. After seven rings, she knew she'd made a mistake. Her uncle was undoubtedly asleep.

"Hello?" There was a sound of irritation in the tone.

"Uncle Alec. It's Celeste." She felt awkward, and a little dumb. "The necklace is beautiful. I just wanted to thank you."

"Necklace?"

She smiled. "You're such a rascal." She hesitated a moment. "The vacation is wonderful, but I can't shake the feeling that I should be in Tampa helping you."

"Celeste, I'm an old man and I'm tired late at night. You're where I want you to be. Already things are calming down in Tampa. With you out of the picture, my investigators can begin to ask questions, to probe around delicate matters. Stay put."

Beneath the gentle admonitions was a tone that Celeste read as fatigue. She was wrong to have called so late, but she couldn't stop the next question. "Have you found anything?"

"Celeste, honey, it's too soon. You left town this morning."

She twisted the phone cord in her hand. He sounded tired. He was in his sixties, after all. "I know, I know," she interrupted. "I'm sorry I called. It's just so hard..."

"Relax, have a good time." He hesitated. "I wasn't going to tell you, but I've discovered a few things about Barry Undine. It's nothing substantial, but at least it's enough to start some additional investigation."

"Barry hated me from the minute I walked into the firm. He's always blamed me for losing his office, but would he frame me?"

"It's hard on a male ego to have a private office taken away—and given to a young woman." Uncle Alec's soft voice was calm and sympathetic. "It would upset me, my dear."

"I doubt you'd blame the woman, who had nothing to do with it."

"I'm afraid Barry feels I used my influence to help you."

There was a pause on the line. "But you didn't, did you?"

Alec's laugh was deep and sincere. "This business has rattled your confidence, hon'. You earned that job and that office on your own, and you'll get it back because you're good. Just get some sun, drink some rum or tequila, or whatever the native drink is down there, and stay off the phone lines. When I have something you need, I'll find you."

"I have no doubt about that," she said, chuckling with her uncle. "No doubt, at all."

"I DON'T KNOW, *señorita*. Six days is a long time in a pit of dirt." Thomas couldn't hide the look of distress on his face. "I thought it would only be for a day." He held a small brochure and several receipts. Looking at the blue carbon, he sighed. "Six whole days."

"A week, eh?" Celeste felt her own hesitation. The proposed dig at the ancient Maya ruin in Chichén Itzá was something of a surprise. Uncle Alec, who changed his starched shirt each day at lunch, didn't seem the type to dream about archaeological digs. It would be six days in the heat, probably without hot water, with bugs and dirt, all for the pleasure of finding someone else's very old bones.

"A week. The arrangements have been made." Thomas was morose. "Maybe you could call your uncle?"

"No." Celeste stood and began brushing her hair. After all the trouble Uncle Alec had gone to to plan such a vacation, she wasn't going to call and complain. Besides, calling Tampa would only stir up all her anxieties about work. Only two nights before, when she'd called about the necklace, he'd promised to let her know when there were any new developments in her case, and he hadn't felt moved to add any details to the Barry Undine angle.

Instead of information, Uncle Alec had sent flowers again, champagne, earrings, and several beautiful *huipils* made by local women. And the necklace, which exactly matched the color of her eyes.

"If Uncle Alec thinks a week in a ditch will do me good, then I'll go." She realized that her voice reflected her lack of enthusiasm. After three days in Cancún, days of sun and water and laughter with Thomas, she was itchy to get home. She was better rested, she had to admit. The inactivity had begun to wear on her, though. She grew more and more uncomfortable with each passing day. Her future was on the line, and instead of tending to business she was set to go on a dig.

"My mother's village is very close to Chichén Itzá," Thomas brightened. "I cannot stay at the dig with you, but I will be close by."

"It'll be fun," she assured him, trying to also reassure herself. "Maybe I'll find the secret of King Tut's tomb."

"Wrong country," Thomas answered, laughing. "But there are many Maya secrets and legends. I will have my mother tell you some of them, if you'd like."

"I'm not superstitious, but I'd love to hear some of the stories."

"We should leave now, if we want to arrive in time to see the ruins," Thomas pointed out. "Travel conditions are not always the best."

"I'm packed, so let's go."

The drive was long, with several checkpoints where armed guards searched the car. Thomas conversed casually with the officials, making small talk about Cancún and the weather. Celeste eyed the automatic rifles with more than a little distrust. Her rural upbringing, complete with the blood lust of hunters, had shown her more than once how destructive firearms could be.

"Don't worry," Thomas reassured her at each checkpoint. "*Banditos,* thieves and dope smugglers are their only interest."

Between the checkpoints, the countryside blurred into a haze of heat, small villages with thatched huts and bumpy roads.

Celeste's first sight of Chichén Itzá was a disappointment. A line of shacks, where vendors hawked all types of tourist goods, stretched beside the parking lot.

"I thought this was going to be a historic ruin, not a tourist mecca," she complained under her breath.

"Not even the merchants can disturb the power of the pyramid," Thomas assured her. "Wait and see."

At the gate he waved aside the offers of several guides, insisting that he would conduct the tour himself. He ignored her low-volume grumbling as she wiped her forehead with a kerchief. The day was already hot, but a breeze occasionally stirred the branches of a few squat trees.

It was the first sight of the structure the Spaniards had named El Castillo that silenced her complaints.

"It's magnificent," she finally said, staring up the side of the ancient pyramid.

"We should find the director of the dig and make sure that the arrangements have been made," Thomas cautioned her. "We want to be sure you have a place to stay, food, the necessities."

"Go ahead," Celeste waved him on. "I'm going to the top of the pyramid."

"*Señorita,* it is a difficult climb. Very steep. Wait until later in the day when the sun isn't so hot. There is much to see besides the temple. The climb will exhaust you before we even begin.''

The steps were steep and narrow, but Celeste could not resist the thought of viewing the ruins from the top of the structure. None of Thomas's arguments could persuade her to wait.

As she started the climb, she looked back at him, a small figure in white waiting in the shade of a tree. She waved, and he returned it with an additional shake of his head.

Halfway up, she realized the truth of the young boy's words. The footing was treacherous and she remembered something he'd said on the long drive—the steps were designed so that no one could descend straight down, thereby turning his back on the gods. The narrow steps forced a crab-like sideways movement, and as hard as the ascent was, going down was going to be even worse.

Her white camp shirt was soaked by the time she reached the top, and tendrils of her hair clung to her neck and chest. The ruins stretched out below her, a place where one of the most civilized nations in the world had once existed. With the thought came a vivid picture of what might have taken place in centuries past. She saw the women walking single-file along the paths and imagined the men in the fields. It seemed an idyllic time, when food and sleep were the rewards for a hard day. There was no stock market, no high-rise towers filled with ambitious traders who would stop at nothing, not even lies! No Barry Undine!

She sat down on the stone altar and leaned her head back to catch a breeze beneath the heavy weight of her hair. She couldn't dwell on the pending SEC investigation. The humiliation and pain would destroy her if she let it. Instead, she would enjoy her surroundings and learn from the past. The sun was so warm, and she was tired from the climb. She closed her eyes and imagined the village of Chichén Itzá as it might have been before the arrival of the Spaniards. She'd read somewhere that the Mayas were very devoted to children.

"Looking at the architectural wonders, it's hard to imagine that these same people practiced ritual sacrifice, isn't it?"

The voice, and the question, startled Celeste. She sat forward and opened her eyes. The tall stranger from the airport stood before her, and there was an unpleasant look in his eyes. She read it first as anger, then disdain.

"I wasn't aware of the practice of ritual sacrifice, and I'm not certain I care to hear about it," she answered, irritated by his tone and by the unpleasant image he'd thrust at her.

"The Maya often went to war so they could take prisoners. The gods were hungry back then, and prisoners made excellent fodder."

He was being deliberately abrasive. "I find that, like the gods, I'm hungry, too. I'll leave you to your *pleasant* imaginings." She stood abruptly. The man, be he tourist or whatever, was baiting her. It was disconcerting to realize he'd been at the airport and now he was here.

"You're along for the dig, aren't you?" he asked.

The question stopped her as she neared the edge of the pyramid. She said a silent prayer that the disapproving man wasn't going to be her companion for a week. "Yes, if it's any of your business." She faced him.

"I'm Mark Grayson. I head the expedition," he said slowly and in a softer tone. He had been surprised by her fighting spirit. If her body belonged to the band of idle rich, at least her mind seemed to function. There was also the matter of her necklace. He'd caught only a glimpse, but it looked interesting—and authentic.

"Do you hold all of us 'tourist archaeologists' in the highest contempt?" she shot at him, pleased to see by the widening of his eyes that she'd accurately hit her target. "I'm delighted to meet you." The sarcasm was entwined in a deliberately sweet voice.

"Not only observant, but also intuitive," he said carefully. "But since you've paid for the privilege of attending a dig, I'm sure my contempt won't bother you."

"Not in the least," she agreed, hiding her fury behind a smile. "Now if you'll excuse me, Mr. Grayson, I'll leave you to your fantasies of human sacrifice."

She started down the steps, her anger making her more reckless than normal. She wanted to put as much distance between herself and Mark Grayson as possible. He was odious. The epitome of machismo. Machismo tamped down with the double load of some twisted intellectual superiority. He made his living from tourists, yet he despised them. She'd seen that attitude in a variety of different guises all her life. Well, it was his problem not hers.

"Señorita!" Thomas was waving at her. "Take care! You will be hurt!" He rushed to meet her, breathless. "You are angry?"

She saw the surprise on his face and suddenly let her anger go. Mark Grayson wasn't worthy of concern. She smiled. "No, just determined to get down so we could eat. I'm starved! How about you?"

"Sí," he agreed, heading for the picnic basket the hotel had packed for them.

Standing on the pyramid, Mark watched the woman and the young boy. He was angry with himself. He'd attacked the woman without any provocation. He'd seen her sitting on the altar, so out of place and yet so natural. Something about the image had angered him enough so that he attacked her. To his amazement, she'd seen through his remarks to his reasons. She'd seen them even more clearly than he.

He rethought the scene, focusing on the figure that dangled from the gold chain at her neck. It was a symbol of the god Quetzalcoatl with a female form emerging from his mouth. He'd heard the local Mayas read the image as one of reincarnation, or more accurately of rebirth of the god. Return of Quetzalcoatl was a common theme in a land where poverty had left little to cling to but old legends.

The woman wore the necklace as if she had the right. That was the thing that had set him off. Her money had certainly bought it, but that didn't mean she had the right to dangle a piece of history as an ornament. Especially not when it was more than likely stolen from some archaeological site.

He shook his head and went to the altar to sit. No matter what he thought, his reaction had been extreme. Never before had he been so harsh, not even with the worst of the tourists who came to dig.

A weary smile touched his lips, crinkling the deeply tanned skin around his mouth. Well, he'd attacked, but she'd defended herself with admirable skill. There was a fire in her soul that matched that in her hair. His smile grew slightly wider.

The best thing to do was apologize. The week would be long enough without a feud running between them. He chuckled as he imagined Roberto's return. His partner would be furious if he knew that Mark had just insulted the most beautiful woman he'd seen in many years. He remembered Roberto's appreciative glance at the redhead in the airport.

Better to get the apology over and done. He started down the steps, counting. The pyramid-shaped structure was reclaimed on only two sides, but originally there had been ninety-one steps on each of the four sides. Ninety-one. The number of days in a season. The Mayas were great calculators of time.

Descending the steep steps in the oppressive heat, he had another thought. Gossip among some of the Maya workmen had it that an important time was drawing near. Though he'd tried to locate the source of the gossip, he'd been unsuccessful so far. The local Indians thrived on omens and signs, the possibility of a supernatural event. One village woman, in particular, had a going business in charms, potions and omens. Normally he shrugged it off. The necklace had triggered his emotional reaction to the talk. When he got close enough to the fiery redhead, he'd have another look at the figure. There was something about it that struck a cord of concern.

Chapter Three

The first sign is awareness. The sun calls the days forth in order. The moon rides the smoothness of the sky. Preparations, long begun, continue.

"Hold on to your iced tea," Celeste warned Thomas as she caught sight of Mark Grayson's long-legged strides. "A very unpleasant man is coming toward us." Without warning, her stomach knotted. She was determinedly on vacation, and she didn't want trouble.

"He was at the airport. You know this man?" Thomas watched the approaching figure with amazement. "He is like the stories of the first Spanish, tall and angry."

"And just as mean as some of the tales I've read," Celeste said in a mock whisper.

"I'm sorry to interrupt your picnic." Mark ignored Celeste's remark. He meant to look at the necklace, but he met her curious gaze instead. Her eyes were an odd shade of green, like polished jade.

Celeste waited, unable to avoid the look he sent her. He wasn't a pleasant man, not by any standards she knew, but he was compelling. She couldn't say why exactly, but she wasn't surprised to find him at her picnic site.

"I've come to apologize for my behavior. It was inexcusable and completely unwarranted. I hope I haven't spoiled your first impression of Chichén Itzá." He tried to examine the jade figure, but it had slipped beneath the collar of her camp shirt.

Lifting a glass of cold tea, Celeste took a swallow before she answered. "I have to admit I was a little taken aback, but no, Chichén Itzá isn't spoiled for me. With Thomas to guide me, I've been fascinated by the history here."

"You're..."

"Celeste Coolridge," she said, automatically extending her hand to him.

He took it with a smile. So, she was a businesswoman. He noticed the lack of rings and the presence of perfect manicured nails. By the end of the week, her hands would not look the same.

She withdrew her fingers from his. "Would you care for something to drink? Thomas and I are enjoying my last day before I become a minion in the efforts to recover the past."

Folding his long legs beneath him, Mark sat down in the shade beside them. His view of the necklace was blocked, but the tea did look wonderfully refreshing. He smiled as he took the glassful Celeste poured from the thermos. "It's been months since I've had iced tea," he said. "Simple pleasures can become very important here."

Celeste could read no barb in his remark, so she let it pass. "I'm excited about the idea of the dig," she said, forcing enthusiasm into her voice. "My vacation is something of a special arrangement, so I didn't have any time to prepare. Could you tell me something about what you're working on?"

"We have reason to believe there's a tomb of one of the great kings of the Maya here. As you probably know, the Mayan civilization started to crumble even before the Spaniards began to exert real power to conquer it. Chichén Itzá has an interesting past because of the infusion of the Toltecs, a more warlike tribe. I'm hoping to find some clues to the past, to several legends in particular, and possibly to some of the answers that have thwarted archaeologists for the past two hundred years." Mark intentionally kept the talk general. He made it a point never to mention the Jaguar's Eye to the tourists who came to dig. The idea of a large ruby might send them into a frenzy of destruction.

"Much of the Mayan history has been destroyed," Thomas said, sipping his tea thoughtfully. "My mother says that what writings are left will never be seen by any white man."

"There is distrust, and it is completely understandable," Mark agreed. He eyed the young boy with respect, as he drank the cold, sweet tea. "Are you full Maya?"

"*Sí.*" Thomas looked around the ruins, his brown eyes seeming to see both past and present. "This is a sacred place to my people, my family."

Remembering Thomas's earlier reluctance to spend much time at the dig, Celeste had a sudden intuition. "Does it bother you to see the ruins uncovered and exposed?"

She felt Mark's gaze on her, and surprisingly there was admiration in his look.

Thomas looked at the ground, picking up the plastic fork and tracing a pattern through the remains on his plate. "For me, no, it is not painful. For some of my people the answer is different. The gods may not wish to be disturbed. There are some who believe that digging up the tombs will change the natural order of time."

"And you, Thomas, what do you believe?" Mark asked, a new gentleness in his voice.

"The road my people must take is in the future, not the past," Thomas said. "If the ruins are restored for the tourists, then many people will come to learn how great the Maya heritage is. We will be respected, maybe."

"I have much respect for the Maya people." Mark pressed the cool glass that held his iced tea to his forehead. "There is so much we can learn from studying Chichén Itzá."

"Some of my people are afraid that the ruins will be taken from us. That we will be made to pay," he waved back to the gate, "as if we were tourists ourselves. It makes some people angry." He cast his gaze down at his plate. "Very angry."

"Can I talk with these people?"

Mark's question was quick, as if an opportunity long awaited had presented itself. Celeste watched the exchange with a whisper of unease touching her skin. So, the dig was controversial. That could account for Mark Grayson's snappy attitude.

She dropped her gaze, flashing an occasional look at Mark. He was not especially handsome. He was rugged, his visage strong and unrelenting. Enduring was the word that came to mind. There was a light in his blue eyes that warned that once his mind was made up, he was an unstoppable force. She shivered a little at that thought.

"I will ask my people if they would like to meet with you," Thomas said, shrugging his shoulders. "Don't expect too much."

"As long as they know I will talk, anytime." He finished his tea and handed the glass back to Celeste. "Thank you." With casual grace he unfolded his legs and stood. He hadn't caught a clear view of her necklace, but he had to go check on the crew near the cenote. "I hope you've accepted my apologies, Celeste, and I'd like to ask you for a drink tonight in my quarters. My partner, Roberto de Solarno, will be there. He'll be delighted to make your acquaintance."

"That would be nice," she agreed. "Maybe you can fill me in on some of the old legends and superstitions."

"Do you believe in such things?" He watched her with sudden interest.

She studied his face before she answered, trying to fathom the meaning behind the words. There seemed to be the hint of a smile at the corner of his lips, but she couldn't be certain.

"I don't know what I believe, until I hear them," she finally said.

"I saw you at the airport when you arrived. I knew at that moment that you would come to the dig. How do you explain such a thing?"

He was definitely teasing her, and she found she liked it. "Let's see, I had the look of a tourist with time and money. I'll bet you see a lot of that type." She laughed at his confirming smile. "Perhaps I won't be as much of a nuisance as you intuited," she added. "Only time will tell."

"Tonight at seven," he answered, returning her smile. She was smart as a whip, and nobody's fool. He was beginning to view her presence as an interesting diversion.

THOMAS'S FAREWELL was a mixture of haste and disapproval. He was eager to see his family, but he was uneasy about leaving Celeste at the ruin.

In the long, hot hours of the afternoon, Celeste had learned that Thomas lived with relatives in Cancún so that he could work the tourists. He was the primary support of his family, sending home most of the money he earned in tips as a Cancún guide or troubleshooter. His flawless English gave him an edge over many of the other guides, and his ability to find things and ease the tangle of arrangements afforded him a good living.

His dream was to go to London and work as a secret agent for "Her Majesty, the Queen." And he took his duties to Celeste with equal seriousness.

"I will be back in three days," he had promised her. "If you're tired of this place, we will go back to the beach."

Celeste had rumpled his hair, trying to stroke away the worry that furrowed his brow.

He'd left with reluctance, but also with a deep need to see his mother and to carry Mark's message to her village. Celeste could see that the rift between the archaeology crew and the village was serious, indeed.

Once Thomas was gone, Celeste prepared for dinner. She'd been given a small hut that offered minimum accommodation and not much more privacy. There was a bed, a kerosene lamp, a chair and a table with a small pitcher and bowl. A brightly woven piece of material was hung over the door opening. She washed and put on a clean shirt, all too aware that the setting sun would bring night. Without electricity, it would be very dark.

She was ready when Mark came for her. Dusk had begun to drop over the ruins and a strange peace seemed to surround them.

"There's a little light left," he said. "Did you see the ball court? The influence is more Toltec than Maya, but it's the largest discovered in Mesoamerica." The invitation surprised even him. Looking at Celeste as she stood in the doorway of the hut, he suddenly wanted to show her a part of the ruins, to see if she could appreciate the things that were so important to him.

"I didn't have a chance to see much," she said, wondering why Mark Grayson was being so solicitous. In the softer glow of twilight, he was almost handsome with his sun-streaked brown hair and piercing blue eyes. "I think I wore myself out climbing that pyramid."

They walked to the ancient ball court in silence. Standing beside one of the walls, Mark's hand drifted unconsciously over the old stone, as if he could touch the secrets and draw them forth.

"Many differences were settled on the ball court," he said.

"Thomas told me that the captain of the losing team was beheaded." She gazed upon the ghostly court, trying to imagine it filled with spectators waiting for a sacrifice. "It's a harsh penalty for poor athletic performance."

"It was the choice of the gods," Mark corrected her softly. "I think you may be reading a type of enjoyment into it that didn't exist. It was simply what they felt they had to do to please the gods and survive. The losers were out of favor. The gods' wishes had been made evident."

"What hungry gods," she said with a twist. "Thank goodness they're gone now."

"The human race suffers from a lot of misguided behavior. We have our own gods, and some of them are ravenous. It isn't all in the distant past, you know."

"Hey, if you're trying to give me an attack of the goose bumps, you've just succeeded." Even though the sun was still above the horizon, Celeste couldn't suppress a shiver.

Somehow his words had triggered a memory of the brokerage firm. Losers weren't beheaded there, but it was almost as bloody. Failure wasn't tolerated.

"Many of the locals chosen for sacrifice felt it was a great honor and went willingly," Mark continued, unaware of her very personal reaction. "The thought of pleasing the gods was part of their upbringing. Because the tribe's survival depended on the sun and rain, the power of the gods, it was a great honor to be selected."

"An honor I could do without."

"Me, too." Mark guided her toward a long wall. In the deepening shadows he pointed out the images of a multitude of skulls. "This is the platform of the skulls. The ceremonial aspect isn't clearly understood."

"Look," Celeste said. At one section of the wall, a vibrant orange flower had blossomed. It seemed to sprout from the base of the wall. "Life in a wall of death," she said, touching the stem of the blossom.

"The Mayas were great believers in the cycle of life. Their calendar was a count of days, a repetitive cycle, with certain days influenced by specific gods. A priest could predict which day would bring good luck or bad because he knew the past. The priests were very powerful." He paused, bending to touch the flower. "It's odd, but in all the years I've worked on this site, I've never seen a flower here. How did it survive the hordes of tourists? They pick and collect everything imaginable."

Celeste didn't answer as Mark guided her to a portion of wall where they could sit. The enormous pyramid loomed only a short distance away, and Celeste watched as the evening shadows began to fill the stone building.

"Did you see the jaguar throne inside?" Mark asked. "You asked earlier about legends, and there are a lot of them attached to that throne. Stories abound about the prophets who sat there. There was also once an incredible carving of a jaguar." He watched her face for interest or boredom.

"What happened to it?"

"Do you want what's been proven, or the legend?"

"How about both," she answered, "but the legend first. I've always been partial to the more romantic renderings of history."

"Not a good sign for an archaeologist," Mark replied, but he was smiling.

His entire face seemed to change when he allowed himself to smile, Celeste noted. He was even more compelling. "Lucky for me I'm not intending to become an archaeologist. Since I'm only a tourist, I'll take the spiced-up version."

"Okay. When the Maya empire began to crumble, there was a faction of high priests who had foretold the destruction. Years of drought had reduced the crops to nothing. Lack of water had also driven the wildlife farther into the jungles. The Mayas were being scorched out of their homes by the sun. No amount of sacrifices could bring the gods to send water. There was also discontent among the old Mayas and resentment toward the Toltecs."

"My history is skimpy, but it seems the Toltecs had the habit of taking over by force. They weren't exactly diplomats," Celeste said. She was fascinated by the story, and by the effect it was having on the man who told it.

"Good history recall," Mark said. "The Spaniards had already arrived throughout Central America, and as you know, if the Indians didn't convert to Christianity, the Spaniards summarily executed them. The Mayas' faith was very strong, very old. It was a conflict that eventually cost thousands of lives. It seems the Indians were being assaulted on all fronts."

Celeste reached far back into her grammar-grade lessons. For a period of time her class had studied the Mayas. "Weren't they basically peaceful? I mean except for the habit of human sacrifice."

"They weren't warlike, which is an issue apart from sacrifice. They weren't prepared to defend themselves, and they didn't know how to change." He fell silent.

"It is remarkable that an entire culture was destroyed."

"Methodically destroyed," Mark said. "The Mayas had much of their culture written. It was burned."

"No wonder Thomas's village is hesitant to allow exploration."

"Yes, they have their reasons. At any rate, legend has it that a small group of Maya rulers determined to preserve the old Maya ways hid the carving of the jaguar. The carving, which is reportedly an elaborate work of art, had one closed eye, to symbolize the folly of the Maya people. The other eye was an enormous jewel, a blood-red ruby."

"I would have thought it would be an emerald," Celeste said. She watched the man across from her. She had the distinct feeling that he believed in the story far more than he would ever willingly admit.

"It would seem so. The ruby, though, could possibly be a symbol of the vengeance that will be extracted against those who attempt to thwart the gods. You see, the jaguar is a symbol of prophecy, of the highest order of priests. There are many other symbols, but the main god, Quetzalcoatl, is represented by the snake."

"I've seen hieroglyphics in books that contained the image of Quetzalcoatl." Celeste was delighted to feel her memory jog so successfully. "A snake is an interesting god."

Mark laughed. "Yes, it wouldn't be the North American creature of choice, I suspect. The Maya people were greatly appreciative of survival skills. Snakes have existed for millions of years."

Celeste joined in Mark's easy laughter. "I've never looked at it that way. So, what happened to the jaguar in your story?"

"The priests removed the eye and put it somewhere in these ruins. I'm not certain about the statue itself. Some say it was destroyed to keep the Spaniards from taking it. Local talk has it that the carving and the ruby will be reunited at some point in time."

"A good point or a bad point?"

Mark shrugged. "I guess it depends on what perspective you have." He hadn't intended to get so involved with the legend. Celeste was simply a very good listener. Too good. "Have you had a chance to go into the interior of El Castillo? The jaguar throne is there, and Roberto and I believe that's where the jaguar carving was once worshiped."

"No. Tomorrow I'll explore some more." While they'd been talking, darkness had fallen around them. Small creatures of the night had begun their music. A long-buried part of Celeste was touched. There had been times when she sat in the dusk with her parents and listened to the sounds of the night. The memory was pleasant.

"There's the observatory and the sacred cenote. You'll want to see both of them," Mark continued.

"The what?"

"The well. It's the source of water here, as it was for the Mayas. There are many legends about it, but we should save them for the daylight." He chuckled. "I don't want you to think that the only topic I can converse on is human sacrifice."

"Then tell me how you became such a dedicated archaeologist." She meant the question to be light, and she was unprepared to see the tension return to his face.

"My father was an archaeologist."

"Did you go on digs with him when you were a child?"

"Every summer. All summer long." His tone softened.

"Is he still working? Is he on this site?"

"My father is dead. He was excavating a ruin on the coast. The expedition was poorly funded and a tomb collapsed. He and two assistants were killed."

"Mark, I'm so sorry." Celeste nosed the toe of her sneaker into the soft sand beneath the wall. "I'm sorry."

"It isn't your fault, Celeste. It's a fact with a lot of expeditions. We make do with what we can get, and we're as careful as possible." He stood suddenly. "We should head back. Roberto will be waiting, and the other members of the team are eager to meet you. There's another American couple, the Tretorns, a few graduate students and some of the locals, if any of them stayed." He shrugged. "We'll have a drink and then dinner, where you'll meet everyone."

They walked back through the deepening night. Without the lights of a city, the darkness was falling in a thick curtain. The stars, brighter than Celeste had ever seen them, winked on. Walking beside Mark, she chanced a look at his profile. The shadowed eyes showed a moment of pain, and she thought of his father, buried alive. No wonder he was sensitive about wealthy amateur diggers.

"So, here you are at last. I was beginning to think you'd taken Ms. Coolridge for a swim in the cenote. I was about to become jealous." A tall, handsome man stepped from the shadows, a drink in hand. "I was delighted when Mark told me you were going to be on the dig this week. I saw you in the airport."

"I'm delighted to be here," Celeste said, taking the room-temperature gin-and-tonic Roberto offered her. "I've already learned a lot here."

"Mark is an excellent teacher, though he seldom takes the time to talk with our other guests." Roberto's eyes flashed at his partner. "I'm glad to see he's finally found a student worthy of his efforts."

"Enough, Roberto," Mark said, not at all perturbed by the teasing. "I was rude to Celeste, and I felt the need to make it up to her."

"Now we're even," Celeste said firmly. "Let's forget about it."

"Mark? Rude?" Roberto was laughing. "I find that hard to believe."

Mark made himself a drink and settled down at a table outside the door of a larger hut. A kerosene lamp had already been lighted and his face was easy to see.

"Roberto constantly likes to point out my shortcomings," he said, then sipped his drink. "Lucky for him, I have a tough hide."

"And an excellent eye for the beautiful," Roberto added, waving Celeste into a chair at the table.

She looked at the two men, so different in tone and temperament, yet such good friends. She sipped her drink and withheld comment.

"So, you are on vacation?" Roberto said, focusing the conversation on her.

"Yes, for a few weeks."

"Do you work?" Mark asked.

Celeste's hesitation was barely noticeable. "Yes, I'm a stockbroker in Tampa." She felt hot and uncomfortable. It wasn't exactly a lie, but she didn't want to go into the details of her professional trials.

"Very fast-paced," Roberto said with interest. "Mexico is just the place to unwind. Here in Chichén Itzá there will be no ringing telephones, no market reports, no pressure."

"Exactly what I need," she agreed, eager to turn the topic away from herself. "Tell me some of the things you've discovered here, so far."

"Mark just excavated a stela on the outskirts of the current ruins. It appears to be a clue to this hidden tomb that he's been hallucinating about for so long." Roberto's enthusiasm was barely concealed, and he walked around the table and patted his partner on the shoulder.

"What kind of clue?" she asked. The gin-and-tonic, once she got used to the idea of the drink without ice, was refreshing.

"It's a glyph," Mark answered, his voice carefully controlled in contrast to Roberto's. "We can't be certain of the value of the find until we decipher the drawings. It might not tell us anything."

"Don't be so modest!" Roberto interjected. "Mark is certain we've found the first vital clue. Tomorrow we'll finish hoisting the column from the ground. It's fallen over."

"It's tedious work, Celeste," Mark warned her as he saw the excitement touch her eyes. "Not as glamorous as it sounds."

"Will I be allowed to help?" she asked.

The two men exchanged glances and Roberto shrugged and grinned.

"There's only you and the Tretorns here this week," Mark said. "As long as the site looks safe, you can help. There are other excavations. Wilfredo has some men near the observatory where we've found some undocumented ruins. There's actual sifting and collecting going on there. It might be more interesting."

"Wherever you think I'd be the most help," Celeste answered, catching the look the two men threw each other. She smiled. Mark and Roberto would soon learn she wasn't some spoiled tourist.

"I think dinner is ready," Roberto said, stepping to Celeste to help her from her chair. "It will be my honor to introduce you." He took her arm and Mark was left to follow them fifty yards through the darkness to a long table set outside what was obviously the kitchen.

In the light of several lamps, Celeste shook the hands of Charles and Rebecca Tretorn. At the end of the table several young people had formed their own conversation group. They greeted her pleasantly and fell back into their discussion.

"The graduate students," Mark whispered to her. "Intolerably self-centered."

"And this is Wilfredo, our local crew boss," Roberto said as a short man of evident Maya heritage stepped to the table from a nearly obscured path.

Celeste held out her hand with a ready smile, but the man hesitated. He was staring at her as if he'd never seen a woman before.

"Welcome," he finally said, barely touching her hand. "Welcome to Chichén Itzá, home of the Mayas."

"Tough day in the bush, eh Wilfredo?" Roberto asked, laughing. "It does make a man speechless to suddenly find a beautiful woman in the middle of a dig."

"*Sí,*" Wilfredo agreed, glancing at Celeste.

"I intend to show that some amateurs can be helpful." Celeste picked up the thread of conversation, hoping to smooth over Wilfredo's obvious awkwardness.

"Oh, I'd say your presence is more than enough," Roberto said with a tantalizing smile. "You will boost morale all over the ruins."

Celeste shook her head. "Beware of the man with the silver tongue," she said, and everyone at the table laughed.

Juanita, the cook, served a beef-and-tomato dish with beans, rice and tortillas. Celeste discovered that most of the local workers went home to the village each night. "They rotate guard duty," Mark explained.

"What do they guard?" Celeste asked, her gaze moving through the darkness.

"It's a routine matter," Mark said easily. He turned his attention to the Tretorns, who were telling Roberto about their shoe dynasty in Houston. Sitting beside Roberto, Wilfredo was unusually silent. The man seemed crazily awed by Celeste.

"Stiletto heels can just do wonders for an ugly ankle," Rebecca Tretorn said, leaning toward Roberto. "No woman with an ounce of chic would wear flats to a business meeting. I mean, really, a woman's legs can be a tremendous asset, don't you think?"

"Absolutely," Roberto said, his white teeth flashing.

"My wife loves her shoe business," Charles Tretorn said, leaning back in his chair and smiling at his pretty blond wife. He was several years older than her. "We call Rebecca the Imelda Marcos of Houston. I do believe she owns a pair of every shoe she sells."

"I do," she agreed. "Why, I brought three suitcases of shoes just to come here."

"I hope not all of them are high heels," Mark said.

Celeste heard the undercurrent of disapproval in his tone and hid her smile behind her napkin.

"Charlie insisted that I bring these horrible old walking shoes. I mean they weigh a pound each, and they dangle on the end of a person's leg like a ball and chain. But he insisted."

"Thank goodness for Charlie," Mark said with a wry smile.

"She seldom listens to me," Charles said softly, resting his hand on her arm with affection. "She's a headstrong woman, but, then, I like a woman with a little spirit."

Roberto's remark was cut short by a shrill scream that erupted in the night.

Celeste shivered as if ice had been poured down her back. The sound was primal, frightening. "What is it?" she asked.

There was a moment of silence before the wild cry was repeated. At the very end of the table, Wilfredo rose slowly and came to Mark's shoulder. He bent to whisper in Mark's ear, darting looks at Celeste.

"It isn't possible," Mark said. "They're extinct here."

Wilfredo bent lower, his words unintelligible but his tone clearly one of concern.

When he stepped back, Mark stood and confronted the silent, anxious faces around the table. "Wilfredo seems to think that the noise we just heard was made by a jaguar. The species has been virtually eradicated in this area. I don't think a big cat has been spotted in the past thirty years. But let's be on the lookout and not take any foolish chances."

"Maybe this dig isn't such a good idea," Rebecca said to Charles. "We could just go back to Cozumel and play on the beach."

"Even if it is a cat, I'm sure that it won't come near a settlement," Roberto said reassuringly. "If it's managed to survive here, it's stayed away from people."

"Unless it is the gods," Wilfredo said in a voice so low that only Celeste and Mark heard him.

There was the sound of running feet, and one of the Maya lookouts stumbled into the lamplight. His eyes were wide with fear. He spoke rapidly with Wilfredo in a language that was part Spanish and part Indian. Though Wilfredo argued, he could not calm the other man down.

"Zeha is leaving," Wilfredo finally said. "He is afraid to stay here with the jaguar."

"That's absurd," Mark exploded. "Are they afraid of the cat, or of the legends?"

"Both," Wilfredo said without flinching. "The jaguar is a sacred animal. It has been foretold that the return of

Quetzalcoatl will be told by a large jaguar with gleaming eyes."

"I'm aware of the legend," Mark said with control, "but surely Zeha does not believe that a jaguar will actually talk."

Wilfredo's eyes seemed to blaze. "The jaguar will foretell the coming of the god and many will die. It is the word of the old ones."

Chapter Four

March 7. The day of Men on the Maya calendar, the tenth in the count of thirteen. The burner begins the fire. The prophet stalks the jungle.

Celeste buttoned the blue shirt and stepped into the sun. It was early, but it was already warm and an eager anticipation of the day had awakened her. Despite the scare from the still unidentified animal's scream that had fractured dinner, she'd slept like a log. Her thighs were stiff and sore from the climb up the pyramid, but otherwise she was looking forward to her first dig experience.

She joined the long table of silent and aloof graduate students for a quick breakfast of tortillas and beans. There were three girls, almost identical with their long hair, deep tans and lack of makeup, and two boys, both with beards. She tried several attempts at conversation, but the students answered in monosyllables. She shrugged, assuming that graduate students, too, looked down on tourists.

"Good morning." Rebecca Tretorn took a seat beside her. "That was the most awful night I've ever spent. I was terrified, and that cot! How could anyone sleep on such a thing? Did you hear any more wild beasts?" Her perfectly made-up face was tense with displeasure.

"None." Celeste smiled. "They could have danced around my bed, I suppose. I slept like the dead."

"Not a very nice comparison," Rebecca said with distaste. "Frankly, I'm ready to call it quits and go home. I mean there aren't even bathrooms. If I hadn't told everyone in Texas about this trip, I would go home. I thought it sounded so glamorous . . . and the idea of finding a treasure was exciting."

Celeste smothered a smile. She didn't want to seem unsympathetic to Rebecca, but she didn't want to discuss the lack of luxuries. She was much more interested in learning a bit about the dig. She used the departure of the graduate students as an excuse to terminate the conversation. "I think we're late." She picked up her plate and stood. "Everyone seems headed down that path, so I think I'll try and catch up."

"Yes, my dear, you should do your best to make a good impression." Rebecca's smile was conspiratorial. "Is it dark Mr. de Solarno or the defiant Mr. Grayson you fancy?"

"I'd say it was more a desire to learn something new." Celeste turned on her heel, a flush of anger spreading from her neck to her face. She took her plate to the kitchen and went back to her hut to pick up a kerchief and a water canteen. Why was it that some women boiled every action down to an attempt to interest a man? Rebecca probably meant no harm, it was just her way. She banished her anger as she left the clearing and began to walk into the tenacious growth that had tangled the ruins for hundreds of years.

The scrubs along the path looked parched. The Yucatán was often dry, a real problem for those who tried to eke out a living on a farm. She scanned the clear path ahead. There was no sign of any of the students, or Mark or Roberto. She slowed her pace, listening for the sound of voices to guide her. A tiny glimmer of irritation touched her. Mark had abandoned her, and the Tretorns and gone off to tend to his dig. He should have left a guide, or at least a map. As far as she could tell, there wasn't a human alive in a five-mile area.

A crackle of brush alerted her, and she turned to the north, relief taking some of the sting out of her anxiety. So there was somebody nearby. She searched the underbrush but saw nothing. Perplexed, she started to walk on.

Once again, the crackle of dry limbs caught her ear and she paused. The local workers were shy, but surely they wouldn't be afraid to come near her. She looked closer, noting that the ground cover was thick but not tall. A man should be easily visible.

Unless he didn't want to be seen.

She turned and began to walk. Her stride was long, her steps rapid. She could feel the acceleration of her heart in her chest, even though her mind chastised her for foolish reactions.

At the sound of a stick popping, she swung around abruptly.

The cat stood completely still, its large body as relaxed as if it were on display. Only its eyes watched her, eyes a bright, fiery green.

For a moment, Celeste thought she was hallucinating. The jaguar was only ten yards away, a huge beast. The only movement was the flick of his tail, which rustled some dry shrubs.

A choking sense of panic swept over her. She stumbled backward several steps before she caught herself and froze. She couldn't outrun the animal. If he wasn't hungry, he might decide to chase her for the fun of it, if she ran. Her best bet was to remain completely still. She'd read somewhere that vicious dogs lost interest in a victim if he didn't move. She could only pray that wild cats were of the same temperament.

In the far distance, Celeste heard the sound of a small motor kick and catch. She heard it with a part of her brain that registered fact instead of emotion. If she screamed, no one would be able to hear her above the noise of the motor. She felt the sweat begin to trickle into the band of her shorts.

The cat shifted his attention to a distant clump of shrubs. He seemed to hear some inaudible sound. He looked at Celeste once more, then slowly began to walk away. His shoulders moved beneath the gorgeous spotted hide. He left, his tail twitching one last time behind him.

When Celeste finally moved, it was to squat, forehead buried against her arm. She was shaking, and a dull sickness seemed to roar in her head. She'd come within a few feet of being breakfast for a truly magnificent animal. Thank goodness the cat had a finicky appetite, a larger-than-life Morris. At the weak joke she smiled feebly and pulled herself erect. She tested a step or two, to make sure her legs wouldn't go rubbery, then moved forward toward the sound of the motor.

"Celeste!" Roberto came toward her, concern on his face. "What has happened? You look deathly pale."

"I had a scare," she said softly, looking around the group of curious faces. All of the graduate students were there, but no sign of Mark, Wilfredo or the Tretorns.

"Mark went to check on our guests. Didn't you see him on the path?"

"No, I must have taken the wrong direction."

"What happened?" Roberto eased her down onto a large rock and motioned the graduate students to go back to work.

Celeste took in the site. There were four poles used as a support system for a winch that was driven by a small motor. She could see the motor was straining to lift a heavy pillar of stone.

"You're going to think I've lost my mind, but that cat we heard last night . . ."

"The noise that frightened Wilfredo's men?" Roberto laughed. "Yes, I recall the noise."

"It was a jaguar. I saw it in the bush."

Roberto's laugh was merry until he looked at her. The laughter died away. "You aren't kidding, are you?"

She shook her head. "I was about ten yards from it. Large cat, spots, very sleek and elegant. It had to be a jaguar."

"But that's impossible." The emphatic words burst from Roberto. He looked at the graduate students who'd given up any pretense of working and were eavesdropping as much as possible.

"Back to work," he ordered, "or you'll get very bad reports from this expedition."

Two of the students grinned, but they returned to the ropes on the stela, bending down to check the knots.

"I'm not hysterical. I saw a real, live jaguar in the weeds." Celeste spoke with calm determination. "He watched me and then walked away."

"We should tell Mark," Roberto said, his brow furrowed with worry. "We'll have to figure out some way to kill it."

"I hardly think so!" Celeste stood. "Mark said last night that jaguars are almost extinct here. I don't know much about archaeology but I do know you shouldn't kill that animal."

"He could hurt one of the workers, or even one of the tourists," Roberto said softly. "This cannot be allowed."

"It's illegal to hurt an endangered species," Celeste said stubbornly. "I'm sure Mark will agree with me."

"I doubt that very much," Roberto said slowly. He matched her steady gaze. "You should know one thing about Mark Grayson. Nothing gets in the way of his expedition. Nothing. Keep that in mind and don't worry about wild beasts, Celeste. I wouldn't want to see you hurt." He took her elbow and started back to the camp.

"I can manage," Celeste said softly but firmly. She extracted her elbow from his supporting grip. "I do want to tell Mark, but I can do it by myself. Maybe you'd better stay here."

Roberto looked at her, then at the stela. He was clearly torn between responsibilities. "What about the cat?"

"I'm sure he's long gone. Besides, I'll take another path."

"No, it isn't safe." Roberto took her arm again. "I will walk you. The students will be safe together. I can see this jaguar is going to complicate our dig even more." There was irritation in his voice.

"Roberto," Celeste said firmly, "I can manage on my own. I insist." She stepped back from him. "I insist," she repeated. "I'll probably meet Mark and the Tretorns on the way."

The sound of a rope snapping was the deciding factor.

"Watch out!" A student threw another to the ground as the rope whipped dangerously through the air. The motor whined in a shrill tone.

"Maybe I should stay." All of Roberto's attention was on the motor. "If they burn up that motor, we may never get another one. This entire rig is impossible."

"I'll be fine," Celeste assured him as she began to back down the path toward camp. She wanted a word with Mark Grayson, alone. She was shaken by the jaguar, but strangely enough she wasn't actually afraid. If the cat had intended to hurt anyone, it had had a perfect opportunity.

The trip back to the campsite was uneventful. As she approached the small cluster of huts, she found them unexpectedly empty. There was no sign of Mark or the Tretorns, or even Juanita, the cook. The camp fire was still burning, but not a soul was in evidence.

She pushed aside the colored cloth to her hut and stepped into the gloom. A splash of water on her face and neck would help her feelings, she decided, going to the washstand.

The ceramic pitcher was cool in her hand as she poured water in the basin and then ducked to splash her face. She was drying with a rough towel when she felt another presence in the room. Without turning, she tensed.

"Señorita Coolridge?"

She almost knocked over the pitcher as she spun around. The woman in the chair was short, squat and very dark-haired. She was perfectly motionless.

"Who are you?" Celeste snapped. The heavy pitcher was her only weapon and she lifted it.

"I am Maria Ibba. Thomas is my son."

Slowly Celeste returned the pitcher to the table. "You startled me," she said. A sudden thought drew her face into a frown. "Thomas is okay, isn't he? He's not injured?"

"My son is happy to be home. He is a child again."

The woman spoke softly, never moving. "I came here without Thomas, because I want to talk with you. My son has talked of only you since he returned. He says you are very smart, very eager to learn. He says you want to hear the stories." In the dim room, she stared at Celeste.

"Yes, I'm very interested." She sat down on the cot beside the woman. "Why didn't you bring Thomas?"

"I wanted to come alone. To see you." She rose suddenly with a flowing grace that belied her shortness and size. "When Thomas described you, I thought he was not telling the truth. I can see that he was." She approached Celeste slowly, extending her hand until she pushed the collar of Celeste's shirt aside. "He told me of the necklace, too."

"It's a lovely piece of work," Celeste said, disconcerted at the woman's strange behavior.

"Where did you get it?" Maria asked, her eyes scanning the artifact.

"It was a gift." Celeste shifted, bringing the collar of her shirt together.

"Gifts can show the future," Maria said suddenly. She went back to her chair and sat down again.

"What do you mean?" With some distance between them, Celeste was beginning to recover her equilibrium.

"Sometimes others see our destiny. They select the gift that shows us the way." She looked at the place where the necklace was hidden beneath Celeste's shirt. "Did you hear the jaguar last night?" she asked.

"Yes. It upset the workers."

She nodded. "The jaguar is very powerful. He has been gone for many years. Now he has returned."

"Then people in the village have seen one?" Celeste leaned forward. Her eyes had adjusted to the dimness of the hut and she could see the resemblance between Thomas and his mother. Both had the same dark and lively eyes, the same intelligence showing. She also noticed the intricate figures woven into the bodice of the woman's *huipil*.

"No, the jaguar has not been seen. Not yet, but it will. Soon he will return to his people."

Celeste hesitated. "Is there a story about a jaguar?" she asked.

Maria Ibba smiled. "The jaguar is a very sacred animal. The Maya people suffer because the jaguar has abandoned us. When the jaguar returns, it will tell of the coming of Quetzalcoatl. This will be a time of great joy for my people."

The morning seemed to hold still. In the distance, Celeste could hear the sound of laughter. Was it Rebecca Tretorn or Juanita? She couldn't be certain.

"Tell me the story," she requested softly.

"It is an old story, about the jaguar who comes to talk with our people," Maria said. "Long ago, when the Maya ruled the world, the jaguar was a prophet. He stalked the jungle and lived like a god, taking what he needed, showing his strength. My people worshiped him for his beauty and speed, for his skill at the hunt. We learned from him how to hide, soundless, in the jungle. There was a time when the jaguar and the Maya were plentiful. But that changed."

Celeste saw the slight shift in Maria's features. She was telling the story, but she was also telling the history of her people. Once the rulers of a continent, now the Maya had fallen to the bottom of the economic heap in Central America.

"One day the jaguar will return." Maria's voice strengthened. "He will bring his beauty and skill back to the jungle. He will bring new answers to the Maya people. The legend says that the jaguar will speak."

"In a human voice?" Celeste was caught up in the story, despite herself.

"That is the legend. I do not believe the jaguar will talk. Not in the voice of a man. But there are those who believe that this will happen. The scream of the jaguar last night. That was a beginning."

"I saw the cat today," Celeste said.

"You saw him?" Maria turned to face her fully. "Where?"

"Near the ruins."

"What did he do?"

"He watched me. I was afraid, but I didn't run. Then he turned and walked away."

"He made no noise or sound?"

Celeste thought for a moment. "No, he didn't."

"He will be back," she said, rising. "I must go."

"I think the cat will move on when he gets hungry. There's nothing out here for him to eat. The underbrush barely supports any life at all, much less enough meat for a big cat."

"He will not leave, Miss Coolridge. He cannot." She smiled. "He has come home."

"To Chichén Itzá?"

"Yes." At the door Maria paused. "Stay out of the jungle in the darkness. I came to tell you a story and you have given me a sign. There is a woman in the stalls outside Chichén Itzá. Her name is Carlotta Bopp. Go to her. Tell her I sent you for a charm. That is all I can do."

"What about Thomas?" Celeste asked. She had the feeling that Maria Ibba might not allow her son to return to guide her.

"Thomas must find his own path. He is a man."

The woman drew back the flap of cloth and left. For a second the hut was filled with bright sunlight, and then it was dark again.

Celeste got up and went to the doorway. She pulled back the cloth, hoping for a view of Maria Ibba walking down the road. The yellow dirt path was empty.

"Celeste!" Mark called her name. "Are you okay?" He strode toward her out of the heat and bush. "Roberto said you had a run-in with some animal."

"Yes, a jaguar." She watched the disbelief spread across his face. "I know it isn't possible. Roberto's already told me that." Her smile was rueful. "Why is it that the Maya are too willing to believe the jaguar has returned—and you and your expedition won't even consider the fact, when it's told to you by a person who is considered very responsible in real life?"

"Real life?" Mark's blue eyes grew suddenly hard. "Your real life as opposed to my make-believe dig?"

"I didn't mean it that way," Celeste said. "I meant in another world, in the business community."

"Tell me what you saw?" he said curtly.

She told him, but left out the visit by Maria Ibba. There was something there that troubled her, an implied warning. She'd been told to visit another woman to buy a charm. Her hand went to the necklace at her throat. Maria had been very interested in the design. And what was it the man who delivered it to her had said? Wear it at all times and it will protect you against your enemies. She heard the vague echo of his words.

"Celeste?" Mark had stepped closer to her. "Are you okay?"

The hardness was gone from his eyes and she saw true concern. "Yes. The cat gave me a scare, but he didn't do anything. He just looked and walked away."

"Can you take me to the place where you saw him?"

"I think so. But why?"

"Roberto was right. We'll have to do something. Maybe trap him and move him."

"Mark!"

"Listen to me. If we don't, then someone around here will just shoot him. These people can't afford to lose a chicken or pig or goat, or whatever they have, to a cat. That's why the species is extinct around here."

"I thought it was because the rule of the Maya ended."

The words had a startling effect on Mark. He walked up to her. "Where did you hear that?"

She stepped away from him, sorry that she had repeated Maria's words. It would only make trouble.

"Celeste, that sounds like something one of Wilfredo's men would say."

"I understand there are a lot of old legends." She held back the fact of Maria's visit. Relations with the villagers were strained. Mark might take it the wrong way. She pointed toward the path where she'd seen the cat. "Let me try and find the spot. I was frightened and a little disoriented, but I think I can manage. I went this way."

Mark walked behind her. "No wonder you got lost. You're headed due north. This is the path to an old site we worked months back. It does eventually wind up at the stela, but it's more direct to the cenote," Mark said.

"I'll remember that," she said, biting back the comment that if she'd had a guide, she wouldn't have gotten lost.

She took him to the spot where she'd seen the cat. "Right in this area, I think," she said.

In the hard-baked earth, there was no sign. Mark searched the area for a while, then gave it up. "Why don't we walk on to the cenote and you can see it? The sacred well has an interesting history."

"What about the cat?"

Mark shook his head. "The best we can do now is to hope he's moved on. He could be thirty miles from here. If he's smart, he'll keep moving until he finds some better territory. There's nothing here to sustain him."

"I hope you're right." Celeste fell into step beside Mark. "He was magnificent."

They traveled through the jungle with Mark explaining in a casual manner along the way. The path was called the Sacred Way and went directly from the center of Chichén Itzá for about three hundred meters to the well.

At the lip of the cenote, Celeste paused. It was a long drop to the water. A very long drop. The area was surrounded by dense growth and a small altar had been cleared. Mark didn't have to tell her that this was the place of ritual sacrifice.

"Why did they do it?" she asked. "I mean throw people into the wells."

Mark moved to the altar and sat down. "The first rule was to appease the gods. I'm certain, too, that it was a convenient way to get rid of political adversaries. It was a risky business, though. If the victim lived, he or she became a prophet. The prophet would know what the gods wanted and expected.''

"Sounds like a position with a lot of clout.''

Mark laughed easily. "That's an understatement. You know, this cenote has been dredged. Hundreds of artifacts were retrieved. Humans weren't the only things they sacrificed to the gods.''

"I wondered why you weren't working here.''

"The cenote has been thoroughly explored.''

"Did you say it was safe for a swim?'' she looked at him expectantly. There was a path that twisted down the steep incline and appeared to go to the water's edge.

"You wouldn't want to stir up any angry spirits, would you?''

For the first time all day, Celeste relaxed. That easy, teasing note was back in Mark's voice. "For a cold swim, I'd risk it.''

"No suit,'' he pointed out.

"It doesn't matter,'' Celeste answered as she moved along the path, spiraling down to the bank of the cenote to a place where others had gone in before her. "Aren't you coming in?''

"I'll watch and make sure you're safe.'' He found a seat on the bank. "Go on. Just remember, there are those who say that the cenote has no bottom.''

The water was icy, and for one moment, Celeste had a terrible sensation that something lurked beneath the impenetrable water. All doubts fled once she was immersed and stroking in the cold water. Even with her shorts and top on, the feel of the water was delicious on her skin.

From his seat on the altar, Mark watched her cut smoothly through the water. She was very graceful, perhaps even more so in water than on land. That was something he hadn't expected. But she was from Florida. Probably grew up in a pool. He watched her flip onto her back and float for a while. Her long red hair shifted out beside her head. Her eyes were closed, giving her the appearance of a deep sleep.

"This is wonderful," she called up to him, but she didn't open her eyes. "Are you sure you won't come in?"

"Maybe later," he said. "At the end of the day. Then I can relax."

"Another few minutes and I'll get out," she promised.

"Take your time." He enjoyed watching her. There was something childlike in her pleasure that he found gratifying. She was on her side now, stroking across the pool.

A movement in the underbrush across the cenote caught his attention. For one eerie moment, he half expected to see a hungry jaguar walk out of the bush. Instead, he caught only the shadow of a human. The man, or woman, slipped away before he could even be certain of the gender. All he knew was that he was being watched, and he didn't like the feeling.

He stood up, intending to explore, but he didn't like the idea of leaving Celeste alone in the water. He encouraged the students and other members of the dig to swim in pairs. It was a good safety rule.

"Celeste." He called down to her softly as he moved around to help her out.

"Okay." She turned her face into the water and stroked rapidly to shore. "I feel like a new human," she said as she took his hand and came out of the water. "What is it?" The look on his face stopped her, as she grabbed the hem of her shirt to wring out the excess water.

"I should get back to the others. Roberto's been working with the stela all morning, and it hasn't been an easy day."

"Of course." She slipped into the leather sandals. "Let's go." She took the path back to camp, aware that her clothes were clinging to her body with a certain unavoidable suggestiveness. They would dry in a matter of moments in the hot Mexican sun.

"What with all of the excitement, I haven't had a chance to learn anything about this dig. Maybe this afternoon I could help Wilfredo or Roberto, or wherever you need an extra pair of hands.''

When Mark didn't answer, she turned around. He had stopped on the path and was staring back at the greenery surrounding the cenote.

''What is it?''

''Nothing.'' Mark answered, moving toward her. He'd seen the figure once again, and he'd seen enough to know it wasn't Roberto, the Tretorns or one of the graduate students. The figure was too short. It had been a squat person, solid and fully fleshed. And Mark had the distinct impression that whoever it was had been spying on Celeste, not him.

Chapter Five

Imix, bad. The 13th Maya month begins. The moment of revelation approaches. Read and prepare. Those who doubt will perish.

"Thomas!" Celeste rose from the waist-deep trench and brushed her hands against her khaki shorts. The only thing accomplished was a cloud of dust rising about her. "Welcome!" She ignored the dirt and went to the boy, giving him a quick hug. "Did you come to see what work I've done? Yesterday I found my first piece of pottery. You would have thought it was a twelve-carat diamond. It was very exciting."

"*Sí,*" he said without his normal enthusiasm. He took in the scene of dirt-streaked workers scraping and sifting. His expression remained despondent.

"Would it be okay if I took a break?" Celeste called to Roberto. He was twenty feet away, excavating a trench with the help of three graduate students and two grousing Tretorns.

"You aren't on the clock," Roberto reminded her.

"Let's take a walk," she whispered to Thomas, drawing him away from the group. She could feel the tension in his thin shoulder. "I was afraid your mother wouldn't let you come back."

"She doesn't know I'm here," Thomas said. "She thinks I've gone to visit my cousins, so I can't stay long."

"You shouldn't disobey your mother." Her high spirits took a tremendous dive. She was delighted to see the boy, but she couldn't encourage him to go against his mother's wishes.

"She's wrong," he said flatly. "She thinks something is going to happen. She thinks it's because of you."

"What are you talking about?" Celeste was more amused than upset. Maria Ibba was a woman of strong convictions and great imagination. The ancient stories governed much of the woman's life and there was nothing Celeste would be able to do to change that. She could only be Thomas's friend, and downplay the situation. "We haven't found much more than that shard of pottery. Mark's been foiled in lifting the stela because the equipment isn't powerful enough, and there's something about the materials that he has to be so careful. Nothing's happening here, except sweat, dirt and insects." She smiled to try and lighten the boy's mood.

"My mother has been acting odd. I hear whispers, bits and pieces, and she talks about you."

"She came to visit me," Celeste said.

"I thought she might." Thomas shook his head. "Be careful, *señorita*. There is a bad feel in the whispers of the village. I am worried for you, for the people who dig in the ruins."

"Will you be able to return to Cancún with me?" Celeste sat down in the shade of a tree and Thomas sat across from her.

"My mother is opposed, but my father says she is being an old woman." He shrugged. "We will see. How is the dig?"

"Hot," she said with a laugh, "but there is a fascination. Working in the dirt, sifting through the sand and rock, the excitement is an undercurrent. There is the chance that the past will come to life in your hands. I really feel like I'm helping. At least I've tried hard." She'd had little chance to talk with Mark, but several times she'd seen him walk by with an approving look in his eyes. She'd shown him how a "tourist" could work.

"Then your uncle was a smart man to arrange this trip."

"Uncle Alec." Celeste said the name with a combination of affection and dismay. "I've been so caught up in the work here that I haven't really even thought about my life in Tampa."

"Don't go back," Thomas said simply. "Stay in Mexico."

"If it were only that easy." She tousled his hair. For a split second the possibility of a life in Mexico tantalized her. She'd found a new value system in the hard work, the minute discovery of a stone blade or trinket. For the first time in years, she felt as if she were truly doing something important and not just profitable. "If I stay here I won't be able to help you get that job in the British Secret Service."

"Then you must go back," Thomas said, his face a wide open smile. "You will sacrifice yourself for me, no?"

"*Sí,*" she said and then laughed. "Can you stay for dinner with us? Juanita is a very good cook."

Thomas shook his head and rose slowly to his feet. "I must go home. But I will be here Saturday if I can. If not, then I will try to meet you at the hotel in Cancún. If I am not there by the following morning, you must arrange for a new guide."

The boy looked so sad that Celeste hugged him quickly. "There is no other guide for me. You have to know that when I return to Cancún I'll probably head back to the States very soon. But I'm sure things will work out. Perhaps, before I go, I might talk with your mother."

"Perhaps," Thomas said, but there was not a hopeful note in his voice. "*Vaya con dios, señorita.*"

"*Buenos tarde,* Thomas."

She watched the small figure in the white shirt retreat into the evening sun. The day had been long, and sitting on the ground she realized she was bone weary. Thank goodness it was time for the evening meal. In the past few days she'd adjusted to a routine of food, work and sleep. If she'd had some hesitation about Uncle Alec's vacation plans for her, she had to admit that he'd picked the perfect scheme. She was too tired to worry about what she couldn't control, and working in the ruins made Tampa and her past life seem a million miles away.

Thomas had said to stay in Mexico. Strange, but the country had narrowed down to the Chichén Itzá ruins. A plot of enduring buildings ... and a man who was as rugged and tough as the terrain. Mark Grayson was like no other man she'd ever known. He worked hard, without expecting personal gain. At least not monetary. He worked because he believed in what he was doing. They'd had little opportunity to talk, but she'd seen him watching her, and she thought she saw respect in his eyes.

"No sandbagging."

She turned to confront Roberto, who had walked to the shade without making a sound. "I got worried about you. I think you may be the hardest working tourist we've ever had."

"Thomas just left."

"He's a cute boy."

"Cute and bright." She sighed. "Is it time to eat?"

"I think so. At least it's time to quit." He offered her his arm and they started toward camp. "I have a confession to make, Celeste."

There was a secretive tone to his voice and Celeste laughed. "I'm not sure I'm the right person, but go ahead and spill it."

"The first night you were in Cancún, I followed you from the airport. I wanted to ask you to dinner, but once you went into your hotel, I decided not to."

"That's strange." Celeste turned to look at him. "Thomas said someone was following us, but I thought it was him playing at James Bond. He has quite an imagination."

"And apparently a good eye for detecting tails." Roberto laughed. "So, I was thwarted on my first attempt. Would you have dinner with me when you return to Cancún?'' He squeezed her arm lightly.

"I didn't realize you ever left the dig," she answered to give herself time to think.

"Seldom, but for a special occasion exceptions are made. It is Mark who refuses to leave. I," he touched her cheek, "realize that a beautiful woman is reason enough. Especially one who works so hard. You have earned my respect, *señorita*."

"Dinner would be fun, Roberto," Celeste said quickly, turning away from his hungry gaze. She liked Roberto and found him warm and charming, but not in a romantic way. "I'll probably be returning to the States the next day, and it would be nice to have a farewell dinner with some of my friends from the dig. Maybe Mark will break his rule and join us." They were almost at the camp clearing and she felt a slight relief. Roberto was one intense man.

"I don't think so," Roberto said with a wicked grin. "I have no intention of asking him."

Before Celeste could offer a protest, Mark stepped to the edge of the camp clearing and motioned them to his hut. He poured three shots of local tequila. "It's been a hard day and there's an even harder evening to come."

"*Sí*, that is true," Roberto said, tapping his glass with Celeste's. "Daniel is expected here in the next hour."

"Daniel?" Celeste was blank.

"Our beneficiary. Our bankroll. The man who calls the shots," Roberto said in an imitation of clipped big-city talk.

The two men looked at each other, exchanging hidden meanings. "Should we tell her?" Roberto asked.

Mark hesitated.

"Is the man an ogre or what?" Celeste asked, unable to resist the air of secretiveness the two men shared.

"Oh, Mr. Ortiz is very cultured, very wealthy. He is an impeccable host, and he will love you," Roberto assured her. "He will want to throw a party in your honor, because you are so beautiful."

"I don't like this," Celeste said, shifting her gaze from one man to another. Mark looked away.

"You will enjoy Daniel," Roberto said, adding a splash of tequila to her drink. His gaze held hers a moment. "He is an interesting man who has accomplished a lot in the business world. He will find you delightful."

"There's a chance you could convince Mr. Ortiz to put a little extra money into this operation," Roberto added quickly.

"Roberto!" Mark's disapproval was evident in his tone.

"It's true." Roberto gave a Latin shrug. "He would give the money sooner, if Celeste asked. If she showed some enthusiasm, talked about how wonderful he was to have an interest, you know the line." He looked at Celeste. "It isn't actually a lie. You have become very involved in this dig. If we had more equipment, more money, we might be able to move faster."

Celeste felt a wave of heat on her face. She turned to Mark. "When did you two think up this plan?"

"As soon as we heard Daniel would be visiting this week," Roberto cut in. "Daniel has a fondness for beautiful women. It wouldn't hurt to ask."

A drum-like beat was throbbing in her temple when she looked back at Mark. "And this was your idea?" So much for the theory that Mark respected her.

"I said that it might prove beneficial for Daniel to see you. You're enthusiastic. You seem to have a talent for understanding the work." Mark picked up the bottle from the table and studied its contents.

"Mark said it would be the first time a tourist ever contributed anything significant to a dig," Roberto said. He went to Celeste and put his hand on her shoulder. "You could help us. It could make all the difference in the world."

Celeste carefully set her untouched drink on the table. Mixed with the drumbeat of anger was acute disappointment. She wanted to be alone. "Excuse me," she said softly. "I need to get ready for dinner."

"Celeste," Roberto said, starting to follow her. "It was only a suggestion."

"I'll think about it," she said over her shoulder. She picked up speed and hurried to her hut. She threw back the cloth and entered the semidarkness with a sense of despair. A wall of anger seemed to smash into her as she sat on the cot. She thought she'd begun to earn Mark and Roberto's respect. Even the graduate students were thawing a little. But it was all a sham. Her real contribution could only come as a cheap hustle, at least that was the way Mark looked at it. She blinked back hot tears. Well, the lesson she'd learned was that archaeological digs were not too much different from selling stocks and bonds. People used other people as much and as often as they could.

She went to the basin and washed her face and hands. Well, she wasn't going to let them know how deeply they'd cut her. She was hypersensitive, after the lies and accusations leveled against her in Tampa. She thought about going back to Cancún in the morning, but she immediately rejected that idea. She'd signed on for six days, and she'd give them six days of hard work.

She left the hut and settled at the table for dinner. Instead of the easy camaraderie she'd developed with Mark, Roberto, Wilfredo and the others, she chose to direct her conversation to the Tretorns. It was easier to let Rebecca run on and on about her shoe business. After all, neither of the shoe-dynasty owners really seemed interested in the dig. They spent most of their time swimming in the cenote or at the local vendors' stalls outside the ruins buying souvenirs. What little work Rebecca did, at Charles's urging, was apathetic. Rebecca had the attitude that only a major chest of treasure was worth any effort at all.

The students and workers had finished eating and left, when Celeste heard a small commotion and knew that Daniel Ortiz had arrived. She wasn't prepared for the elegant, silver-haired man who stepped out of the darkness and into the circle of lamplight at the table. He was close to her uncle's age, a man who wore his successes with ease and confidence.

"This is Daniel Ortiz," Mark made the introductions, starting with Charles. At Celeste, he hesitated for a brief moment, then spoke briefly of her work as a stockbroker.

"I see that my plan to allow tourists to participate in the dig was a good one," Daniel said in English which rose and fell with the rhythm of a man whose native language was Spanish. "It's always pleasant to be right."

"Our progress is hampered by a lack of equipment," Mark said before Daniel Ortiz could even find a seat. "We need more money, Daniel. We're operating on a shoestring, and that's a dangerous way to run a business."

"This isn't a business," Daniel said calmly, accepting the drink that Roberto brought to him. He settled down across from Celeste. "This is a hobby. I've never made a penny from this expedition and I don't expect I ever will. You know that, Mark. I fund this thing because I want to, and I give it as much money as I can. I'm not a Rockefeller, though."

"You have plenty of money for..."

Mark was cut off by Roberto's smooth interjection. "We're hoping to lift the stela this week, Daniel. I hope you can stay tomorrow and watch. The work has been very disappointing, especially for Mark. He's obsessed with this ruby, as you well know. If we could find that stone, you might actually see some returns on your investment."

Daniel laughed. "I really don't care if I make money or not. I just can't afford to lose an unlimited amount." He turned to Mark. "I give you what I can. It's the best I can do for now."

Mark nodded. "It's frustrating. I feel that we're close to a breakthrough." He took a swallow of his drink.

"So, have any of your people fallen victim to the curse of the Jaguar's Eye?" Daniel asked. He raised both eyebrows. "I've been doing a little research myself. The ruby is supposed to be hexed, you know."

Around the table Celeste and the Tretorns moved in closer. "What ruby?" Rebecca asked, showing more interest than she had in days. "No one mentioned there was a ruby to be found. I knew there was treasure here, though!"

"You haven't told your guests what they're looking for! An incredible ruby!" Daniel said in amazement. "Tell them, Mark."

Mark slowly looked around the group, his gaze lingering on Celeste for only a split second. She could see his discomfort.

"Those of you who've been in the inner pyramid have seen the jaguar throne. There was also a carving at one time." His gaze slipped back to Celeste. "The eye had special significance. It was believed that the ruby disappeared when the Maya lost favor with the gods. When the ruby is returned to the jaguar carving, then the fates will turn for the Maya. They will prosper once again. This is all in combination with some fertility beliefs, and of course the reincarnation of Quetzalcoatl."

"And what about the curse?" Rebecca asked.

A chill flicked across Celeste's skin as she listened. All of the old legends were filled with gods and magic. They were fun to listen to, but there was something a little macabre about them.

"It is said that the person who finds the ruby has a chance at becoming a god, or a terrible death," Mark finished lamely.

"I don't believe you have a prayer of finding the ruby," Daniel said. His gaze shifted to Celeste and held. "But I have to admit that at least you have some beautiful help in the search."

"Miss Coolridge is a very hard worker," Mark said quickly. "She's distinguished herself. It is unfortunate that we haven't made any really interesting discoveries while she's been here. I'm afraid she'll lose interest and leave."

"Not a chance," she said clearly. If he thought he could dismiss her so casually, he was mistaken. "I'm here for as long as I said. That's something you should know about me, Mr. Grayson. I don't quit.''

Her words held a clear challenge that strained the atmosphere.

"My, my, a woman with spirit," Daniel looked across the table at Mark and lifted one eyebrow. "Could it be that something more than the dig is frustrating you?" He laughed and was joined by the Tretorns and Roberto. Only Celeste and Mark did not join in.

"I am only teasing my most serious archaeologist," Daniel said after a few moments. "I apologize, Miss Coolridge, if I used you to take a shot at Mark. He is too much the dedicated worker, too little the man."

"So I've been told," Mark said in a light voice. If he felt any anger at being the butt of the joke, he didn't show it. "But let's hear what brings Daniel to Chichén Itzá."

"I find the work of uncovering the ancient past endlessly fascinating." He turned to Celeste. "But the real reason I'm here is a personal mission." He patted his coat pocket. "I have a message for you, Miss Coolridge."

"For me?" she was startled enough to lean forward. "From who?"

"Perhaps we could take a walk." He stood and held out his hand to her.

Feeling that all eyes were boring into her, Celeste stood also. She caught a satisfied look in Roberto's eye and wondered for a brief second if she'd been set up. There was no time to hesitate. Daniel took her arm and began to walk toward the ruins.

"Your uncle asked me to deliver something to you," he said as soon as they were out of earshot of the others. He reached into the white linen jacket he wore and pulled out an envelope. He handed it to her as they continued to walk.

"Thanks." Celeste held the letter, consumed with curiosity but unable to read in the darkness. "How do you know Uncle Alec?"

"As I mentioned earlier, real-estate development is my business. Though San Diego is my base I have an interest in properties throughout the United States, and in Florida, in particular. That's a market that will always grow."

"But how did Uncle Alec know to send a message by you?" She'd never heard her uncle speak of a Daniel Ortiz. The connection eluded her.

"Alec called me about some properties he wanted to sell several months ago." He paused. "I suppose that I was actually the one who gave him the idea for your vacation in Mexico. I hope you haven't been disappointed."

"Not in the least." Celeste stepped back a pace. "It's been invigorating." She couldn't help but wonder how much Uncle Alec had told this man about her troubles. She didn't care to press the issue.

"Well, I've monopolized you long enough. I'm sure you're eager to read your message." He turned back toward the camp. "You're lucky to have someone like Alec Mason to look out for you."

"I know," Celeste said, feeling much better as they drew nearer to the clearing. "By sending me to Chichén Itzá, Uncle Alec has opened an entirely new world to me. It is very exciting, and worthwhile, I believe. Mark is terribly dedicated."

"I know that," Daniel said, then added a chuckle. "He's obsessed. But then his father was like that. Such a loss."

"You knew him?"

"Yes, I was one of the backers of his expedition."

"Then you're aware of the dangers of poor equipment?" The question popped out of her mouth before she had time to consider the consequences or implications.

"Yes. Marcus Grayson was a personal friend of mine. To his credit, Mark has never mentioned the accident in a request for funding."

"Would you have helped?" she asked bluntly.

He shook his head. "No. As I told Mark earlier, I give what I can to keep the expedition operating. Since you have such an interest, maybe we could drum up some additional backers."

Celeste's stomach took a sudden turn. This was too much the scene Roberto had suggested and she'd stumbled into it in all innocence. "Mr. Ortiz, the work being done is valuable. That should be reason enough. My interest is insignificant."

"Perhaps," he agreed, "but you are a businesswoman, Miss Coolridge. In selling stocks and bonds you have certainly become wise enough to allow each man his own reasons for buying...or contributing."

"You're right, of course." She slipped her arm from his at the edge of the camp. "Thank you for delivering my letter. When will you be returning, in case I have a reply for my uncle?"

"Tomorrow or the next day." He lifted her hand and kissed it with a swift, sure motion. "It would be a pleasure to carry your answer." He turned on his heel and went toward Mark's hut. Celeste was left standing alone in the clearing.

The kerosene lanterns had been extinguished, except for one on the main table. She sat in one of the wooden chairs and lifted the unsealed flap on the envelope.

My dearest Celeste,
New developments have taken an unexpected turn. Beware of Barry Undine. Use extreme caution in everything you do. I am relieved that you are safely out of the country. I am afraid Barry may be an extremely dangerous man. Stay at the dig, and stay safe. Call when you return to Cancún.

                                                    Love, Alec

She folded the letter and held it in her hand. Barry Undine. She saw the broker's angry face thrust at her as she prepared to leave the building. She'd suspected his ethics, and his temper. But to find that he was actually involved in framing her... The only problem was how he'd done it. She opened the letter and read it again. She felt as if a tremendous weight had suddenly been lifted from her shoulders.

Uncle Alec was clearing her name. Soon she could return to her job in Tampa.

The sensation of jubilation lasted only a few seconds. But did she want to return to that life? Certainly she wanted her name cleared. As for the rest—the pressure and tension and long hours of watching financial markets move and shift— was that what she really wanted?

"I don't know," she whispered into the night. She looked up at the black sky with millions of stars. Since coming to Chichén Itzá she'd found a new purpose in her life. It wasn't that she thought she might become an archaeologist. What she had discovered was that there were other jobs, other careers, that gave as much or more satisfaction. There was a different pace to life that allowed her to look around at the beauties of her world.

"Celeste?"

She clutched her letter and whirled around. In the dim light, she saw Mark Grayson's lanky body.

"I wanted to talk with you about what Roberto said. It didn't come out exactly right."

"You've always been totally honest about your opinion of tourists, Mark. I don't know why I was shocked. Forget it."

He stepped closer until the lantern's glow fell on his penetrating eyes. "It isn't okay with me. I won't be viewed as some sexist because that makes it easier for you to leave here. I was unfair to you when we first met, but I didn't plan on sending you up as the sacrifical lamb for Ortiz!"

For some reason his angry words calmed Celeste. His emotion seemed real and honest, and she waited to hear what else he had to say. "Go on."

"Roberto thought it would be a good idea if you asked about additional funding, that's true. I disagreed. In theory I understood what he meant to accomplish, and I agreed with him. It's just that it sounded sordid and manipulative, and I didn't want you linked with anything like that."

"I see," she said.

"I thought Roberto had put the plan out of his head."

"You thought wrong," she said, thinking about her conversation with Ortiz. There was no point relaying it to Mark. Daniel didn't seem interested in granting additional funds and with Mark as touchy as he was, he might get irritated by the fact that his father's name was mentioned.

Mark moved to the seat beside her. "You've done some hard work this week. Not even a run-in with a jaguar could scare you away." He smiled and leaned forward to rest his elbows on his knees.

"I've enjoyed the work, and found a measure of...peace here." She looked into the night. "I've two days left, and I'm hoping you get the stela up."

"Tomorrow," Mark promised. "Instead of working with Roberto, come with me tomorrow. I want you to be there when we lift it."

"I'd like that," she said.

The sound of running feet came through the silent night, and the moment of intimacy was shattered. Mark turned expectantly to the sound that came from the north.

"Mark! Mark!" There was panic in the voice that Celeste recognized as Wilfredo's.

"I'm here." Mark stood swiftly and grasped the lantern. "Wilfredo, what is it?"

The Maya foreman rushed into the clearing, his eyes wide open with fear. "It's Timma. He's dead."

"Dead?" Mark took a step forward and moved the lantern closer to Wilfredo's face. "How?"

"It looks like some animal has attacked him." Wilfredo looked behind him in the darkness. "It is the work of the jaguar."

Chapter Six

The sequence of thirteen is complete. It is the day of Cauac, a bad omen. It is cold. Beware of cold places that do evil. When cold spreads at dawn, a time of fog and many clouds, the curse of doubt will fall upon the people.

Mark knelt beside the body and felt for a pulse at the throat. In the glare of several flashlights, Celeste could tell it was hopeless. Timma was dead. The jaguar had done a thorough job. She averted her eyes from the body and focused on Mark. He was swamped by dismay and, if she knew him at all, a feeling of responsibility.

"Mark," she said softly, touching him.

He felt Celeste's touch on his shoulder and he stood. There was nothing he could do. Timma was beyond all help. One of his employees was dead.

Wilfredo covered the body with a blanket. In the background, Rebecca Tretorn gave a gasp and turned her face into her husband's shoulder.

"This is going to make trouble," Daniel Ortiz said, breaking the silence of the night. His face appeared beaded with sweat. "This is horrible. I'm not sure where we stand legally. I'll have to call the insurance agency right away."

"I doubt Timma's family has the sophistication to think of a lawsuit," Mark answered angrily. "I wouldn't worry about that."

"That isn't what I meant. Wait a minute, Mark," Daniel said.

Mark didn't answer. He took Celeste's arm and turned her back toward the camp as Wilfredo and another worker shifted the body onto a wooden stretcher. Timma had been killed while on guard duty beside the stela.

Mark's long strides moved them ahead of the rest of the group. When they were out of earshot, Celeste slowed her pace slightly.

"You were a little hard on Mr. Ortiz. After all, he's a businessman." She spoke quietly, aware of how deeply Mark felt his responsibilities toward his employees. She could not forget, either, that Mark's father had died on a dig.

"For Daniel, the bottom line is the most important factor. We've been consistently shorthanded. Overworked. Tired to the point of being careless. You're right; Daniel's a businessman. But sometimes . . ." He took a deep breath. "Some things should be more important than money."

They walked for several moments in silence. "What will you do?" Celeste asked. She could feel his sorrow and frustration. There was little she could do, except offer her support.

"I'll go into the village and tell his family. Tomorrow we'll hunt for the cat. I was careless not to pursue this matter when you saw it. I never believed a wild animal would stay around a place as populated as the ruins." The edge of frustration cracked his voice. "There's a highway not half a mile from here."

"What can I do?" she asked. In the few days she'd been at the ruins, she'd never seen Mark Grayson hesitate with an order. Now he did.

"There's a chance the local help will all quit. I know you came to dig, but could you give Roberto a hand in the morning with breakfast? Then plan on meeting me at the stela. I have an idea."

"You can't lift it without help." Timma's tragic death was affecting Mark's reasoning ability. "Maybe we should wait a few days, until after the funeral or..."

"I can't wait. Nothing will stop me." The grim determination that was part of his character was back in clear view.

"What about the villagers?" she asked. She was worried about the repercussions. There was already trouble. The killing of Timma, especially by a jaguar, would only stir up old fears and resentments. "This could be ticklish, Mark."

"I know." He slowed his pace. "I also know I can't quit working. Maybe you could help me explain. The villagers like you. Thomas has seen to that. They need to understand that Timma's death really doesn't have anything to do with the dig."

"I'll go with you to the village. Maybe Thomas can help." Celeste felt a clinch of apprehension. Roberto had warned her of Mark's obsession with finding the Jaguar's Eye. Now she was seeing it.

"I'd appreciate that," he said, catching her hand and squeezing it. "We also can't let this get blown out of proportion in Daniel's eyes."

"Is there a chance?"

"Yes," Mark said. He turned back down the path. In the distance the low but urgent sounds of Roberto and Daniel talking came to them.

"I'll do what I can," Celeste said. "I don't know how much help that will be."

"If we can move that stela," Mark said, thinking out loud.

"Yes, the stela," Celeste answered. A chill touched her bare arms and legs and made her shiver. She wasn't certain if it was caused by Mark's attitude, or by the thought of what might be the cost of exposing the stela.

AT TIMMA'S HOME, Mark spoke softly with the widow in Spanish and explained what had happened. He left Celeste with the woman as he went to help make the necessary arrangements.

The news spread rapidly through the village, and soon Celeste found herself an unnecessary stranger in a communal scene of grieving and sympathy. In the small, round house with earthen floors, she felt worse than useless as woman after woman came inside. Timma's widow cried silently but with a total despair that tore at Celeste.

The women clustered about, offering condolences and prayers. It took a while for Celeste to understand that the women were talking of the misfortune as if it were an act of fate, or an act of the angry gods. The turn in conversation made her feel ill at ease. She was preparing to edge toward the door when the colorful cloth that served as a door was pushed aside.

Maria Ibba entered the room on a sudden hush. Celeste met the woman's eyes, and the silence in the room deepened. She felt the sidelong glances cast her way from everyone in the room. She was an outsider at a time of grief, but was it more than that?

"Hello, Maria," she said softly. "How is Thomas?"

"Leave my son alone," she said, but her voice was lacking hostility. "I do not want him to suffer because of you."

"I would never do anything to hurt Thomas." She was shocked by the implication, and confused by the way Maria looked at her, with pity and a strange respect.

Maria's dark gaze held hers. "I know that, *señorita*. There are many things beyond our control. Timma is dead because he did not believe in the old ones. He was warned not to take the money of foreigners, not to destroy the home of the gods. He wouldn't listen."

"Timma was on guard duty. He was alone and he was attacked. The victim could have been Mark or me or any one of us," Celeste said in halting Spanish. "This was an accident. A tragic accident."

The cloth door rippled, and a tall, dramatic woman draped in multicolored shawls entered. She paused for a moment at the door, assessing the room, and then went to the widow and offered words of sympathy in a low, throaty voice. She left the crying widow to turn to Celeste.

"You have brought bad news," she said simply. She stared at Celeste with open curiosity.

"It was a tragic accident," Celeste said. "We're very upset."

"You are upset." There was anger in the voice. "This woman has lost her man. How will she feed her children? Who will comfort her at night? What is an accident to you is the end of her life." She waited for an answer.

The direct accusation stiffened Celeste's will. "Her husband did not die because Mr. Grayson was negligent. Timma could have been attacked and killed while walking along the road. The things you say are unjust."

"But he wasn't!" The woman moved closer, her dark eyes gleaming with hostility. "He was killed while helping the white man rob the ruins. The gods have shown us their anger."

"Carlotta," Maria Ibba stepped forward and took the other woman's arm. "Señorita Coolridge is only a visitor at the ruins."

"They are all visitors in my homeland," Carlotta said angrily. "She is the most dangerous of all." She brushed back Celeste's collar in one swift movement. "She wears the snake as if it were her right!"

Celeste forced herself not to flinch. "The necklace was a gift. I'm sorry if it offends you. I'm not aware of the meaning that it has for you. I was told it would protect me from my enemies." She took a breath. "I don't know what will happen in the future at Chichén Itzá, but I know Mark wants to help the Maya people. I should leave now." She went to Timma's widow. "I am terribly sorry," she murmured before she walked out the door.

In the cool night air she was able to breathe at last. Her fingers touched the jade figure of the snake at her chest. Why had a necklace generated such hostility from Carlotta Bopp? It was an interesting work, but certainly not that valuable.

At the edge of the yard she heard a small hissing noise. The sound made her feel as if a snake had crawled inside her skin. She kept walking. The last thing she needed was a confrontation with another of the Indians. She needed to find Mark and get back to camp.

The noise came again.

"Señorita!" The voice was that of a young boy.

"Thomas?" She examined the darkness but saw no sign of him.

In a moment he slipped toward her from the shelter of a small tree. He nodded toward the house. "Carlotta Bopp is very angry. She is one of the ones who want the archaeologists to leave Chichén Itzá."

"Who is she?" Celeste asked. The woman had been formidable.

"She has a stall where she sells to the tourists. She is very powerful in the village. Many people listen to her. You must be careful. I think she is jealous of you."

The words rang in Celeste's head. She'd had another message only a few hours earlier warning her to beware of a Tampa stockbroker. Barry Undine at least had a reason to be jealous. Carlotta Bopp was coming from left field. "Thanks for the warning, but I'm sure things will be fine," she said to Thomas. He looked far too worried for a twelve-year-old. "Mark will work it all out."

"Saturday," Thomas said, touching her arm. "We will go back to Cancún. This will all be over. I must go home before my mother finds I am out."

"Good night, Thomas," she called to his disappearing back. She felt a pang of guilt that Thomas had overheard his mother. The boy was incredibly loyal, and he was pulled in two directions now.

Somewhere in the small village a baby cried in the night. Celeste felt very much alone and unprotected. Outside the boundaries of the settlement was a wild animal that had killed a man. She, who'd always been surrounded by the trappings of civilization, found that she was afraid.

She said little to Mark when he picked her up to return to the ruins. He, too, was silent. The tragedy of Timma's death overwhelmed them. At the opening of her hut, Mark touched her shoulder and turned her to face him.

"I'm not unaware of the needs of the villagers. It's just that if I don't unravel the mystery of the Jaguar's Eye soon, I might not have a chance. I get the feeling that this entire expedition is coming down around my ears."

"I'm not here to judge your priorities," Celeste answered. She had to be truthful. She was troubled.

"Thanks for your help. For your concern." He touched her cheek with the tips of his fingers.

"You're welcome." She could hardly speak over the tightening of her throat. His fingers were rough but gentle. His touch was unexpected, so much softer than she had expected. She realized suddenly that she had thought of his touch. At some point, she'd imagined it. It was a disturbing idea, and she turned slightly away.

"See you in the morning." He bent quickly and kissed her cheek. Then he was gone into the night.

"Celeste!" The word floated to her from the camp clearing and she recognized Roberto's voice.

"Yes?"

"I'm standing guard, so don't worry. Try to sleep."

"Thanks, Roberto." She entered her hut and prepared for the long night.

Not even the strenuous work she'd endured brought sleep, and Celeste found her body tired and her mind exhausted when the sun rose the next morning. She hurried to the cooking hut and helped a bleary-eyed Roberto put together breakfast.

Neither Mark nor the Tretorns ever appeared, and Celeste hurried through the mealtime ritual as fast as possible. She had a moment's hesitation about setting out alone for the stela. She found Roberto's gaze on her speculative. He reached into his belt and drew out a gun.

"Take it," he said. "Mark asked me to give it to you."

"What about you?" She knew how to use a pistol. Her father had taken her target shooting as a child, and she'd often shot skeet with Uncle Alec and his clients.

"I'm not going into the jungle today," he said. "And re-member, if the jaguar shows himself, kill him. There is no room for compassion now."

She nodded, tucking the gun into her own belt. "Thanks."

Hurrying down the path, she felt the gun against her hip. She wasn't certain it made her feel any safer. It was with great relief that she found Mark, coated in thick dust, lean-ing on a shovel at the stela.

The column was six feet long and at least three feet wide, a massive hunk of stone with a delicate composition. Ce-leste eyed it with doubt. No matter what master plan Mark had come up with, the stela was going to be hard to maneu-ver. Not even the powerful motor Mark had shipped in from the States had been able to budge it.

"I suppose you've got Hercules tucked away somewhere in the jungle," she said, walking to Mark's side.

"We're not going to lift it," he said. He bent over the large stone monument and adjusted a rope.

"Thank goodness for that. Maybe it will stand up on its own," Celeste answered.

"Don't think we've given up." He stood and motioned her closer. "We're going to roll it over. A simple solution that has eluded me in my single-minded pursuits."

"Roll it?" The stone looked as if it would take a team of elephants to budge it. "I don't know..."

"Leverage is the proper word." He reached for the rope pull on the motor. "Leverage, and the fact that I spent the entire night digging under it by lamplight. If we can just get enough leverage to get it started, it should roll." He jerked the cord and kicked on the motor.

As Celeste watched, the slack went out of the rope. A long pole was thrust into her hands and she took it. At Mark's direction, she placed it against the stela with another rock for leverage.

"Now push down on the pole," Mark said as he took up a similar stance and threw his weight.

To Celeste's amazement, the heavy stone pillar moved a notch. She pushed the tip of her pole under it further and strained down. The stela rolled a fraction of an inch.

"We can do it," Mark said, his shoulders bulging from the effort. His foot slipped in the dry dirt and he almost fell, but he recovered and pushed harder.

Inch by inch the stela started to roll. When it was a quarter of the way, it suddenly shifted and rolled on its own. The release of the pressure sent Celeste and Mark sprawling in the dirt.

"I should have thought of this weeks ago," Mark said as he scrambled to his feet. "I was afraid the sudden movement would crack the stela. Once that happened, it might disintegrate." He was moving over the stone surface, making sure that it was intact. It took a moment for him to notice that she was still sitting on the ground.

He stretched out his hand and pulled her up, and together they moved to examine the stela.

The first figure Celeste saw made her draw in a sharp breath. The carving was crumbling in places, but the image was still clear. A serpent god slithered along the pillar. From the open mouth, a woman emerged. Her hand went to her chest.

"It's my necklace," she said, her voice a whisper. The discovery was somehow sinister, and her hand clutched the necklace where it dangled beneath her shirt.

"Yes," Mark said. "I knew your necklace was old, but I had no idea." He knelt down beside the pillar and brushed the dirt away. "Now we have to decipher what these glyphs mean." As he gently brushed, his hand uncovered more and more of the intricate figures. "These predate the Toltecs by years!"

"What's this?" Celeste asked as she brushed at a figure on an altar. She wasn't certain if the woman was a sacrifice or asleep. Behind her the serpent god was shedding his reptilian scales to emerge as a man.

"Looks like a reincarnation or rebirth scene," Mark said, puzzled. "This is something that's going to take a lot of work."

"Look at this!" Celeste took the hem of her skirt and cleared away an image that now held more significance than ever before. The jaguar seemed to stare at her from the stone. In its mouth was a man.

Moving up and down the stela, she and Mark uncovered new glyphs. "These have a meaning, but it will take some time," Mark said. There was excitement in his voice. "To think, we could have rolled this thing all along. Roberto is right. I get so narrow and focused that I miss the forest for the trees. I should go and get Daniel. This might take his mind off the tragedy."

"I'd also like to talk with him before he heads back to Cancún." She'd had little time to think about Uncle Alec's latest message. It had been encouraging, and she needed to send a response. Maybe things were going to work out all around, for her and Mark.

"Thanks for helping me with this." He stood over her, his hands on his hips and a real smile on his face.

She was struck by the generosity of his smile and the warmth in his eyes. "Thanks for asking me to share." The fleeting touch of his fingers on her cheeks, his lips against her skin came back to her. She was attracted to him and there was no point denying it to herself. Flush with success and warmed by the early morning Mexican sun, she had a sudden desire to kiss him. Instead she dropped her gaze to the ground. "Where is Roberto? I should have thought he'd be here."

"He was going to, but he decided to talk with Timma's widow today. The woman is going to be in trouble without her husband to support her. If there's anything we can do, we will."

The words Carlotta Bopp had spoken the night before came back to Celeste. They'd troubled her all through the dark hours, displaced for only a brief time in the excitement of finally revealing the secrets of the stela and the sudden feelings she'd acknowledged about Mark.

"What will she do?"

Mark shook his head, and his face returned to lines of worry and sorrow. "She has three children." He sat down on the stone beside Celeste. "You'll soon go home to your career and future." He looked in the distance toward the village. "These people will struggle on, I suppose. It is the way of life. That kind of struggle must be alien to you."

For a moment Celeste thought she'd heard him wrong. When his words sank in, her anger moved from her heart to her tongue in a matter of seconds. "No, someone like me could never understand struggle," she said, standing up. "I make a lot of money, so I'm compensated. I wouldn't know struggle and disappointment." Before he could respond, she walked away.

HER OUTBURST HAD been an overreaction, she knew. She slowed to a walk and tried to sort through the confusion of feelings that sweltered within her. It was all too much. Instead of going back to camp, she changed her course for the cenote. Mark didn't encourage solitary swimming, but she wasn't in much of a mood to worry about pleasing Mark Grayson at the moment. Besides, she had Roberto's gun and she needed a swim, time to cool off and relax. The cenote was the perfect answer.

Part of the path was flat and barren, but the Sacred Way also tunneled through jungle that was lush and thick. Among the verdant leaves and vines, Celeste found she was calmer. She'd lost her head for a moment back at the stela. She'd let fancy and fantasy color her thoughts. It was the sense of betrayal she'd felt when she realized his opinion of her was still that she was some spoiled and pampered rich woman. It was that juxtaposed on top of the way she'd been feeling about Mark. She'd been thinking like a fool.

The path narrowed and she found herself listening for the calls of the birds in the dense growth. She could see motion, but it was difficult to sight the tiny bodies with feathers that blended so well with the brilliant foliage.

An iron grip captured her wrist and jerked her fiercely off the path. Her scream was caught in her throat, held captive by another hand that covered her mouth.

"Whatever you're up to, Celeste Coolridge, you're going to stop it now."

The voice came from behind her, and it was very familiar. She struggled to turn around, but the man held her in a grip so tight she couldn't breathe.

"You're trying to ruin me, and I won't have it. You and your uncle! I'm not going to let you get away with this."

With all of her strength she brought the heel of her booted foot into his shin. With a yelp he released her and stumbled back.

"Barry!" She turned on him, fury making her green eyes glitter dangerously. "Don't you ever touch me again." She wanted to slap him, but she decided that keeping a safe distance was the better choice. She circled him, never showing him her back as she worked her way around to the path. She had no doubt she could outrun him on a clear trail.

He smiled. "You're a dangerous woman."

"A lot more than you ever imagined," she said. "What are you doing here?"

"Trying to keep you and yours from ruining my career."

"What are you talking about?"

"Don't play innocent with me, Celeste. Your uncle has been working on me since you left town. He's got the whole brokerage firm talking and wondering. I want it stopped. I won't take a fall for you!" He ground the last sentence through clenched teeth.

"You've lost it, Barry. The pressure has finally gotten to you. I don't have any idea what you're talking about, and I don't want to know. If anyone's trying to pull a fast one, it's you." She felt a moment's elation. "What happened? Did my uncle catch you with your fingers in the pie?"

The expression of hatred was more than she'd bargained for. She backed up two steps involuntarily. "Go back to

Tampa and leave me alone. How did you get here, anyway? How did you know where I was?"

For the first time Barry Undine seemed to regain his confidence. "Oh, I know things, Celeste. I know plenty. I have my ways."

"What'd you do, break into Uncle Alec's office and rifle his desk?" She saw that her accusation was right on target and she wasn't surprised. "Leave now, Barry, before it's too late."

"Is that a threat?" he asked, his smile widening.

"Take it however you want. Just leave." She stepped back onto the path and headed for camp. She was shaken, but she didn't want to show it.

"I'm on to you, Celeste." Barry lunged for her.

She drew the gun Roberto had given her from her waist and pointed it. Her hands were rock steady, as she'd been taught. Her knees were slightly bent. "Don't make me do something I'll regret," she said.

"You're capable of anything," Barry said softly. "I always thought it was possible, and now I believe it."

"I'll do whatever is necessary to defend myself," she said. "Remember that."

"I will. Don't doubt it, I will. And remember that I'll do the same."

Barry's voice followed her down the path, and she had the terrible feeling that all of the troubles she'd left behind in Tampa had suddenly caught up with her.

SHE ARRIVED AT the camp with one intention in mind—to find Daniel Ortiz and have him send a telegram to her uncle. The fact that Barry was in Mexico gave her some hope that her uncle had made a lot of progress in clearing her name of the insider-trading charges. Barry had panicked. She wanted to tell her uncle that, and let him know she would be on the next available flight home. It was time to leave Chichén Itzá, in more ways than one.

When she got to the camp, she found only Rebecca.

"The charming Mr. Ortiz has returned to civilization," Rebecca said in response to Celeste's question. "He said that Timma's death had to be reported to the proper authorities. He also mentioned something about seeing what could be done to have that jungle cat removed from this area." She watched the disappointment on Celeste's face. "If you ask me, he was nervous, too."

"A man was killed last night. That's enough to make anyone nervous," Celeste answered. She was tired and upset that she had no way to get a message to her uncle.

"It was more than that. The way he was acting, you'd think he was responsible for Timma's death."

"I'm sure Mr. Ortiz was upset. We all are." She went into the cooking hut, pausing for a moment with her hands on her hips. She hoped Rebecca would take the hint and leave, but she heard the other woman's footsteps behind her. At loose ends, she began to make sandwiches.

"Domesticity is an interesting trait for a woman like you," Rebecca said as she leaned against the wall of the kitchen.

"Since you're leaving tomorrow, could I get you to take a message for me?" Celeste ignored Rebecca's barb. She sliced a tomato and arranged it on the sandwiches, then cut them in half.

"Aren't you leaving, too?" Rebecca picked up a half of sandwich and slowly bit into it.

"I had thought of staying, at least until Mark and Roberto could get more help. This business with Timma will have a negative impact. I think even some of the graduate students will leave."

"Charles and I aren't going." Rebecca smiled and took another bite of sandwich. "If there's a valuable jewel there, we want to share in the profits. Since you and Mark were out at the stela, I'm assuming you made some progress."

For some reason Celeste hesitated. "That legend is probably a crock and you know it. Even if it isn't, the jewel belongs to the Mexican government, not the finder. Those are the laws."

"A lot of finds aren't reported," Rebecca said. She took the last bite of sandwich.

"Mark isn't that type of person, and you know it."

"Who says Mark will find it?"

"Maybe you could round up the graduate students for me?" Celeste asked. "Lunch is as ready as it's going to get."

"Oh, by the way. Some Indian woman was here looking for you. She left this." Rebecca reached into the pocket of her jumpsuit and pulled out a carved figure. "It favors you tremendously, don't you think." She handed the wooden carving to Celeste.

Celeste took the intricately carved figure of a woman with great care. She went to a window to get better light. The figure was beautifully rendered, and someone had gone to a lot of trouble to paint the hair a shade of red that exactly matched her own color.

"Did Maria leave this?" she asked, turning back to Rebecca. She slipped the carving into her own pocket.

"No, it was that Bopp woman. Very imposing. Rather ominous, if you ask me. She said she wanted to see you. I believe she said it was urgent."

Chapter Seven

Thunder comes from the north. It is not the rumble of the clouds, but the gnashing of the serpent's teeth. The rattling of his feathers will create an evil wind.

Carlotta had not designated a meeting place, but Celeste knew where to find her. She walked out of the ruins and toward the line of merchants' stalls.

"I wish to see Carlotta Bopp," she said in halting Spanish to an old man sitting beside a multitude of hammocks. The shop contained *huipils,* shawls, dresses and shirts, shoes and an assortment of fresh produce in varying stages of ripeness. Celeste's Spanish had improved a lot since she'd arrived in Mexico, but she still had to struggle to make herself understood.

The old man pointed to the back of the shop. Barely visible past mountains of multicolored bolts of materials and row after row of T-shirts was a door. Celeste went to the rough wooden plank and pushed it open. The room she entered was filled with towering aisles of goods. Chairs, broken furniture, piles of cloth were scattered about, so that she wasn't certain which direction to take. Her stray thought was that Carlotta Bopp had an impressive inventory.

"Thank you for coming." Carlotta stepped in front of her. She motioned Celeste to follow.

At the back of the room there was a small table and two chairs facing each other. Carlotta took one and motioned

Celeste into the other. "We must talk." She nodded slowly. "We have much to say to one another."

"Your English is perfect. Did you study in the States?" That fact had been bouncing in Celeste's mind since she met the woman.

"In England."

So that was the trace of formality she heard. "How did you come to be in England?"

For the first time Carlotta smiled, and Celeste saw what a tremendously appealing woman she could be. "I was married. I went with my husband, an engineer. It was what my parents wanted."

The explanation took the steam from Celeste's questions. The woman sitting across from her had regal bearing and impeccable English, but she was a part of Chichén Itzá. Celeste found it difficult to imagine her in slacks or an American-style dress moving through the streets of London.

"You find it shocking?" Carlotta asked, amused instead of offended.

"Not shocking, exactly."

"I found it shocking. I was very young, only seventeen. I had little choice in the matter. My parents thought they were saving me from a life of poverty, so they essentially gave me to Sidney. He tried to take care of me, but I could not live away from my heritage. When I could bear it no longer, I left the children with him and I came back."

The crowded room held a deep hush. Celeste did not feel pity for the woman. Carlotta Bopp did not allow anyone to pity her.

"I did not ask you here to talk of my life," Carlotta said, breaking the golden afternoon silence. "I want to ask you to stay at the ruins. For a week or so, until the trouble about Timma begins to calm."

"What trouble?"

Carlotta shook her head. "Some of the villagers are disturbed. They are also afraid. Police officers came and took Timma's body from his widow. That is a bad sign for the village people. The officials can be very harsh, even when there is no reason."

"Since he was killed by a jaguar, I don't see how the authorities can make much trouble. It's a simple case."

"There have been no jaguars in these parts for many years. At least no normal jaguar." She smiled, but her eyes were humorless. She spoke in deadly earnestness. "They see the fact that Timma was mauled and savaged by a cat as a sign that the gods are growing angry. They think it is because the ruins are being explored."

"I've heard you say that," Celeste remarked.

Carlotta nodded. "It is true. I have said it, and I believe it. But I also don't want to see more bloodshed and trouble. I love my people. If there is a riot, or some action, it will be my people who suffer. The white man is above the law. He has money to pay the authorities. If there is trouble, we will suffer."

"And you anticipate trouble?" Celeste felt as if a tight band had been placed about her chest.

Carlotta's black eyes met hers. "I am certain of it. If you go."

"Why me?" Celeste wanted to get up and pace, but something about Carlotta Bopp made her sit still. The woman had power and authority.

"Some of this you must blame on your little guide. He has done nothing but talk of you all week. He says you are just, that you will not allow the others to harm us. He says you will see that the jaguar is captured but not harmed. The animal is sacred to us."

"I have no control over these things!" Celeste touched her chest and leaned forward. "I'm a paying guest. Mark has very little respect for people like me."

Carlotta smiled. "That may indeed be true, but it is not what my people think. I promise you, if you go, there will be bloodshed. You must decide."

"I have trouble in my own life," Celeste began in a hesitating voice. "I must go home and see to it. My future depends on it."

"And the lives of many here depend on you." Carlotta watched her closely. "Each man and woman must follow his destiny, Miss Coolridge. I cannot tell you what to do. I left my three children and a man who loved me to come here to sell trinkets to the tourists. No decision is ever easy. All are selfish to one degree or another."

Stunned, Celeste folded her hands on the table.

Carlotta reached out and took Celeste's right hand, gently pushing open the fingers to reveal the palm. She studied it for a moment and then put it down.

"Do you read palms?" Celeste asked. She'd always had a certain amount of curiosity, but no opportunity to explore the world of the psychic or palmist.

"No," Carlotta said softly. "I do not read for people. My mother did. She was respected and had much influence. She taught me, but I do not read." The entire time she spoke, she stared at Celeste's hand, which was lying palm up on the table.

"I must go," Celeste said, rising. "I will think about what you've said. I'll talk it over—"

"Please keep this conversation as a confidence. Mr. Grayson is a man of iron. He will resent any idea that you are of importance to his future."

Celeste recognized the truth of those words and she gave a bitter smile. "Did you see that in my palm?"

Carlotta did not stand, but she seemed to grow taller in her chair. "I saw an opportunity for greatness. I saw great honor and prestige. You have the hand of power and the mark of one who serves, like a queen."

Celeste wanted to laugh, but the other woman's expression would not allow it. The words were not sinister, but they had a frightening sound to them. "Not in this lifetime," she said, forcing a small chuckle. "My friends would never allow such a thing. They already say I'm too hard to deal with."

"You cannot escape your destiny," Carlotta said. "You will see that."

Celeste started for the door, but then turned back. "Why did you leave this carving for me?" She pulled the figure from her pocket and handed it to Carlotta.

"I did not," Carlotta answered. "It is very beautiful, very old. The pigments are lustrous, very natural," she said. "Someone has created you before you were even conceived."

For a moment the strange words gave Celeste pause. She looked at the figure again. "Thank you." She opened the door and stepped back into the hammock shop. The old man was gone and there seemed to be no one tending the goods.

"Celeste!" Carlotta hailed her. "Wait. There is something I would like you to see. It is an ancient ceremony of celebration. No one other than the Mayas has ever seen it."

"Why are you asking me?" Celeste asked. She felt a knot of discomfort in her stomach.

"You are special, whether you accept it or not. It would honor us if you came." Carlotta stepped closer. "But you must come alone. It is for no other eyes."

"All right," Celeste said. "When?"

"Tonight. I will send a messenger for you." Carlotta turned back into the shade of her store and disappeared.

WIPING THE SWEAT from his brow, Mark dropped the sketch pad in the dirt and collapsed beside it. The last strong rays of the sun were flattening on the horizon. He'd been sketching the intricate carvings on the stela all day—and trying not to think of Celeste. He had a pretty accurate rendition sketched out, but it had taken hours. Photographs would work, and he would take them, but he liked his own sketches best. He could get the shadings down more accurately. Instead of the satisfaction that should have come from his work, he found that he was discontent and irritable.

He knew the source, and it was one redheaded woman with a short fuse. That was the problem with the wealthy tourist type. They never gave a man a chance to explain.

They made demands, and then they lost their tempers when those demands weren't instantly met.

He wiped his forehead again, knowing that he was not being fair to Celeste. She'd worked like a dog, never complaining and doing whatever menial chore had come her way. He'd watched, from a distance, her long tapered legs and slender back bending and lifting. She was one of the most attractive women he'd ever seen, and it was as much her willingness to help as her physical attributes. But those physical attributes were hard to miss. Even in his disgruntled state, he couldn't suppress a smile. Roberto could hardly work when she was around. His partner spent a good deal of time staring at the amazingly oblivious Miss Coolridge.

He picked up the sketch pad and looked at the intriguing and mysterious figures. He should be jumping for joy, but he wasn't. There was something about the figures that was unsettling. They were of Maya design and conception. Some of the symbols were well-known and almost universally interpreted. The glyphs of the Mayas, though, typically followed a theme, and he could find nothing that connected the series of what were essentially panels.

He flipped through his sketches, convinced his work was acceptable. Still, he couldn't shake the feeling that something was wrong. He couldn't say exactly that the images on the stela were ominous, but they were...mocking? The idea made him pack up his gear.

He'd planned on sharing the discovery with Celeste, and now that was ruined. That was the particular bug eating at him and he ought to accept it. If he knew anything about tourists, Celeste was packing to go back to Cancún. Well, most of them didn't stay four days. She was a marvel of discipline and sacrifice.

The last bitter thought made him smile with a tight expression. He was back to his cynical ways. And it was just as well. That tiny fissure Celeste had chipped in his attitude would cause nothing but trouble if he allowed it to grow.

THE WOMAN WHO appeared at Celeste's window long after the dinner dishes had been washed and put away was someone Celeste did not know.

"Carlotta says come," the woman whispered, hanging back in the shadows as if she were afraid to be seen.

Celeste rose from her cot and moved toward the shadowy figure. "Where?"

"Las Monjas," the young woman said in a voice like the whisper of corn silk. *"Ahora."*

"Las Monjas?" Celeste felt a moment of panic. She wasn't familiar with the place. *"No comprende,"* she said.

The young woman wavered at the window, as frightened as a rabbit and as ready to run. "The nunnery," she answered in stilted English. "The nunnery," she repeated before she sprinted away into the night.

Celeste felt in the waistband of her shorts for the gun Roberto had given her earlier. She had every intention of going to the nunnery, one of the oldest buildings on the Chichén Itzá site. She wasn't going unarmed, though. It wasn't the jaguar that worried her as much as it was the thought that Barry Undine was out roaming the jungle, ready to jump out and frighten her half to death.

The entire camp seemed peaceful and sound asleep as she left her hut. She knew the ruins directly south of the camp, but the nunnery was a long distance away. She'd had precious little time to explore much of anything, she'd been so busy sifting dirt.

Whatever ceremony Carlotta wanted her to see, she hoped it was action-packed, or otherwise she might fall asleep in the middle of it.

She hurried by the west side of El Castillo, all too aware of the magic that the structure could cast over her imagination. That was one reaction to her experiences at Chichén Itzá that she would never have anticipated in a million years. She, the math whiz who'd never been able to concoct more than a few declarative statements, was suddenly able to imagine life among an extinct culture. When she was standing on top of El Castillo, she could close her eyes and see the Mayan town alive and thriving.

She forced her feet along the path, reluctant to leave the pyramid behind, but also eager to see what Carlotta had in store for her.

The first sound was a flute-like noise. It was distant, yet clear and distinct. Then she heard a percussion instrument supporting the lighter melody of the flute. For an acute second, Celeste felt as if she'd dropped through some hole in time. As she slipped through Chichén Itzá, some areas clear and others overgrown, she wasn't certain what sight might greet her. The music seemed to precede her, as if the musicians were just ahead, moving through the jungle at the same pace she traveled.

She caught the dense shadow of the high priest's grave to her right, then the house of the corn grinders. From listening to Mark and Roberto, she knew that the Red House was one of the oldest structures in the ruins. She was in the most ancient section of Chichén Itzá, the part which bore the trace of the Mayas more than any other. So much of the tribe had been absorbed by the Toltecs and Aztecs and abolished by the Spaniards.

She found her feet moving in rhythm with the beat of the drum. It was slightly irregular, almost but not quite like the pulse of her heart. She let the music draw her down the path toward the far southern boundary of the ruins where the structure known as the nunnery remained.

Celeste's knowledge of the ruins was limited, but she remembered Mark's comment that the nunnery had apparently been used as a palace by members of the royal Itzá family.

As Celeste saw the building and walked toward it with a sure step, the music stopped. She paused, taking in the structure, which was almost as long as a football field and three stories high. She felt uncomfortably alone in the sudden stillness of the night.

"The masks are of the rain god," Carlotta said from the shadows. She stepped forward and took Celeste's hand.

"There is much you should know. There is much I would like to show you."

"I want to learn," Celeste said. "I don't have long to stay in Chichén Itzá, but I'd like to learn as much as possible. The ruins have captured my imagination. Carlotta, I know you're opposed to the ruins being disturbed, but think about what an impact coming here has had on me. For the first time, I have an interest in the past, in your past. By coming here, I have begun a long journey that will take me to many places. Chichén Itzá will affect others the same way. People will learn to appreciate and respect your history."

"It would be simple if we were old bones and broken bits of pottery," Carlotta said. "Then people could study us without damage. But we are not those things. We are a people with a future as well as a past." She took her elbow and began to lead her up the steps. "Enough about that. Let me show you how the Mayas prepare for the coming spring."

THE TENSION IN Mark's shoulders forced him to bend his head and roll it from side to side. He was exhausted from studying the sketches he'd made of the stela. He needed a break, and he needed to talk with Celeste. She'd given him no opportunity at the evening meal.

He rose, taking a moment to splash cold water on his face. In the week that Celeste had been at the dig, the nights had grown warmer and warmer. Or maybe it was just his imagination.

He was at the door of his hut when he heard the sound of urgent whispering. With great care he looked to make sure Roberto was sound asleep. His partner was out like a baby. Mark resisted the urge to wake him and slipped into the night. It took a moment for his eyes to adjust, but once he was used to the dark he had no trouble spotting the slender young woman at Celeste's window. The girl hurried away into the shadows, and in a moment Celeste appeared.

She started down the path toward the ruins, as if she knew where she was going. Mark followed fifty yards behind, always careful not to snap a twig or give his surveillance away.

He didn't examine his reasons for following her. He'd never warned her properly about running around alone in the dark jungle. He'd never considered it a real danger, until Timma's death. But again, he'd never had the villagers slipping into the camp to visit the tourists, either. Celeste had developed some strange rapport with the Mayas.

He followed Celeste for an hour, wondering where she was going with such long-legged determination. In the older section of the ruins, he felt less and less comfortable. This had been the site of his first excavations. They'd found little. Some broken pottery, obsidian knives, vessels suspected of being the receptacles for the hearts of sacrificial victims. And there had been the strange figure of a woman, which he'd found in the observatory. He'd never classified it as a find, because it was left there, as if it were a gift. There had been nothing Mayan about the slender woman with flowing hair. He'd recognized the age, but suspected it was the totem or keepsake of some conquistador rather than an Indian.

The observatory was on his left, and he had a strange moment of intuition. There was a figure on the stela that could be connected with astronomy. When he got a chance, he was going to investigate the observatory with the sketches in hand.

He heard the music, halting for a moment to ponder its significance. There was only the flute-like instrument and the drums. He'd never heard those instruments near Chichén Itzá before. Among the merchants' booths, there was always the sound of a portable radio playing popular music. The sounds coming from the old nunnery were ancient, a strange blend of jungle melody and beat. Celeste had disappeared down the path to the nunnery following the silent figure of the Indian girl.

He stopped for a moment, recalling the uncanny way Celeste had been accepted by the villagers. Thomas was partially responsible. It was clear the boy had developed strong feelings for Celeste.

As Mark moved closer to the nunnery, he grew more careful. He felt some guilt at sneaking around in the dark spying, but he had to make certain Celeste was safe.

He had Celeste in sight again at the steps of the nunnery when Carlotta Bopp moved out of the shadows. They spoke for a moment and then climbed the steps and entered the building. He could hear the whisper of their conversation, but he could not make out the words. The music started again, and the two women disappeared into the darkness. In the distance he could see the flare of torches and he moved toward those.

His heartbeat accelerated. Was it possible that Celeste had been invited to witness a reenactment of some ancient ritual? It was remarkable! He'd heard whispers of such rituals, but he'd never believed that a member of his team would ever be asked to participate. He inched in closer.

CELESTE SHED HER feelings of discomfort. Carlotta made her feel welcome, and a part of the small circle of Mayas. She thought she recognized a few of them, but she couldn't be certain. They wore strangely decorated masks. Carlotta had explained a few of them, the rain god, the god of corn, the goddess of fertility.

"We do not practice the ancient rituals, but we honor the gods by masking," Carlotta said. "We wanted you to know our gods, to meet them so that you might recognize them."

"I'm honored," Celeste said, taking a seat in the circle. "Mark would be very interested in this, I'm sure."

"He is not invited," Carlotta said coldly. "He will never be with us. It would be dangerous for him to come here. The gods would punish him."

"I am honored," Celeste said.

Carlotta motioned for the music to increase. Several children, brightly costumed and painted, darted into the nunnery and performed a fluid, ritual dance.

Celeste had no comprehension of what the dance might mean, but it was beautiful to watch. The children seemed completely absorbed in the movements.

"Is Thomas here?" she whispered to Carlotta. She thought she recognized Maria, but she couldn't be certain. The light was poor and the feathers and skins of the costumes concealing.

"If he is here, he is no longer Thomas," Carlotta said. She motioned for silence.

Celeste watched the dances and listened to the music. Once again she found herself caught up in the fancies of the past. The dancers, men, women and children seemed to tell her a story. There was the smell of herbs burning, a pleasant, spicy scent. She sat cross-legged and relaxed.

She felt the sting of a pebble against her arm. The pain was sharp, but quickly gone. There was the same sting on her leg. Someone was throwing things at her. Slowly she examined the area behind her, but she could see no one. She turned back to the dancers, only to feel another sharp sting on her back.

Shifting her position slightly, she was able to look behind her into the darkness. At last she caught a flash of light on the crystal of a watch. The only man at Chichén Itzá who wore a watch was Mark Grayson.

Anger flared. He'd followed her, uninvited. She rose slowly, motioning to Carlotta that she was going outside for a moment. She hoped the others would not grow suspicious. All through the evening villagers had come and gone from the circle, some to dance, some to bring food and drink, which was passed around the circle. She had to send Mark on his way before the villagers found him and he further ruptured the atmosphere between the two camps.

Carlotta's gaze returned to the dance and Celeste backed into the shadows. She moved blindly, without any idea where Mark might be hiding.

The touch of his hand on her shoulder was sudden. Before she could react, she felt his arms around her, pulling her out into the night. When they were safely in the bush, he released her.

He'd held her longer than necessary, he knew, but he'd enjoyed the feel of her in his arms. He'd enjoyed it far too much. He'd almost forgotten his reason for interrupting the dance.

"What are you doing here?" she accused. "You weren't invited."

"You sound like Carlotta," he said.

Caught squarely in that observation, Celeste didn't say anything.

"I followed you to make sure you were safe, and then I got caught up in the ritual. What is it?"

"A celebration for the ancient gods. Sort of a way to say they still know them, I think. Carlotta said this dance wasn't actually part of the ancient rituals. I got the impression this is something the villagers do to stay in touch with the past, even though so much of the ritual has been lost or forgotten."

"Carlotta has done what she can to preserve the past. Just remember, some of those gods demanded human sacrifice. I'm delighted Carlotta hasn't taken things that far."

"Be serious, Mark," Celeste snapped. "Carlotta is well educated. She isn't some savage ready to cut out hearts and throw people into cenotes."

"I was only kidding," he said.

"It's out of character." She was still irritated, as much at herself as at him. When she'd felt the pebbles, she'd also felt a moment of elation that Mark was nearby. She'd wanted him to share in her night of discovery. The question was why? Why should she care? It was annoying.

"I didn't drag you out of the party to trade barbs. There's a figure there. It seems to be male. Black paint with yellow. If you could get close enough to notice any details, such as jewelry, the types of feathers. It might be helpful. I'm too far back to see."

"The stela!"

"He might be on it. This might be a clue, if you can get Carlotta to help."

"Okay," she agreed, rising. "I'll do it. It must be hard for you to ask a tourist for help."

"You're more than a tourist, Celeste. A lot more." He rose to stand beside her. "You misunderstood me earlier today. Tomorrow, I'd like a chance to clear that up."

"Tomorrow," she agreed. "Let's go back."

Without making a sound they moved toward the nunnery. When they were still fifty yards from the dancers, Mark grabbed her hand. She turned to him, knowing this was as far as he could go.

The pressure of his fingers was warm, inviting. Celeste smiled, knowing that he couldn't see her face in the darkness.

A low rumble came to them, like distant thunder. A fine sprinkling of dust made them look up just as there was a growl of rock breaking. Before either could move, a large hunk of stone split from the overhead structure and tumbled down on them.

Chapter Eight

The sound of dancing feet has told the news. The god with plumes and scales is aroused. Challenged in his own domain, he grows angry and sends the smallest of his legions.

Celeste felt the hands on her arms and legs and knew she was being pulled from beneath the stones. Part of the ceiling of the nunnery had collapsed. Mark was somewhere nearby, and she moaned his name.

The only response was the sound of whispers. Carlotta and the villagers had come to save them. Celeste tried to mumble her thanks, but her throat was closed with the gritty dust of destruction. She wanted to sleep.

A cool cloth on her face brought her completely awake. She was surrounded by the masked figures of the dancers as she lay in the path outside the nunnery. Mark was beside her.

"You have angered the gods," Carlotta said, "by bringing him to our ritual. What you did was wrong."

Mark was lying very still, but Celeste could see his chest moving softly. He was breathing. He was alive.

"He came on his own," she answered. "He followed me. He didn't mean to do anything wrong."

"So that is why the gods let you live." Carlotta nodded. "Just remember, in all cultures, even the innocent pay a price for mistakes."

She turned and walked away, followed by the villagers.

Celeste shifted closer to Mark. Dawn was breaking in the east, and the dim light was enough for her to see that his eyes were open.

"Are you hurt?" he asked, shifting to his side with a moan.

"Not really. We were lucky." She sat up and found the base of a small tree to lean against. "How about you?"

"No broken bones, but a whack on the head. I've been in that building a million times. It was structurally sound. There was no reason for this to happen. Not unless someone deliberately weakened a stone."

"That's ridiculous. Carlotta was angry that you'd watched, but I hardly think spying on a harmless dance is worthy of being crushed. Not even in the old Maya laws."

"You're right," Mark said, pushing up on his elbows. He rested a moment and then stood, extending a hand to help her up. "But let's take a look anyway."

Against her better judgment, she followed him into the nunnery and up a set of stairs to the second floor. In the dawning light she could better make out the faces of the gods carved high along the top of the walls.

"They aren't very happy, are they? Never a smile."

"Godhood is serious work," Mark said.

She heard the humor in his voice and turned to him. "Better be careful. Joking may become a habit and you might actually become a pleasant conversationalist."

"Thanks," he said, faking a bow. "Roberto said my manners had improved since your arrival."

"I think it was the recent blow to your head," she answered. She followed him to the stone arch, which was now obviously broken. Rubble was everywhere, and Mark skirted it carefully, signaling her to stay back. When he was at the main support, he let out a low whistle. "It's been deliberately chiseled," he said. "I knew when I'd examined this building last year that there wasn't this type of flaw."

"The villagers wouldn't do this," Celeste said stubbornly.

"Know of any other suspects?" Mark asked in an off-handed way.

Barry Undine's name leapt into her mind. "Yes, as a matter of fact I do."

Startled, Mark came back to her side. "Want to share the information?"

Celeste hesitated. "Not at the moment. But I promise you, as soon as I check it out I'll let you know."

"I don't like the tone in your voice, Celeste," Mark said. "What is it you aren't telling me?"

"A lot," she answered, her steady gaze holding his. "I don't want to tell you now. There are some things I need to take care of in my own life. They don't belong here in Chichén Itzá, and I don't want them here. Let me take care of them in my own way."

For a long moment Mark looked into her eyes. He could read the determination that bordered on stubbornness, and he knew better than to take a frontal assault on her. "I don't like it, but I have to respect that request. Let's get back to camp."

"Maybe we could keep this incident to ourselves," Celeste said slowly.

"That's funny, I was going to suggest the same thing." Mark patted her shoulder. "How about a quick detour before breakfast?"

It was odd, but after a night without sleep and being battered half to death by a falling stone arch, Celeste wasn't tired at all. "To where?"

"El Castillo. I have a theory about the glyphs."

"Really!" Celeste felt the excitement flow between them. "What?"

"That may be the colors on some of the glyphs . . ."

"Colors? I don't remember any colors."

"There were a few bits of residue, primarily black. Remember that dancing figure?" He waited for her nod. "They're barely traces really. But I can have the flecks examined to make sure. Anyway, if the colors are clues to points of the compass, then maybe we can get an idea of where to begin."

"Okay," she agreed eagerly. "I see where your mind is headed. From the top of El Castillo, we can get a good view of all directions."

"Right." He picked up his pace and pushed down the path toward the pyramid.

The morning sun was not yet hot as they hurried up the side of the structure. "I'm going to be thin and have toned legs," Celeste said as she puffed behind Mark.

"I wouldn't recommend any changes," Mark said, holding out a hand to pull her up the last few steps. "If we can imagine how the jungle growth was, and maybe the paths that were in use. If we can recreate the village life in our minds, we'll stand a better chance of figuring this out."

"Do you really believe there's a giant jewel, or is that just some hype to make the expedition more palatable to Daniel?"

"The Jaguar's Eye is real." He reached out to brush aside a curl of hair that had fallen across her cheek. "I believe in it, not because I want to discover treasure. But such a discovery will guarantee the protection of this ruin and others like it. Chichén Itzá is already a tremendous archaeological find, by any standard. But if great wealth were discovered, it would gain popular support. Funds would be spent to preserve it. It would become significant. The idea of finding 'treasure' has great appeal."

"Greed motivates a lot of actions," Celeste said, thinking suddenly of Barry Undine.

Mark noticed the way her mouth hardened, but he didn't press the point. She would tell him when she felt like it. If he'd learned anything about Celeste Coolridge in the past week, it was that she faced life on her own terms. It was a trait he highly admired.

It was another crystal morning that promised a blazing day. As they stood, surveying the site where another culture had worked and played, she felt surprisingly at peace. Her own turmoil subsided. Time was so fleeting. To think that a civilization had lived and disappeared. It made her own troubles seem remarkably insignificant.

"Well?" Mark said.

"Well," she answered. "I suppose someone would have to bring water and food."

"The women," Mark answered.

"And someone took care of the children."

"The women."

"And someone hunted game." She was getting desperate to find a job for the men.

"The Mayas weren't great hunters."

"That's probably because the women didn't do it," Celeste said under her breath.

Mark's laughter was rich and deep. "We sound like one of the worst television sitcoms ever made," he said. "Nothing but stock characters and typical scenes. Let's think. Give your imagination a chance."

"You're the expert. I think it would help to have a better understanding of the deities and their religion."

"Almost every day there was some ritual or event. The Mayas had an incredible pantheon of gods. You're familiar with Quetzalcoatl. There was Tlaloc, the rain god; Yum Caax, the god of maize. Many of the gods are shared with the Toltecs and Aztecs. These gods controlled all aspects of everyday life, and they were sometimes benevolent and just and sometimes not."

"Go on," she urged.

"All of the people sacrificed in small ways. It wasn't uncommon for the Mayas to bleed themselves for ritual purposes, or for health reasons. The priests and prophets were extremely powerful and they could demand blood, dances or food to appease whatever god they thought had been offended."

"So the priest would sometimes attend to village matters from up here, at the altar on El Castillo?" Celeste asked.

"That would make sense." With her encouragement, Mark settled in to creating a daily pattern of life as he imagined. As he talked, Celeste began to fill in the details of the home. It was like the first time she'd climbed the pyramid, when she'd become captivated with scenes of the village as it must have been.

An hour passed, and then another. They moved from north to east to south and then west, using a mingling of fact and imagination to conjure up the paths and people of a different culture. It was only the unforgiving blast of the sun that brought them back to the reality of their own time. They returned, both shaken by the shared experience.

Breathless, Celeste shrugged. "Well, that was something," she said. "I feel almost lost, coming back to the present." She tried to laugh, but she was too deeply affected. "What is it about this place that latches on to me like that?"

He looked down at her bowed head, at the tousled red hair that spilled down her back and hid most of her face. He knew what she was feeling. It was almost as if they'd been intimate. The thought was so natural, so much in keeping with what he wanted, that his fingers went to her chin and lifted until their gazes met. He kissed her without hesitation or further thought. Her lips, warmed by the sun, were not to be denied.

It was a moment of crazy abandonment for Celeste. She gave herself to the feel of Mark's lips with the same passion she'd given to creating the Maya village with him. Reality was swept away. There was no ancient civilization, no present. There was only the two of them, bonded together in a kiss that was as powerful and enduring as the magnificent stones that supported them.

Mark was not surprised that Celeste's passion matched his. He'd already begun to recognize many of those qualities in her. The same needs he saw in himself. His hands claimed her back, the swell of her hips as he pressed her to him. Her long hair, blown by a kind wind, teased his face and neck and unleashed another surge of passion.

The distant sound of shouting at last reached his ears. Celeste heard it at the same time, and they reluctantly broke apart. Below the pyramid, the first buses of tourists were coming through the gates. The daily life of Chichén Itzá was in place. The world they had created for several hours was abruptly gone.

"Mark." Celeste wanted to say something, but she didn't know what. To say that she'd never experienced such a kiss before was trite and stupid. Either he sensed it or he didn't. He brushed the hair from her face and smiled. He was such a handsome man when he allowed his eyes to lighten and his lips to turn up with those strange little quirks at the corners.

"The first time I saw you on this pyramid, I had the strangest sensation that you belonged here. The idea infuriated me." His smile grew more ironic. "Did I recognize, even then, what you could do to me?" He took her hand and turned away, leading her to the steps. "We need to talk, but not here." He started down, and with the treacherous descent, neither could talk.

There were almost at the bottom when Celeste felt a fiery sting on her back. The pain was repeated three more times.

"Wait up, Mark," she said. "Something's biting me."

She balanced on the last step beside him while he inspected her back. She felt his fingers picking something away.

"Ants," he said. "A really large type that I haven't seen around here. When we get to camp we'll put some alcohol and witch hazel on the bites."

"It's okay, just a few bites," she said, twisting her arms behind her to rub. "I couldn't be certain what it was. It might have been a spider."

"Only a few ants," he said, touching her back lightly, "but don't scratch them." His hands paused at her neck. "Weren't you wearing that necklace?"

She touched her neck. "I was. I had it on last night, I know. I haven't thought about it today."

"Could you have lost it when the stone fell on us?"

She thought a moment, her hand still at her throat. "No, I had it when we were climbing the pyramid. I remember touching it." She looked up at the tall building. "I'd better go take a look before the tourists come."

"Wait," Mark said. "I'll send Wilfredo up there. He can climb twice as fast as you."

"I am tired," she agreed, "but it's my responsibility." She started up the steps.

"Wilfredo," he said gently. "He'll enjoy an excuse to sit for a while on El Castillo."

"Are you sure?"

"Positive." He pushed her toward the camp just as Roberto came out of the bush.

"I've been looking everywhere for you," Roberto said, arching his eyebrows. "I woke up and the two of you were gone."

"We had an adventure," Mark said with a smile. His eyes told Celeste that he had not forgotten their agreement to keep the events of the night a secret.

"I think I'll head on to camp," Celeste said. She felt awkward. "If there's anything I can do to help this morning, let me know."

"Sure," Mark called after her. "Ask Wilfredo to retrieve your necklace. He'll be delighted."

As soon as she was gone, Roberto put his hand on Mark's shoulder. "There was a man in camp this morning. He said he used to work with Celeste. He said she was a thief and a liar, and that he intends to prove it."

"Celeste?" Mark was too amazed to get angry. "That's absurd."

"I thought so, too, until he gave me this." Roberto pulled the figure of a redhaired woman from his pocket. "The man said she had it in her room and that she tried to sell it to him."

"The figure I found in the observatory," Mark said. "Celeste had it?"

"It was in her hut."

"That doesn't prove anything," Mark said slowly. "Someone could have put it there, you know."

"What about that necklace? It's ancient. We both figured it came from some ruin when we first saw it. I don't
know what to think," he said slowly.

"I only know Celeste isn't a thief." Mark settled on a
large rock to think. "Who was this man? Where is he? Why
did he follow her here?"

"Those are questions you'll have to ask Celeste," Roberto said. "Just be alert." Roberto touched Mark's chest.
"Guard your heart, my friend. I see that you are falling in
love with this . . . tourist," he smiled to wipe away the sting.
"I thought you were immune to such behavior."

"I did, too," Mark said. "Celeste is different."

"I hope you're right. For now, though, we need to talk
about the expedition. The Maya workers are back, and we
need to get busy." He gave a list of workers and sites, jot-
ting notes on a piece of paper as they talked.

"What should we do with the Tretorns and Celeste?"
Roberto asked after everything else had been settled.

Before Mark could reply, Wilfredo rounded a corner on
the path. He was holding Celeste's necklace and his eyes
were wide. "Señor Mark, did you notice the ants?" he asked
as he held out the jade necklace.

Mark took the jewelry, but his gaze was on Wilfredo's
face. "What ants?"

"Army ants have invaded El Castillo. They have swarmed
the altar, just as the legend says!" He was excited, almost
breathless.

"We were up there only an hour ago. There weren't any
ants then." Mark felt that strange sense of foreboding shift
in even closer. Ants were common in the climate, but there
was something in Wilfredo's expression that warned him
this was no ordinary event.

"The altar is covered. I must go to the village. It is a
sign."

As Wilfredo started to pass by, Mark grabbed his shirt.
"Wait," he said. "What is this about, Wilfredo? What
sign?"

The Maya's face became impassive. "It is part of the legend, *señor*. The villagers will want to know."

"We want to know, too," Roberto interjected. "You've worked these jungles for thirty years. Surely you've seen ants before?"

"On the altar of Quetzalcoatl!" Wilfredo said, the excitement burning brightly in his eyes once again. "It is one of the signs that the god will return to us. It is a sign."

On a sudden suspicion, Mark forced his voice to stay very calm. "This is part of the jaguar legend, isn't it? The cat, and now the ants."

"Yes!" Wilfredo said. "Carlotta said it would happen. There has been no rain for many weeks. The crops are begging the face of the sun for a trace of tears. Carlotta has said the events are coming true. Now the villagers will begin to believe her."

Mark's grip on Wilfredo's shirt tightened a fraction. "Wilfredo, if the villagers get worked up, there could be trouble. Let me take a look at those ants before you rush to tell Carlotta Bopp, okay?"

Reluctance was plain on Wilfredo's face. "I should tell them," he said slowly.

"I'm not saying you shouldn't tell them. But if you'll give me a chance to look first, I'd appreciate it. Let me check, and then you can call the village up to examine the ants if you want."

"They will come," Wilfredo said. "Many of them have not been to the ruins in years. For this, though, they will come." He was smiling again.

"I'll walk Wilfredo back to camp and return Celeste's necklace," Roberto said. "Be careful on the pyramid, Mark. It's hot now. Heat stroke isn't out of the question."

"I will." Mark turned and started back toward El Castillo. He had no doubt he would find the ants, just as Wilfredo had described them. The question was, where had they come from so suddenly? He and Celeste had been all over the top of the pyramid and had seen nothing suspicious. A tiny voice in the back of his mind nagged at him, though.

Had he been paying more attention to Celeste than to his surroundings? That was a distinct possibility.

In the heat he made his way up the steep, narrow steps that led to the top. He passed several eager tourists who'd gotten halfway up and decided to stop for a breather. At the very top, he went directly to the altar, or what had once been cold stone. The entire surface was swarming with huge red ants. They moved in columns, back and forth, marching in what seemed a witless maneuver. Mark checked the area around the altar, hoping to find the nest. If it was there, it was hidden by the ants. There didn't seem to be an opening that he could see. There were only the ants. Millions of them crawling the altar in what Carlotta Bopp would interpret as a direct sign from the gods.

Chapter Nine

*The sun stretches across the sky without wavering.
Night is denied, and the quest of the one god is delayed. His armies are slain, but his works are soon
protected.*

The long afternoon hours wore on Celeste like pumice. With
Rebecca sitting beside her talking nonstop about her ex-
travagant life in Texas, Celeste gritted her teeth and lifted the
sift box again and again. The work had never seemed so tedious or so futile.

Part of it was the fact that both Mark and Roberto had
disappeared shortly after Wilfredo returned with her necklace. Something was happening, she could sense the elec-
tric charge among the three men, but she had no idea what
it was. They'd scattered, leaving her and the Tretorns to
work beside the graduate students at the excavation site.
Mark had given express orders that no one was to go near
the stela. That was the area where the cat had attacked once,
and he wanted no more tragedies. Celeste felt, too, that
Mark did not want anyone snooping around his find.

Mexican authorities had arrived and were supposedly
setting traps for the animal. Juanita, Wilfredo and the other
Mayas were unhappy about the appearance of the authorities. They held no hope, or fear, that the jaguar would be
caught. He was not a flesh-and-blood creature, but a myth-
ical animal far too wary to fall into the traps of a human.

For the jaguar's sake, Celeste hoped the villagers were wrong. If the animal was not caught and moved to a less populated area, someone would eventually kill him. No one would risk such a dangerous animal on the loose.

"What's wrong, dear?" Rebecca asked. "That was one of the biggest sighs I've ever heard. You aren't ready to call it quits and go back to the beaches, are you?" There was an edge of challenge in her voice that made Celeste want to dump the sift box of dirt on her head.

"No," Celeste forced herself to answer. "Tomorrow should have been my last day, but I'm staying to help out. Just like you and Charles." She looked pointedly at Rebecca's perfect hands. There wasn't even a chipped nail or a half moon of dirt.

Rebecca smiled. "It wouldn't do to go back to Texas looking like I'd escaped a chain gang. I have a bridge game a week from Friday. Appearances aren't so crucial for you broker types...thank goodness."

"Yes, some of us find that mental abilities are more important than perfect nails." Celeste smiled. "I thought you'd prefer one of the resorts along the beach. Servants, shops, restaurants, etcetera. Why are you staying here?" Did the Tretorns actually believe they'd discover fabulous treasure and that Mark would let them walk out with it? Surely Rebecca had stayed long enough to provide the necessary chatter for her social functions. Why were they staying? It was a small, vaguely interesting puzzle.

"Perhaps I have a crush on Mark Grayson, *too*," Rebecca answered and smiled sweetly.

Celeste felt her skin temperature change. It dropped to cool, and in a matter of seconds it shot to the top of the chart, a case of pure, absolute fury. Rebecca's remarks were not only insulting, they were taunting. Instead of lashing out, she checked herself firmly.

"You'd better be careful, I might go after Charles," she said, a look of calculation on her face. She wanted Rebecca to consider that possibility—just for a moment. "He's a very nice man. So attentive to you."

"Go for it," Rebecca shrugged, not the least bit perturbed. "Of course if you want financial stability, you'd better move along to someone else. I run the shoe business, and that's the part of Charles's portfolio that makes the money. Without me, he's just another shoe outlet."

Celeste bit back a retort. Before she could say anything, Rebecca continued.

"How has Mark taken the fact that your old beau has set up camp here?"

"What?" Celeste almost dropped the sifting box.

"You didn't know?" Rebecca was clearly enjoying the stir she'd created. "He was talking with Charles. He said you two were an item back in Tampa, and that he'd tracked you down here to convince you to marry him."

"Barry?" It couldn't be anyone else, but still she didn't believe it.

"That was his name. A handsome man with those cool blue eyes. He was very attractive. Of course not as rugged and challenging as the leader of our expedition, but on the whole a lot more secure, I'd say."

"You talked with Barry?" She felt her heart beginning to accelerate in a combination of fury and doubt.

"Only for a moment. He said you'd both worked at Stuart McCarty until recently, when you left. He said you'd found out about a little infidelity. Grow up, Celeste. Men are men." Her eyes opened wider than normal, giving her face an innocent cast. "And women are women. I realize Mark is fascinating, but honestly, he could be dirt-poor the rest of his life."

Celeste's mind had stopped back at the idea of a "relationship" between her and Barry. A few possibilities came to mind, none of them pleasant for Barry.

"Whatever that man said, I've never been involved with him. Not in a romantic relationship, not in a social situation, not even in a financial deal. We are poles apart when it comes to ethics and behavior. Barry Undine is a cretin."

"Where anger erupts, true love once flowed," Rebecca said, then gave a burst of laughter. "Will you go home with him?"

"Only if I'm dead," Celeste said briskly. "Where is Barry? Is he staying here, in Chichén Itzá?"

"I don't know," Rebecca said. "Why don't you put that little boy who hangs around you to work. Mexican children have an uncanny ability to learn what they want to know."

"Yes, most children share that trait," Celeste said stiffly as she put down her equipment. "I've had it for today."

"Well," Rebecca cast a glance around, "since the boss isn't here to impress, it won't hurt for both of us to quit early. Charles napped this afternoon. I think I'll wake him and we'll do a little shopping. There's a place with the most wonderful hammocks. The woman who owns the shop also sells charms and potions. Her prices are higher than the others, but her goods are better. We've already talked her down a bit. By today, we should be able to get five or six hammocks for a song."

"Maybe you should buy several dozen and take them back and sell them in your shoe store," Celeste said, without bothering to hide the sarcasm. "You could probably make a five or six hundred percent markup."

"That's an idea. The string hammocks would make a fabulous display for summer casual shoes." Rebecca jumped out of the trench. "I'll talk to Charles."

As she hurried away, Celeste shook her head. Why had Barry Undine lied to the Tretorns about his relationship with her? The truth was far more damaging than any lies he could concoct. It would have been far simpler if he'd told the facts. So why hadn't he? As much as she dreaded it, she was going to have to tell Mark about Barry's presence in Chichén Itzá. If the man was lying to the Tretorns, there was no telling what else he might be up to. Besides, it was time to tell Mark the entire story about Stuart McCarty.

Until Mark and Roberto returned, there wasn't much she could do. She prepared a light dinner and ate alone, reading an old archaeology magazine that Roberto had loaned her that dealt with the gods of the Mayas.

She had pushed aside her plate of cold fruit and salad when the three officers wearing uniforms of Mexican police officials came into the clearing.

"I am Capt. Emanuel Guirdion," the one with the most medals and ribbons told her. "I have come to investigate the death of the worker."

"It was terrible," Celeste said. "He was on guard at the stela when the jaguar attacked him. I'd seen the cat earlier, but it made no attempt to hurt me. We assumed that it had moved on to a more remote area of the jungle."

"There is no evidence of a jaguar," he said, his eyes watching every nuance of her expression. Behind him the other officers remained completely impassive.

"But I saw it myself," she said. "In broad daylight. There was no mistake. I saw that animal."

"My men have combed the area for miles. There is no jaguar. Such talk only creates problems, *señorita*."

"Problems?" She felt a tickle of threat in the man's tone.

"*Sí*. Now we have to discover who killed the man you called Timma. And why."

"No one killed Timma," Celeste said indignantly. "He was on guard duty when that animal attacked him. Surely you could tell by the way he was mangled that some beast killed him."

"A very clever beast." The policeman finally smiled, and it was scarier than his intense frown.

"What do you mean?" Celeste motioned to the officer to step toward her hut. Whatever he was getting ready to say was going to be shocking and unpleasant. She preferred to hear it in private, without having to worry about the Tretorns or anyone else listening.

"The man who died was not mauled. His body was examined by Dr. Abbrico, our medical investigator. At first it appeared that he was attacked by a large animal. Upon investigation, it was discovered that he died of a stab wound in the heart. After he was dead, his body was lacerated and the claw of an animal was dragged back and forth across his skin to make it appear that he was mauled.''

"Who would do such a thing?'' Celeste looked from the captain to the other two lower ranked members of the Mexican guardia. "Why?''

"Those are the questions we must have answered, *señorita*. Where are Mark Grayson and Roberto de Solarno?'' Captain Guirdion asked.

"I don't know,'' she said, her voice a little shaky. "They both left this afternoon and neither said where they were going. They should be back shortly.''

"We will wait.'' He motioned the two men to separate. They disappeared into the gathering darkness.

"But I saw that cat!'' Celeste insisted. "It was not more than twenty yards from me, standing in the path as if it had followed me.''

The officer looked at her. "I believe you *think* you saw a jaguar. But I know that you did not.'' He nodded his head in a clipped, military fashion. "We will wait for Señors Grayson and de Solarno. I have some questions for them.''

"I'll bet,'' Celeste said under her breath as the man walked away, his back rigid and unbending. She wasn't certain she believed what he'd said about Timma. Who in his right mind would murder a gentle man whose only goal in life was to work and provide for his family? He had no wealth, nothing that would benefit another to take. It was a ridiculous set of circumstances.

It was also very late, and there was still no sign of Mark or Roberto. She was beginning to let the seeds of worry sprout. Barry Undine was crazy. What if he'd hurt Mark, to get even with her?

Sleep was impossible, and she took a flashlight and decided to explore the area of the ruins near El Castillo. There was a three-quarter moon, or nearly so, and the night was bright. The men of the guardia were stationed nearby, probably roaming the ruins as they waited. Since coming on the dig, she'd been so busy working that she'd had little time to appreciate the old stone carvings. The Platform of the Jaguars was nearby, and she'd never really looked at it.

The path was easy to follow in the silvery moonlight, and whenever a thought of the mysterious jaguar came to mind, she simply pushed it aside. She believed it had been there, but she also believed the policemen were accurate in saying it was gone. The animal's behavior was decidedly odd. If it was a killer, it could have had her on the path to the stela. It had shown no interest in attacking her. In fact, the animal was passive. But if the cat hadn't killed Timma, then someone in the camp or the village had to have done it.

She strolled into the ball court, remembering her first visit with Mark. Rebecca had called him a challenge. She'd been taunting Celeste, but her choice of description was accurate. Mark was a challenging man, in more ways than one. She looked up at the pyramid and the memory of the full passion of his kiss made her shiver in the cool night air. In that brief, intimate moment, they'd shared something very special.

He was a man of strong convictions, and that appealed to her. He was a challenge, as Rebecca termed it. There was no denying she was sexually drawn to him. The memory of his hand in her hair, his fingers pressing into her back as he pulled her tight against him aroused her. She smiled in the moonlight. He'd tapped into a hunger she'd hidden even for herself. She wanted the touch of his hands and lips, the feel of his skin against hers.

She walked to one of the carved serpent figures, touching the cool stone as she tried to examine it with her eyes closed. What did Mark feel when he touched the stone? For a moment she lost herself in imaginings, wandering through the past and present trying to understand the man who had so unexpectedly ignited her passions. Never in a million years would she have dreamed that thoughts of a dead civilization could have captivated her so totally.

She opened her eyes and tried to imagine the ball court in action. From the best she'd been able to learn, there were rings in either end of the court where the players tried to

The Jaguar's Eye

score. In her mind it was a combination of basketball, hockey, baseball and jai alai. The Maya rulers watched the game seated on a small dais while the common people sat in the stands made of stone on the side. Underneath the current of well-understood athletic competitiveness was the conclusion of ritual sacrifice. At the end of the game, someone died. Not for the first time, Celeste wished she'd never picked up that tidbit of knowledge. From all she'd learned and seen, the Mayas seemed such peaceful people. Why had they created such bloodthirsty gods?

The sound of a motor rumbled from the parking area near the front of the ruins, and Celeste knew either Roberto or Mark had returned. Whoever it was, she wanted to get to him first and tell him what the police officials had said. As she started toward the front gate, she was surprised to see the Jeep creep through the gate with the lights off. In the moonlight she caught a glimpse of Mark as he drove right past her and headed toward the pyramid. She followed, her curiosity fully awakened.

Feeling a little guilty, she hung back behind a tall column as she watched Mark unload several containers from the Jeep. He began the long climb to the top of the pyramid, struggling under the weight of his burdens.

Amazed, Celeste watched a few moments, then picked up a plastic jug he'd left and started after him. Whatever he was doing, she'd save him a trip by carrying the jug, and she'd also tell him about the police.

With less weight to carry, she found it easy to keep pace with Mark as he climbed. She reached the top only a few moments after him. She followed him to the altar, where he put his burden down and turned on a flashlight.

As Celeste drew up behind him, she saw what the beam of light revealed. Millions of ants were crawling over the altar. The scene was something from a mad science-fiction story. There was no sense in the muddled mass of ants tumbling over each other and falling, only to get up and climb again, crushing other ants beneath them.

"Mark!" she murmured. "What are they doing?"

He started and turned to her, pushing the flashlight almost in her face. "Celeste! You scared me half to death sneaking up like that."

"I didn't sneak, I followed you." She pushed the light down. "Those ants. What's wrong with them?"

"I don't know," he said slowly. He swung the beam of light around to the base of the altar. There were millions of dead ants. "They're crushing each other to death. I've tried to find where they came from, but there isn't an obvious nest."

Celeste rubbed one spot on her neck where she'd been bitten. "They weren't here this afternoon. Maybe one or two, because I got bitten, but not like this." They stood a good five feet away and watched the insane antics of the small creatures in the beam of the light.

"I had to get some poison," Mark said. "I hate to do it, but if those ants swarmed a child, or even an adult, they could kill it."

"I wish I'd known you were going into Cancún. I desperately need to talk with my uncle."

Mark bent to mix the chemicals. "Is something wrong?"

"I'm not certain," she said. "Mark," she started to tell him, but remembered the police officers waiting for him and changed her mind. "I'm worried about my uncle, that's all. Listen, there are three police down at camp looking for you." She told him what they'd said about Timma.

Mark continued to mix the chemicals, and he did not comment.

"Aren't you going to say anything?"

"Timma was murdered. That's absurd. There's no one in this camp capable of murder. What motive?"

"Exactly my thoughts," Celeste noted. "What motive?"

Mark distributed the poison and began gathering the empty jugs. "I'd better deal with those officers. They have almost total authority here. There are several things I need to tell them, too." He looked at her. "One of our most valuable artifacts is missing."

"What?" Her brow furrowed. "Tell me what happened." She made a tender move to touch his face, but he unexpectedly turned away and began to pick up the empty chemical bottles. "We'd better deal with those police," he said and started down the steps. "Be careful. It's steep and treacherous in the dark."

She followed him, feeling each step with her foot before she shifted her weight. It was extremely awkward and exhausting, but her thoughts were on Mark's behavior. Had he deliberately avoided her touch? Maybe it had been unintentional. He was terribly upset by the news of Timma. And those bizarre ants! She shook her head and walked behind him.

At the camp, he turned to her. The kerosene lamps were still burning brightly, and the captain sat alone at the table. When he saw Mark and Celeste, a knowing smile came to his lips and he rose with his miitary posture intact.

"I'm sure the *señorita* has told you about the discoveries of our doctor."

"Yes," Mark said. He put the empty bottles down.

The policeman's gaze flicked to Celeste and back. "Perhaps we could speak alone."

"Celeste, would you mind?" Mark looked beyond her toward her hut.

"But I..." she started to protest, then turned on her heel and left. The idea of being dismissed in such a manner, especially when she'd been trying to help out as much as possible angered her. She was fuming when she threw back the cloth door and fell onto the cot.

As her temper cooled, she tried to listen for the sound of conversation coming from the clearing, but Mark and the captain had lowered their voices or moved into Mark's hut. It was no use. If the captain had more details for Mark, she'd have to wait until the morning to find out about them.

MARK WAS UP before dawn the next morning. With a broom he went to the pyramid and swept away the dead ants. Once the tiny bodies were gone, the altar looked as if the swarm had never occurred. It was extraordinary. While he was in Cancún he'd put in several calls to entomologists at the University of Southern California. He wanted a reason for what had happened. He wanted a lot of answers. At the top of the list was who had killed Timma? After his conversation the night before with Captain Guirdion, he did not doubt that the young Maya had been brutally murdered. The officer had given him details he'd spared Celeste, and Mark now had even more questions.

Had Celeste actually seen a jaguar, or was that part of the story she'd made up to justify Timma's death? The captain had drawn a very clear implication in that direction, and Mark had defended her without reservation. He could not believe she had done anything wrong, at least not on so little proof. He was anxious for Roberto to return from Cancún, but he knew his partner would not make it back before late afternoon. Mark smiled at the consistency of Roberto's nature. No matter how bad things were at the dig, Roberto would be able to push aside his worries for an evening of flirtation and fun. Then he would sleep late, get up and conclude his business and come back to the dig. It was useless to get upset or anxious. Roberto would return in his own time.

With the ants gone, he felt a measure of relief. At least now he could tell Wilfredo not to rush into the village and set off even more alarms. He could sense the whole situation escalating. Somehow he had to keep it under control. A few more "signs" from the gods, and the villagers would be ready to storm the ruins and run off the tourists and archaeologists.

In the dry dawn, he started toward the stela. He'd had little time to consider the mystery of the glyphs, but he was determined to spend the day photographing and cataloging each of the fascinating figures.

At the thought of solving the mystery, he felt a rush of excitement. He wanted to find the ruby, to prove he'd been right for one thing; but more than that, to establish Chichén Itzá as a major resource of Mexico. He left the broom at camp and got his sketch pad and tools as he went toward the stela.

The mystery absorbed him as he cut through the undergrowth. For the first time in days, he had few other thoughts. For several hours, the tragedy of Timma's death could be suppressed. The only thing he couldn't completely shake were his thoughts of Celeste. When she'd appeared behind him on the pyramid the night before, he'd almost had a heart attack. He'd been thinking about her so intensely. Being on top of the pyramid had brought back the afternoon. He could still taste the freshness of her lips. He had wanted her with a longing that was completely shocking. What had she touched that no woman before had been able to reach?

He pushed through the last of the underbrush and dropped his pack on the hard earth. He wanted to view the stela from all different angles with the camera. He picked up the Nikon and shifted into position. At first he failed to register what he saw through the lens. He dropped the camera and looked. Where the ancient carvings had once been so clearly detailed there was a fine powder of crushed stone. He rushed forward, brushing away the chips of stone and debris and found only a beaten surface. The horror of what had happened finally forced its way into his brain. Looking in the brush, he found the sledgehammer not five feet away. It was one of the tools from his own expedition.

He moved quickly down the stela, but not one of the figures remained. Whoever had used the sledgehammer had been effective. The stela was totally defaced. He sat heavily on the stone column, unable to move or think. The destruction sickened him. The craftsman who'd worked on the stela had spent months crafting the intricate puzzle. In a few moments, someone had destroyed it.

Anger replaced the sickness and he gathered up his equipment and the sledgehammer and went back to the camp. He heard Rebecca Tretorn laughing and talking as the graduate students silently ate. Juanita was serving break-

PLAY THE "LUCKY 7" SLOT MACHINE GAME!

AND YOU COULD GET FREE BOOKS, A FREE VICTORIAN PICTURE FRAME AND A SURPRISE GIFT!

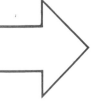

NO COST! NO OBLIGATION TO BUY!
NO PURCHASE NECESSARY!

PLAY "LUCKY 7"
AND GET AS MANY AS SIX FREE GIFTS...

HOW TO PLAY:

1. With a coin, carefully scratch off the silver box at the right. This makes you eligible to receive one or more free books, and possibly other gifts, depending on what is revealed beneath the scratch-off area.

2. You'll receive brand-new Harlequin Intrigue® novels. When you return this card, we'll send you the books and gifts you qualify for *absolutely free*!

3. If we don't hear from you, every other month we'll send you 4 additional novels to read and enjoy. You can return them and owe nothing but if you decide to keep them, you'll pay only $2.24* per book, a savings of 26¢ each off the cover price. There is *no* extra charge for postage and handling. There are no hidden extras.

4. When you join the Harlequin Reader Service®, you'll get our subscribers' only newsletter, as well as additional free gifts from time to time just for being a subscriber.

5. You must be completely satisfied. You may cancel at any time simply by sending us a note or a shipping statement marked "cancel" or returning any shipment to us at our cost.

This lovely Victorian pewter-finish miniature is perfect for displaying a treasured photograph— and it's yours absolutely free—when you accept our no-risk offer.

PLAY "LUCKY 7"

**Just scratch off the silver box with a coin.
Then check below to see which gifts you get.**

YES! I have scratched off the silver box. Please send me all the gifts for which I qualify. I understand I am under no obligation to purchase any books, as explained on the opposite page.

(U-H-I-01/91)180 CIH RDE7

NAME

ADDRESS   APT

CITY   STATE   ZIP

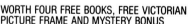 WORTH FOUR FREE BOOKS, FREE VICTORIAN PICTURE FRAME AND MYSTERY BONUS

 WORTH FOUR FREE BOOKS AND MYSTERY BONUS

 WORTH FOUR FREE BOOKS

 WORTH TWO FREE BOOKS

HARLEQUIN "NO RISK" GUARANTEE
- You're not required to buy a single book—ever!
- You must be completely satisfied or you may cancel at any time simply by sending us a note or a shipping statement marked "cancel" or returning any shipment to us at our cost. Either way, you will receive no more books; you'll have no further obligation.
- The free books and gifts you receive from this "Lucky 7" offer remain yours to keep no matter what you decide.

If offer card is missing, write to:
Harlequin Reader Service, 3010 Walden Ave., P.O. Box 1867, Buffalo, N.Y. 14269-1867

fast. At the edge of the clearing he swept the camp with his gaze. Celeste wasn't there.

Gradually all conversation halted, and he realized everyone was staring at him. He threw the hammer into the clearing and turned and went to his hut.

"My, my," Rebecca said softly. "I believe we witnessed our fearless leader in a huff."

"We'd better check that stela," one student said, motioning to the others. "I get a feeling something really bad has happened."

They left silently, hustling their breakfast dishes into the cooking area for Juanita to wash. In a few moments, only Rebecca Tretorn was left. She sipped her coffee, smiling into the morning sun.

She was still sitting there when a haggard Roberto entered the camp area. "Where's Mark?" he asked.

"I believe he's in his hut, sulking," she answered. She gave his rumpled clothes a curious look. Roberto was known for his passion for crisp seams and neatly ironed clothes. "You're up either very early or very late."

"Where's Celeste?" he asked, ignoring her remarks.

"She didn't show for breakfast. She said something about going to Cancún."

"Is she leaving?" Roberto's voice was sharp.

"Dear me," Rebecca said. "It would be better to ask her. No one asked me to assume the role of social hostess, so I've failed to gather all the pertinent information you seem to require."

Roberto shook his head in disbelief. "This isn't a game, Mrs. Tretorn. Is Celeste planning on leaving?"

"I don't think so. There were three policemen here last night and she talked with them. It was a very big secret, but as is true with all secrets, they slip out. There's some funny business over that Maya man's death. Maybe Celeste has decided this isn't the place to vacation. Maybe it isn't good for her health."

Chapter Ten

March 13. Imix, bad. The thirteenth Maya month begins. Messages are received.

"Are you certain?" Mark paced the dimly lighted hut. "There's no doubt?"

"I spoke with her boss. He was evasive at first, but then he admitted that Celeste was suspended, pending an investigation. He would give me no more details."

At last Mark dropped onto his cot and put his head in his hands. "Someone destroyed the stela last night, Roberto. They smashed it with a sledgehammer."

"My God." Roberto began pacing. "And what is that about Timma's death? Mrs. Tretorn made some remark."

"He wasn't killed by a jaguar, he was stabbed in the heart and then the murder was disguised as an animal attack. I guess whoever did it thought he'd be buried locally without an examination." Mark stood and walked to the door of his hut. "This is like a nightmare."

"We should stop Celeste from leaving," Roberto said softly. "And I suppose we should contact the authorities."

"No." Mark turned to face his partner. "We have no real evidence that Celeste has done anything wrong. It isn't unbelievable that she would wish to speak with her uncle."

"What about the carved figure? You can't ignore that."

"Did you see her take it?"

"The evidence is circumstantial, that's true," Roberto said, "but we've been at this dig for nearly two years. Nothing like this had ever happened before, and it started the minute she walked into the camp."

"We've never had tourists like Celeste...or the Tretorns," Mark agreed. "Let me confront her. Let me ask about the figure and about her job in Tampa. At least let's give her a chance to explain."

For a long moment Roberto watched his friend. "You are a strange man, Mark. You won't take off a few hours to take a woman to dinner. You stay out here alone and work for months on end. Now, suddenly, you're willing to defend this woman you've known six days and mostly watched from a distance." He smiled. "Yes, I've seen you watching her, even though she hasn't. Why are you doing this?"

The question was softly spoken. Mark considered for several moments. "I don't know," he finally answered. "I sense something about her, something that's different."

"It could be that she's a thief," Roberto said bluntly.

"No," Mark shook his head. "I've known thieves before, both male and female. I cannot believe that of Celeste."

"Make me a promise, then," Roberto said. He went to Mark and put his hand on his shoulder. "Talk with her. If you don't get some satisfactory answers, then promise me we'll go to the authorities. Mark, a man has been murdered. Celeste may or may not be involved. After all, she's the only person who claims to have seen that cat. That's pretty suspicious, you have to admit."

"I'll talk with her," Mark agreed. He moved toward the door, but Roberto's firm grip stopped him.

"Of all the women you could pick, don't set your heart on the one who will break it. For such a brilliant man, you have no wisdom in the way of life."

"But I have you for guidance." Mark managed a smile and ducked through the doorway. He had no worries that Celeste would leave the ruins. She'd mentioned going into Cancún to call and check on her uncle. That sounded a little flimsy, based on what he'd just learned about her. Maybe she did need to make a call to the States. Maybe it was about her uncle. He headed toward the gates where the busloads of tourists would soon be arriving. He had no trouble finding Celeste. Her beautiful hair, glinting a million shades of copper, was easy to spot.

She was leaning against the rental car in disgust as he approached. The hood was up, and he wondered how much a woman like Celeste might actually know about combustion engines.

"Somebody took the distributor cap," she said as she saw him. "I'd believe it if they took the battery, or maybe the tires, but the distributor cap?" She tried to make a face, but it didn't hide her frustration and anger.

"Sounds like someone wanted to keep you here." Mark offered the comment in a casual tone. "Who would that be?" He had a terrible thought that Roberto might be the one.

"That cretinous toad Barry Undine comes to mind," Celeste said. "He came here to torment me, and he's doing a good job of it."

This was the opening Mark had been waiting to hear. "When Mr. Undine showed up in camp, he leveled some pretty serious charges against you, Celeste."

She felt her heartbeat quicken, and she looked into Mark's eyes. Did he believe she was guilty? She couldn't tell. The dark blue depths were totally without emotion. He was watching her, waiting for her reaction. Which meant he must have some doubts about her. The pain was almost physical.

"Well, accusations are easy to make," she managed, lifting her chin in defiance. Accusations had almost ruined her life in Tampa, and now they were hovering over her again. This time there was more at stake than a job, though. There was something between her and Mark, something that had the potential to develop into a rare and wonderful relationship. But only if he believed in her.

Mark felt his spirits drop a notch. She wasn't denying anything; she was positioning for a better offense.

"He didn't show me any proof. He only said you'd been suspended on a charge of insider trading." He said it slowly and clearly.

She knew Mark was waiting for her to tell him it wasn't true. She could sense it in the way he looked at her, and it made her furious. She was able to judge him as an honest man, a stubborn man, but one with good character. Why couldn't he do the same for her? Would she have to go through the rest of her life reassuring people she wasn't a crook?

"I need to call my uncle." She turned away from him and picked up her overnight bag from the seat of the rental car. "Can I use the Jeep or the Rover?"

"I'll come with you. I need to visit the authorities."

"If you don't trust me to bring the vehicle back, that's fine, come with me," she said coldly. "I thought for a little while that you might be different from all of my friends in Tampa. I honestly thought you might be a man who made his own decisions and opinions. Believe what you want about me, Mark. Just don't ask me to reassure you or make you believe in me." She felt the approach of tears and she turned angrily on her heel. "I have to pick up some things from one of the vendors. I'd like to leave as soon as possible."

"Señorita Coolridge!"

She heard the woman calling her and looked into the distance. Already heat devils were spiraling up from the dirt road, but she could make out the figure of a woman running toward her, the bright colors of her full skirt swirling in the distorted distance.

"Maria?" she called out. It looked like Thomas's mother.

"*Señorita,* you must come. It is Thomas! He has the sickness and he's calling for you."

"Jump in," Mark said, motioning to the Rover. He helped Maria into the front while Celeste took a seat in the back.

"What's wrong with him?" Celeste asked, fear making her suddenly aware that medical help was a long way away. "What kind of sickness?"

"We don't know. He was well yesterday. Last night he disappeared. He is a boy of that age, wandering in the night, wanting to be alone. My husband said to leave him to his freedom. We found him this morning, sitting in the shade of the flame tree. He was dizzy and ill and he kept calling your name. He has gotten worse." She started crying, and Celeste reached over the seat and touched her shoulder.

"He'll be okay. Thomas is young and strong. We'll get him to a doctor."

"Please, *señorita*. You must save him." She turned back to Celeste, her hands clutching Celeste's clothes. "You can save him."

Celeste caught Mark's eyes and saw the same puzzlement she felt. How could she save anyone? She knew a few basic emergency medical procedures, but she was no doctor.

As soon as they got to Maria's home, Celeste halted at the size of the crowd. Young children were playing in the yard while mothers stood in clusters, talking. "If Thomas's illness is communicable, we're going to have an epidemic," Celeste said to Mark under her breath. "This is terrible."

"I'll try to convince them to go home," Mark said doubtfully. "See what you can do for the boy. You have to make them understand that he has to be taken to the hospital."

"Right," she agreed, moving through the women into the house.

She found Thomas in a small bed. Only Carlotta Bopp sat beside him. A sweet odor like incense burned in a small pot beside the sickbed, and several dozen candles were lighted. In the dim room, Celeste could see that Thomas was very pale. Sweat covered his brow, and Carlotta was soaking a cloth in cool water and wiping his forehead. His breathing was shallow and strained.

"Can you save him?" Carlotta asked.

"Me?" Celeste was more taken aback than ever. She'd never expected Carlotta to yield her power with such a question. "I don't know anything about medicine."

"Touch him," Carlotta said, moving away from the bed. "He has been calling your name. Touch him."

Celeste sat in the chair beside the young boy. He looked terribly frail and small. She placed a cool hand on his forehead and called softly to him. "Thomas, it's Celeste. Can you hear me?"

There was no response, and Celeste heard a muffled sob. She looked up to see that Maria had entered the room and was standing at the end of the bed with Carlotta.

"Thomas," Celeste tried agin. His body was frighteningly cool, his breathing fast and shallow. She pulled back the sheets and unbuttoned the top of his shirt, moving it away from his skin. "We must warm him," she said. "Bring hot water bottles or towels. Anything hot and a lot of it." She tried desperately to remember what she knew about respiratory failure and what appeared to be shock. Keep the patient quiet and warm. That was all that came to mind. She knew a little about artificial respiration, but certainly not enough to keep Thomas alive if he went into respiratory failure. She had to figure out what was wrong with him.

The two women hurried from the room to bring more water and Celeste pushed aside Thomas's shirt. She quickly drew off his cotton pants, leaving him in his underwear. As she moved the pants down his left leg, she saw the wound. Two clear and distinct puncture marks. As her hand brushed across it, the boy cried out.

"Thomas," she said urgently. "Talk to me. It's Celeste."

"The jaguar came," Thomas mumbled. "He came from the jungle, his eyes burning like two fires."

Carlotta and Maria returned with steaming towels and several hot-water containers. Celeste showed them the ugly wound. The tissue around the puncture was red and inflamed, and obviously extremely painful. While Maria began to bathe her son's upper body, Celeste applied a cool

compress to the wound. A terrible suspicion was beginning
to form in her mind, even though she fought against it.

"The messenger of Quetzalcoatl has found him," Carlotta said into the silence. "He is marked."

"If you're saying he's been snakebitten, I think you're
right," Celeste said. "Could I have a strip of cloth or a
handkerchief, something to use to wrap around his leg?"

"No snake," Maria said, panic taking over her voice.
"He will die. No snake." She started a hurried prayer in
Spanish.

Celeste felt the situation slipping from her control. Where
was Mark? "Maria, I need a cloth, a belt or something.
Please, it is important." She spoke calmly and slowly.
"Carlotta will help you." She glanced at Carlotta, hoping
for some support.

Without ever taking her eyes from Thomas, Carlotta
reached into her skirts and tore a long piece of material. She
handed it to Celeste. "Save him, if you can. You are the only
one who has the power."

"That's because I'm trying," Celeste said carefully.

"I saw the jaguar," Thomas mumbled. "He called for
Señorita Coolridge. He said her name, and said she is the
one we wait to serve."

In the hush of the sickroom, Celeste felt the hairs on her
arms begin to prickle. "He's delirious," she said. "He's
dreaming, and he doesn't know what he's saying."

"Señorita!" Thomas cried, trying to sit up. "The cat
wants you. He is the messenger, and he wants to tell you that
Quetzalcoatl is coming." He fell back on the bed.

"We must take him to the hospital," Celeste said, filling
the void in the room. Both women were staring at her with
fear and awe.

"Celeste?" Mark entered the small room, seeming to take
up more than half the available space.

"Look at this, Mark," Celeste said, moving away the
compress to show the wound.

"Let me see that!" Mark bent closer, pressing around the
inflamed area until Thomas cried out. He looked at Maria.

"Boil some water. Get me a sharp knife." He turned to Celeste. "Take the Rover back to the camp and bring me the medical kit—and a bottle of brandy, whiskey or whatever you can find." He lifted her by the shoulders. "Quick! The boy's been snakebitten and we have to work fast if we want to save him."

"The hospital?" Celeste said helplessly.

"There's no time," Mark said as he pushed her toward the door. "If you want Thomas to live, drive like hell and bring Juanita back with you, if you can find her."

Celeste flew from the room, her heart hammering. Thomas would not die. He could not. He was strong. But the image of him, so frail and young, crumpled in the bed made her cry out. She whipped into the Rover and raced toward the ruins.

"Juanita!" she cried repeatedly as she ran toward the camp. The cook heard the fear in her voice and fell in beside her as she got the medical bag and a bottle of brandy. Together, without Juanita asking questions, the two women hurried back to Thomas's bedside.

Mark had already applied a tourniquet, lanced the wound and removed as much poison as possible. From the kit he withdrew a small vial of powder. With a syringe he injected sterile water into the powder and with a few vigorous shakes, he had antitoxin serum.

Maria started to cry as he prepared the injection, but Carlotta spoke to her in rapid Spanish while Celeste and Juanita assisted Mark by holding Thomas. With great care, Mark released the tourniquet every few moments.

"It's hard to tell how much venom he's already had. If we can control the flow of what remains on a steady basis, he should be okay. If he gets too much, his respiratory system won't be able to take it."

"Get more hot water," Celeste ordered Maria. "Hurry now. We must keep Thomas warm."

Maria scurried out of the room, her terror relieved for the moment because she had a task to perform.

"You are very wise," Carlotta whispered to Celeste. "You care for the boy, don't you?"

"Very much." She felt a lump rising. This wasn't the time to cry. Mark was battling for Thomas's life, and she had to help.

"We talked about destiny, remember?" Carlotta smiled and motioned her out of the room.

"Yes," Celeste hadn't followed her shift in topic. She was confused, and it showed on her face.

"Perhaps you were here to save Thomas?" Carlotta lifted both eyebrows.

"Thomas might not have been here if it weren't for me. He probably would have been in Cancún making money."

"But you saved his life."

"Technically, Mark saved his life," Celeste pointed out.

"It was you he called for, *señorita*. It was your touch that made him speak. The jaguar spoke of you."

"That's ridiculous," Celeste snapped. "Thomas was delirious. He didn't know what he was saying. He called for me because . . ."

Carlotta smiled. "Because he knew who could save him."

"I'm not some voodoo queen." Celeste couldn't keep the harshness from her voice. "Please stop this, Carlotta. I have nothing to do with life here at Chichén Itzá or the village. I'm a visitor. I'll be going home in a few days."

Carlotta's expression did not change. "Maybe not."

Celeste turned away from her and reentered Thomas's room. She was determined to ignore Carlotta and her foolishness. "His breathing is a little easier," she said. As she bent to look at him, she saw Mark staring at her.

"What?" she asked.

"What were you and Carlotta discussing?" he asked.

"She has some absurd notion that I cured Thomas, that he called me because he knew I could." She felt her ears tingle even as she talked. "The villagers have taken to me in an odd way, partly because of this young man." She brushed the hair from the boy's forehead in a soft gesture.

"I think the worst is over. Do you know where he was when he was bitten?"

She related the story to him as she'd been told.

"That's extremely odd. Pit vipers, which include rattle-snakes and copperheads, are the most common poisonous snakes around here. Judging by the fang marks, it was a medium-sized snake of that family. I took a chance and treated him for that. It looks like we were lucky."

"Lucky it was in the fleshy part of his thigh," Celeste agreed.

"It's strange, though, that the snake didn't give a warning. If Thomas were sitting under a tree, say asleep, the normal behavior for the snake would be to bypass him. It's very odd."

"Señorita Coolridge," Thomas mumbled, starting to struggle again.

Celeste and Mark held him firmly. "What is it, Thomas?" she answered. "I'm here. I'm with you."

"The jaguar spoke your name," he cried.

"It was a dream," Celeste said firmly but with a soothing tone. "Everything is fine, Thomas. You must rest. It was all a dream."

He seemed to drift back into a deep sleep, and his breathing had become much easier. Mark continued to apply and release the tourniquet.

They stayed with Thomas until he was resting peacefully. Mark washed the wound and applied antibiotic salve.

"Lucky you keep a well-stocked medical kit," Celeste said as she helped him repack. "I'd never have thought of anti-venin."

"Snake bite is extremely rare. But when it happens, there's nothing like the right treatment. I probably would never have packed it, but when I was a child on one of my father's expeditions, we had an incident."

"And?" Celeste prodded.

"The worker died. My father did everything he knew, but it was useless. The man's breathing stopped and he died."

"How old were you?"

"About ten or twelve. It was a long time ago." He picked up the bag. "Let's head back to camp."

"What about my trip to Cancún?"

"I can't stop you, Celeste, but I'd like to talk with you first."

"Talk or accuse?" She wanted the protection of anger, but it was gone. Her fear for Thomas had wrung everything out of her.

"Talk," he said. "There's nothing I want to accuse you of doing. There are some things that need an explanation, but I know you'll have one. You'll agree that some very strange things have happened here since you arrived. After this morning, though, I can see clearly that you aren't involved."

"What made you change your mind?" She wasn't ready to give in to a pat answer.

"You said earlier today that you could see me for what I am. I believe you. Somehow, you've been able to tolerate my aggressive comments and behavior and look beyond that to who I am. I saw you this morning for what you really are, and it wasn't a thief or a con artist. It was a woman who cared greatly for a young boy who is no relation to her."

He put both hands on her shoulders. "There's something special about you. I know it, just like I knew that stela held the secret to the Jaguar's Eye. I never lost my faith in you, not really. I'm willing to risk believing in you."

He didn't have to tell her that it had been a long time since he'd believed in another person; she already knew it. Perhaps not since his father's death. She smiled at him, touching the rugged contours of his face with her fingertips.

"I didn't do what Barry accused me of doing. I didn't trade on insider information. I think he might have done it and set me up. That's why I have to talk with my uncle."

"I believe you," he said. He shifted her closer. "We'll go into Cancún together, as soon as I talk with Roberto. When I said I needed to talk with the authorities, I meant it." A frown hardened his gaze.

"What is it?"

"Someone destroyed the stela."

The shock made her speechless. She knew him well enough to know that he wasn't kidding. Mark Grayson had never been accused of having the most developed sense of humor, and he'd never kid about something so important to him. "Was it completely destroyed?"

"There's not an image left. Whoever did the work with the sledgehammer did a thorough job."

"Oh, Mark, I'm so sorry." Her arms went to his shoulders in a movement of support. "What will you do?"

"Make a report to the authorities. That's all I can do. After all those weeks of work and sweat, now the riddle is destroyed."

"Can you remember any of it? I have a clear picture of some, like that serpent."

His arms closed around her. For a moment he allowed himself the luxury of her in his arms. She had a willowy grace that delighted him. "I have some drawings," he said, breathing in the smell of her hair. She washed it every evening in the cenote. Her skin was deliciously soft, like her lips. When he held her, he was able to believe that somehow things would work out.

"Have you any idea who might have vandalized the stela?"

Her question brought him back to reality with a sudden jolt. "No," he answered. "Well, yes and no. I suspect it's someone from the village. I haven't a clue, though. It certainly makes Timma's death more connected to the dig, I'm sorry to say."

"You think it was one of the villagers who wants the dig to be abandoned." She made a statement instead of asking a question.

"That's a logical train of thought. Who else would do it? One of the students? The Tretorns? Roberto? You? Maybe even in a fit of sleepwalking? Not too likely."

She had to agree he had a point. The trouble was that as much as the villagers wanted to send the expedition away, would they deface the remains of the past? On top of that,

Carlotta was trying to stop any altercations between archaeological members and villagers. It didn't make sense that someone would destroy the stela. She held back her thoughts. After all, she was new to the dig. There were many things she didn't know.

"What about my friend, Barry Undine?" She lifted her head from his shoulder to watch his eyes.

"Why?"

Mark's simple question opened a lot of others. "Maybe to pin something on me in Mexico. If I can't go home, then I can't pursue the idea that he's responsible for a lot of the accusations that have been made against me."

"That's one possibility," Mark agreed. "Roberto found a small carved figure in your hut."

"The woman with the red hair!" Celeste was relieved. "I wondered where it had gone." There was a half-beat pause. "What was Roberto doing in my hut?"

"Looking for the figure. It disappeared from the small store of artifacts we've unearthed."

"And Roberto thought I might have stolen it." She was too worn down to be angry. "Even Roberto thought I was guilty." She dropped her hands from his shoulders and started to turn away.

"He had to check it out, Celeste. That's part of our trade. We look for facts, not assumptions or emotions or feelings or intuitions. The figure was missing. Barry Undine had accused you of being a thief."

"Then you condone what he did—going into my hut and sneaking through my things. Why didn't he ask me outright? I would have told him that the figure was given to me."

"Given? Who gave it to you?"

His tone infuriated her. "Carlotta Bopp. She left it with Rebecca to give to me. Next you'll be accusing her."

Mark's hand on her shoulder was firm. "Wait a minute before you let that redhead temper drive you away." He eased her around to face him. "I'm not accusing anybody of anything. Not yet. There are some strange things happening. You've already agreed to that statement. I have to say your relationship with the villagers is odd. I've seen the way they look at you, with some type of, well, almost reverence or awe. There's a lot going on here, including the arrival of Undine, and it all needs to be sorted out. But I told Roberto not to go into your hut. I thought we'd agreed to ask you first. That's Roberto's way, not mine."

"Did you ever think that maybe Roberto was trying to frame me?" The question popped out of her mouth.

"What?"

"First he tried to set me up with Daniel Ortiz, like some cheap gambit. Now he's sneaking through my personal belongings and finding stolen objects. I get the feeling someone's trying to frame me for something."

Mark's hand tightened slightly on her shoulders. "You're right. Not Roberto, but someone."

"Who? And why?"

"Someone wants to stop us from finding the Jaguar's Eye, Celeste. That has to be it. We must be getting closer and closer to the secret."

"Or the curse."

Chapter Eleven

*Those whom the gods have chosen cannot avoid the
moment. There is an art to falling through the sky.
Survival is not the issue.*

Celeste and Mark were halfway back to camp when they
heard Roberto's furious shouts.

"This is a mistake! Release him immediately!"

Mark hurried to the central camp, with Celeste close on
his heels. In the center of the clearing beside the table, Wilfredo stood as a captive of Captain Guirdion and two officers.

"They've arrested Wilfredo for Timma's death," Roberto said angrily. "These men are imbeciles!" He pointed at
the police officers.

"Captain, could I speak with you?" Mark asked in a
courteous voice. He shot Roberto a warning look that ef-
fectively silenced his complaints. With a gracious gesture,
Mark motioned the captain into the shelter of their hut and
dropped the cloth.

Celeste, Roberto and Wilfredo were left standing in the
hot sun with the two police officers eyeing them uneasily.

"I did not do this thing," Wilfredo said, his eyes plead-
ing with Roberto. He made no effort to struggle against the
officers who held his arms behind his back. "Don't let them
take me. My family, what will they do if I go to prison?"

"You aren't going anywhere," Roberto promised him, his eyes still flashing a dangerous blaze. "Mark will convince the captain that this is all a mistake. Relax." He turned to the officers. "Wilfredo is very respected in his village. His character is well known and many will speak for him. He is not a criminal."

The two officers, without the vigilant eye of their superior, relaxed their hold on Wilfredo's arms. At the release, he straightened and gathered his dignity. His fear seemed to lessen, and he spoke to Roberto again.

"I did nothing wrong. I would never hurt Timma. He was my friend. It was the cat, even if no one wants to talk about it."

"I heard shouting. What's going on?" Rebecca wandered to Celeste's side. "I see you've met the charming officials. They were here earlier and couldn't find a soul to talk to except me. The captain told me it was a simple crime of passion. Wilfredo has been seeing Timma's wife, or so it seems."

"I don't believe that for a minute," Celeste retorted. The idea was repulsive, especially after she'd witnessed the grief of Timma's window. "They've made that up, just so they'd have an excuse to arrest someone."

"Then who did kill Timma, since you consider yourself Agatha Christie?" Rebecca asked, her voice arch with her own brand of humor. "I'm going shopping."

"I don't know," Celeste shot at her retreating back. "I haven't ruled you out as a suspect yet." She went to stand beside Wilfredo. "That woman is capable of anything," she muttered.

"Why does she hate me?" Wilfredo asked.

Celeste didn't have that answer, so she turned a question to one of the guards. "What is the evidence against Wilfredo?"

"We have a witness to the crime." The officer seemed almost apologetic.

"Who?"

"He is protected by law until the trial," the other man answered.

"You can't arrest a man without telling him who his accuser is," she reasoned, appalled because she knew they could do exactly that.

"Speak to the captain," the officer said, motioning to his partner to be silent.

"I will," Celeste said, drawing Roberto aside. Her own anger with him for searching her hut had evaporated. There were more important things to consider. "There's no witness. They're making it up. Did you see the way they acted?"

"I don't know." Roberto was watching the two officers and Wilfredo. "They already know about someone destroying the stela, too. Since they've arrested Wilfredo, there's a good chance they'll blame that on him."

"You mean they'll just say he did it!"

"It happens," Roberto said, shrugging. "Not only in Mexico, either. People are often wrongly accused."

"Don't I know it," Celeste said. A long sigh escaped her. "I've already talked with Mark and told him I'm innocent. I want to tell you, too. I didn't take that carved figure." She started to tell him about Carlotta Bopp, but things were complicated enough with the villagers. "Where will they take Wilfredo?" she asked.

"To Cancún, for the time being. I'm not exactly certain what the procedure will be. It could be months before a trial date is set. Even longer. The prisons are an atrocity." He was worried, and he didn't bother to hide it. "Wilfredo doesn't know how to survive in that type of environment."

"We can't let this happen," Celeste said suddenly. "It's one thing to be accused of a white-collar crime in Florida. A murder charge here, what could that turn into for Wilfredo? His family might starve while he's gone."

"What can we do?" Roberto asked. "Mark is talking with the captain, but believe me, I tried. The man is unreasonable."

"Let's give Wilfredo a chance."

"What are you talking about?" Roberto eyed her with new interest.

"He knows this area. If he had a moment's distraction, he could get away. He could hide out until they find the real murderer."

"That's absurd, Celeste." Roberto's eyes were intense. "If you interfere with these officers, they can very easily arrest you."

"It's a risk I'll have to take. Wilfredo didn't do anything, and I'm not like some people I know. I've been exposed to people who sit back and let others be unjustly accused. I'm not going to let them haul him away from his family for years."

"Celeste!" he cautioned her.

"Officer," Celeste motioned one of the men over to her and Roberto. "I need to go into Cancún to make a telephone call. Would it be possible for me to ride with you and catch a bus back tomorrow?"

The man looked toward the hut where his superior had disappeared. "You must ask the captain. It is possible."

Celeste smiled. With her heel she stepped on Roberto's instep, nudging him toward the other guard. She stepped closer to the guard near her.

"Could you ask the captain? I'd like to pack a few things, if I can ride with you." She darted quick glances to make sure Roberto had engaged the other officer in conversation.

"I should not interrupt the captain," the man said. He looked from Celeste to the hut, apparently torn between a desire to help Celeste and the thought that he might anger his superior.

"He'll understand how impatient a woman can be," Celeste said with a small chuckle. "I'm sure the captain comprehends the ways of tourists. We have a bad reputation, but we rely on the authorities to help us."

"Americans are very impatient, at times," the guard agreed.

"Ask him, *por favor,*" Celeste said, using her brightest smile.

Reluctantly the guard approached the hut. Celeste turned to find that Roberto had stepped between the other guard and Wilfredo. "Oh, Roberto, I forgot to tell you about the distributor cap!" she cried, starting to hurry toward him. As she got close, she tripped. With a cry she dove headfirst into Roberto. Thrown off balance, he toppled into the officer. In that split second of tangled legs, Celeste managed to look up and catch Wilfredo's eye.

"Run!" she grunted, giving him a signal to leave.

Wilfredo needed no second invitation. He sprinted for the jungle and disappeared down one of the paths before either officer could raise an alert.

"Help!" Celeste squawked, rolling and tangling herself among the men. She thrashed helplessly, clutching at legs and holding them until the officer she'd sent on an errand ran back to assist his partner. By the time they were untangled and standing, Wilfredo had a good three-minute start.

"This was deliberate," the captain shouted as he rushed from the hut and confronted the four of them. He looked toward the jungle where Wilfredo had disappeared. "It is pointless to chase him now. He knows the jungle too well. But he will not escape justice."

"Captain," Mark said, "Wilfredo is innocent. It might seem that a criminal has escaped, but he did not kill Timma. He will help you find the real murderer."

"You will be punished," the captain said to his men, completely ignoring Mark. "And you," he looked at Roberto and Celeste, "have interfered with the law. You haven't helped your friend. We will find him."

"Wilfredo would never hurt anyone," Celeste spoke up. "Someone else killed Timma." Her red hair blazed in the sun, but her skin was milky white with anger. Mark was giving her a warning look, but she was too mad to pay heed.

"The answer to your question is no. You may not go into Cancún. You are not to leave the ruins, Miss Coolridge. I will post a man to make sure that no one leaves. I will also collect the keys to your vehicles.''

"With pleasure," she said, digging into her pocket for the key to the rental car. "Someone has already helped himself to my distributor cap. You might as well have the key." She dropped it in his palm.

"Captain Guirdion, there are times when we need a vehicle," Mark said. "A young boy in the village has been snakebitten. There are emergencies when we need transportation."

"Then my officer will decide. Give me the keys."

Mark gave him both sets.

"No one from the group will leave. No one. Is that understood?"

"Are we under arrest?" Celeste asked.

Mark walked to her side and gripped her arm tightly. "Shut that mouth," he whispered in her ear. "The man has had it with you."

Captain Guirdion smiled at her. "Would you like to be?"

With Mark's fingers burning through her flesh to the bone, she shook her head no. She couldn't open her mouth or she'd yell with pain.

"Good," he answered and started walking away. Both officers followed him, their heads bowed. In the tension-filled circle of the camp, Roberto finally sighed. "That was close." He looked at Celeste. "Maybe you don't understand. That man has complete authority. He could have hauled you away, American or not. You made him look bad in front of his men."

Now that the crisis was over, Celeste felt her legs go rubbery. She stumbled, and only Mark's tight grip kept her from falling. "I've never been one to do such things," she said. "I don't challenge authority," she said, laughing weakly.

Mark's hands slipped beneath her arms and helped her to a chair. "The tigress has collapsed," he said. His hands lingered on her shoulders, giving her a gentle massage as Roberto went to find a drink.

"What you did was inexcusable," Mark whispered, "but you might have saved Wilfredo's life."

"He was innocent," Celeste said. She was feeling better, but the temerity of what she'd done made her tremble. "I couldn't let him be taken after what Roberto told me. It was wrong." She rested her head on her hand for a moment. "I only hope I haven't made matters worse for Wilfredo. If they catch him..."

"That captain is right about one thing. If anyone knows that jungle, it's Wilfredo. He'll be okay for months, hiding there."

"The thing we have to do is find out who killed Timma," Celeste said. "I need to get a message to my uncle."

"None of us can leave," Mark reminded her. "I wouldn't go against that order, either."

"Thomas," Celeste said. "As soon as he is well, he can contact Uncle Alec. How long will that be?"

"Several days, at least," Mark said. "I doubt that any of us will be going anywhere for that length of time."

"Since we're virtually imprisoned here, what can we do about the stela?" she asked. "You said you have sketches."

"Good idea." He motioned toward Roberto who had brought three cool drinks. "Let's get the sketches of the stela and see if we can figure any of this out."

"Where are the Tretorns?" Celeste asked suddenly.

"Shopping," Roberto said drolly. "Where else?"

"I think it might be a good idea if they didn't know you had any sketches," Celeste spoke slowly, looking from one man to the next.

"Why is that?" Roberto's question had an edge. "Are you on to something?"

"More than anything, it's Rebecca's attitude. She was needling me, and I made some smart reply back about going after Charles. She said to go for it. She meant it, too. The implication was that he didn't provide for her and she was not opposed to being rid of him." She drew a breath. "It's just something about them. They came here expecting to find a treasure, as if they already knew about the Jaguar's Eye."

"Daniel might have mentioned it," Roberto said. "He's known my hopes, but he never pays any attention to what we tell him. He could very possibly have implied that we find treasure every day."

"I don't know," Mark said carefully, "but your suggestion to keep the sketches secret is a good one. The fewer people who know they exist, the less chance that someone will try to destroy them the way the stela was destroyed."

"Good idea, so dash off and get them," Roberto said, slipping into the seat beside Celeste.

Mark returned with the sketch pad and they carefully reconstructed the design of the stela across the top of the table. The three of them studied the drawings, always listening for the sound of anyone approaching.

"If white is north," Celeste said, latching onto the theory Mark had told her before, "then maybe we should start with this figure." She pointed to the drawing of a prophet on a dais. "Maybe this is the teller of the riddle."

"Maybe," Mark agreed, excitement in his voice.

"What is this one?" Roberto pointed to a drawing that looked like piles of clouds filled with many different animals.

"The Maya version of heaven?" Mark asked.

"How does that figure?" Celeste bent closer.

"My theory is that this is a story, sort of a prediction, if you will. I'm not certain, but I believe that the Mayas realized their civilization was beginning to crumble. The Toltecs had made Chichén Itzá their own in many ways, but there was still a small section of those who clung to the old Maya ways. As the Empire began to fall apart, I think they removed the large ruby from the figure of the jaguar. They hid it, believing that they would eventually return to power and the stone would be replaced".

"So how does the glyph figure in?" Celeste asked.

"Well, this could very easily be the scene of the Maya creatures waiting in heaven for the day when they could return in glory."

"Sort of a resurrection," Celeste said in awe.

"It is amazing how constant themes run through culture after culture," Roberto said. "Take a stab at this one, Mark?" He pointed toward the serpent, the largest figure, with the woman emerging from its mouth.

"To me, that's the reincarnation symbol of Quetzalcoatl. I could be way off, but it would seem to be that. It's an old symbol, but I've seen it more than once. Take Celeste's necklace, for instance. If that necklace came from another Maya city, then the theory of reincarnation might well have been very widespread. There may have been many believers that the god Quetzalcoatl would return, either in the form of a woman, or through the help of a woman, or something like that."

"The figure!" Celeste said suddenly. "That carved figure! The pose is very similar to this!" She pointed to the woman standing on the serpent's tongue.

"She's right," Roberto said, leaning closer. "There is an uncanny resemblance. Very strange coincidence. Mark was never certain if he'd found the carving, or if someone might have left it there for him."

Celeste felt a cold chill touch her back. "That's creepy, Roberto. If someone is planting clues for Mark, then someone wants us to find the solution. You have to ask why? If there's a fabulous jewel involved, then why haven't they gone after it themselves?"

"Why indeed?" Mark asked. He looked up, scanning the jungle. "Somebody's coming," he said, gathering the sketches. "We'll work on this later tonight."

"I thought the lot of you would be in jail," Rebecca said, strolling into the camp with Charles, who was carrying a bundle of packages. "I thought for certain we'd be able to pack it up and go home with a clear conscience. In fact, why don't we?" She looked at Charles, who shifted uncomfortably.

"I'm afraid Captain Guirdion has removed that option," Mark said slowly. "He's asked all of us to stay here, until Wilfredo is found."

"How did they lose him?" Rebecca asked, her voice lifting on a note of humor. "They had him securely when I left."

"Well, they lost him," Roberto said, flashing a smile to cover the sharpness of his words.

"And we are somehow involved in that escape?" Rebecca asked. "The details on this should be very entertaining." She looked at her husband. "Charles, this is proving to be more of an adventure than either of us anticipated."

"CELESTE! WAKE UP!" The urgent words seemed to come as part of a dream and she fought against them.

"Celeste!"

She sat up in the narrow cot. Mark was calling her. Something was wrong. She swung her legs to the floor and pulled a thin robe over the T-shirt she'd fallen asleep in.

"Mark?" she said, carefully approaching the window. The constant song of the small insects was undisturbed. "Mark?"

"I thought I was going to have to come in and wake you," he said, moving to the unglassed window. "Meet me outside for a walk."

"Okay." She pulled on a pair of shorts and sandals and ducked through the door. The night was pleasantly cool, but the chill she felt racing across her skin came from the anticipation of being with Mark.

He took her hand as she came out of the hut. "Let's go to the observatory," he said. "I've been studying the sketches and I think I've solved one part. Remember the one with the moon and the prophet-like figure on the dais? There were scrolls and emblems along the bottom. I think they might be some sort of astrological calculation."

Celeste checked the sky. It was brilliant with stars and a waxing moon. "You want to check the calculations at the observatory."

"Right."

"Let's go."

Together they slipped through the darkness. Mark knew the trails so well that he guided her without a light. The silvery glow of the moon gave enough illumination for the long trek.

Once inside the building, Mark brought out a flashlight to help her up the winding stairs to the circular tower. There was already a telescope in place.

"I came here earlier, and when I actually felt like I was getting close, I went back for you and to study the sketches once more. I think the glyph has something to do with the equinox." He studied the sky and Celeste leaned against a cool wall.

"I didn't know you were also an astronomer," she said.

"I'm not. That's the trouble. If I were, I'd be able to solve this particular riddle a lot faster. Anyway, I think it's the equinox and the south, something about the direction south."

He stood, stretching his back. "The Mayas were considerably shorter people," he said.

"I'm glad you're tall." She waited for him to come to her, knowing that he would. They'd delayed it as long as possible.

Mark pulled her away from the wall and into his arms. He kissed her without hesitation, a long, slow exploration of her lips. Celeste responded with eagerness.

"I couldn't stop thinking about you," he said when he finally ended the kiss. "I don't often give in to impulse, but tonight I'm glad I did."

"Me, too." She leaned against his shoulder, still a bit unsteady after the passion of the kiss. In a strange twist of events, she found herself without anything to say. Being with Mark was enough for the moment. She needed time to calm herself. Her heart was racing, and she knew that if he kissed her again, she would want more.

He stroked her hair, letting the silken strands slide through his fingers. "I'm glad Captain Guirdion has ordered you to stay," he said.

"I was going to, anyway." Celeste looked up at him. The hardness had disappeared from his eyes.

"Why?"

"I don't know, Mark. At first it was pride. I was going to show you that I could work as hard as anyone else, regardless of my financial sheet."

"And now?"

"Part of it is that I want to help solve the riddle. Another part is that somehow I've gotten caught up in the lives of the people here." She hesitated, then smiled. "And a big part is that I want more time to get to know you."

He kissed her, slipping his hands beneath the big T-shirt as he pulled her against him. His fingers circled her waist, then moved slowly up her ribs.

He lifted the shirt over her head. The moonlight from the opening in the observatory shimmered down on her brilliant hair and milky skin, picking up the points of the jade figure that dangled at the top of her breasts.

Taking her hand, Mark led her to a slice of moonlight that fell across the floor.

"Just a moment," he whispered. He slipped away from her, and Celeste heard the ragged sound of a match dragging across a rough surface. In the small burst of light, she saw Mark was holding a candle.

Placing the candle on a stone shelf, he went to her. He brushed her hair back off her shoulders, kissing her neck.

Her fingers nimbly unbuttoned his shirt and then pushed it back down his arms. Her hands sought the contours of his chest, feeling in the semidarkness of the stone room.

"We could go back to your hut," he suggested.

She shook her head. Her heart was thundering, and she couldn't delay. Their two very different lives had crossed and given them a chance. She didn't believe in superstition or luck, but she did know that she wanted him. She'd also learned that attempts to plan the future were impossible.

Somehow, she'd grown to love Mark Grayson. Maybe it was the magic of a Mayan moon, or the simple fact that for the first time in ten years she'd been able to look past the printout of a stock company. Whatever had happened, she didn't want to question it or deny it. She wanted to revel in it.

She circled his neck with her arms and kissed him. "Let's stay here," she whispered.

MARK WATCHED the candle, which had sputtered to a short stub. In another hour it would be gone, but by then it would be daylight. Celeste was curled against him, her head pillowed on his arms. He could feel her breath on his chest, and he knew that she wasn't asleep.

"I think I've broken every one of my own rules," he said with a touch of humor. "I wonder if I can claim bewitchment."

"That would put me in the uncomfortable position of being labeled a witch," she answered, nuzzling his chest.

"I think you might be." He kissed her hair, inhaling once again the fresh scent that always seemed to linger in the long tresses. "In fact, I'd be willing to swear to it."

"Sounds interesting." She was more content than she could ever remember. Mark's arms offered her a security she'd never known.

"You have to stay at Chichén Itzá," Mark said, hugging her. "Now that you've bewitched me, you have to stay and help me."

"For a while," she answered, feeling the first tug of concern. "There are some things in Tampa I have to go back and face."

"Then I'll go with you, as soon as we can."

"Would you?" She sat up on her elbow. "You'd leave the dig to go and help me?"

He reached out to touch the frown line on either side of her mouth. "Of course. What do you think? I'm dedicated to my work, but not so much that I would allow someone I love to suffer through an ordeal alone."

She kissed him, slow and long, then lifted back to look at him.

"I do love you," he said. "I think one reason I was so hostile toward you at first was because I realized you were different. I'd done a pretty good job of avoiding all emotional entanglements, and I sensed that you might be the one who could knock down all of my elaborately created blockades."

"You were pretty thorny," she said.

"And you gave it back." He sat up and shifted so that he could rest against the wall. He maneuvered her across his lap so he could look at her. "That's what scared me. You didn't take it for a moment, you just dished it back. But then you worked so hard."

"That was my strategy. I wanted to prove that I wasn't some spoiled brat. I've always worked hard, and I hated it that you thought I was one of those people who had everything handed to them."

"You won my respect. You've stuck through some pretty awful incidents. A lot of other women would have gone home. Not you. Not even poor Timma's death could daunt you."

A frown touched her face. "What about Timma? Have you thought very much about what happened? I've gone over it again and again. It doesn't make any sense."

"I've thought about it a lot. He was relatively new on the site. He'd been working about ten months and was one of the younger men. He came in the morning, and except for the evenings he had guard duty, he went home. It really doesn't make any sense, but I know Wilfredo didn't do anything to him."

"I know." Celeste felt a deep sadness. "There seems to be such tragedy with this site."

"I saw Wilfredo earlier tonight." Mark reached across the floor to his pants. "He gave me something for you."

"For me? Is he okay? Will he be able to manage?"

"He's fine. He's very smart in the ways of the jungle. They won't catch him, and he's providing for his family as best he can. Of course I'll send over whatever I can to help out, too." He pulled a small object from his pocket. He picked up her hand and slipped a ring on her finger.

In the dim light, Celeste stared at the figure of the jaguar, ready to pounce. The ring was bronze, and the cat carved into it was in a crouched position.

"It's remarkable," she said. "Wilfredo didn't have to do this, though. He should sell this to buy food for his family."

"He said he could never sell the ring. It's part of the Maya culture. That's why he wanted you to have it, Celeste. He feels you saved his life."

"I only did a little stumbling, which is something I do naturally enough without a reason." She held her hand up and admired the ring. "When his name is cleared, I'll give this back to him."

"Wear it until then. It will please his wife if she sees it." Mark lifted her hand, kissing the palm. "It's almost dawn, how about a swim in the cenote?"

"That sounds wonderful," she said, pulling her T-shirt and shorts on lazily.

Mark snuffed out the candle and ducked out the entrance to the observatory. Celeste was behind him, feeling her way in the total darkness that followed as soon as the candle went out.

There was the sound of a groan, and something heavy struck the ground.

"Mark!" She stood perfectly still, listening for him. There was no answer and her eyes had not yet adjusted to the dark.

She stepped forward and her foot struck something. Kneeling down, she felt his body slumped on the ground. "Mark!" Her fingers searched his chest, his head. "Mark!"

The hands that grabbed her from behind were very strong. She struggled, but a cloth was pressed against her mouth and nose, and the sweet odor of some chemicals took her breath away. She felt herself falling, but she couldn't stop. Suddenly the darkness was too heavy to fight.

Chapter Twelve

March 14. The second day of the thirteenth Maya month. Ik. A bad day. The season for rebirth approaches and the ground remains hard.

The bright yellow light seemed to bore into Celeste's eyes and she turned her head, feeling the now-familiar sensation of sickness. Her stomach felt as if she'd suffered severe food poisoning. A headache throbbed at the front of her skull. She forced her eyes open and tried to bring her surroundings into focus. The thatching of a roof told her she was in a building of some sort. When she turned her head, she saw tropical flowers cascading down trellises to the floor. The structure had no walls, only a brilliant swirl of blossoms and vines dripping from the roof.

She was lying on a cot, a very comfortable piece of furniture compared to the one in her hut. Birds were squawking and singing only a few feet away, and she was utterly miserable.

She moaned and sat up. The pain in her head jabbed all the way down her spine, but she forced her feet to the floor. Something had happened, but it was hard to remember exactly what. She focused on her bare legs.

A flash of blue caught her eye. She bent down to examine her skin and almost yelled. Her left ankle was circled with a drawing of a blue snake that coiled around her leg and moved up her calf. As she reached down to touch it, she found the same blue pattern on her left wrist with the snake extending up her arm. Her first reaction was to rub at the brilliant blue, but it would not come off.

Where was she? She looked around the enclosure and knew she had never seen it before. The dirt floor was covered with flowers and aromatic leaves. She felt as if she'd stepped into a bridal bower in some primitive culture. That thought sent a clenching twist of panic through her. Where was Mark? The events of the past night came back to her slowly. They'd gone into the observatory and made love. On the way out, someone had attacked them. She remembered touching Mark's unconscious body, and then hands had grabbed her and she'd been drugged.

That accounted for the headache and nausea. She pressed her palms against her temples and squeezed. Had Mark been drugged, too? Or had he been injured? Was he somewhere nearby? If she moved around, maybe the remnants of whatever drug they'd used would clear. Ether? Chloroform? She didn't know. Whatever it was left a humdinger of a hangover.

Struggling to her feet, she made it to the side of the strange room. A thick wall of unrecognizable jungle met her gaze not more than ten yards from the building. She could be anywhere. She didn't even know how long she'd been knocked out.

Fear nibbled at the nape of her neck, and she felt a surge of self-pity swelling up. She fought against both emotions. Mark might be injured. His life might depend on her actions. She had to get up and get moving before whoever had abducted her came back. As far as she could tell, she was unguarded. Maybe she could find Mark and they could both escape.

She stumbled down the length of the strange room. There was no sign of anyone else. If Mark had been taken, he wasn't in the same location. She moved along the perimeter of the room, finding only thick jungle wherever she looked. It was as if she'd been dropped into the middle of nowhere by a helicopter. There seemed to be no paths, no way out.

Dizzy and nauseous, she sat back on the cot to gather her wits. She explored the snake pattern on her left arm and leg, wondering what it might mean. The craftsmanship was fascinating. The snake's scales were uniform, almost glistening. The blue was a bright shade, and the design was primitive but very skilled. On her arm and leg, the snake's mouth was open, as if it were getting ready to speak. In both cases, the tongue was extended.

The extreme insanity of what had happened struck home with a jolt. She touched the snake design on her leg. Someone had waited outside the observatory until she and Mark came out. Mark had been attacked, and she'd been drugged and kidnapped. In the period of time she was unconscious, someone had sat beside her and drawn and colored her flesh. The idea was horrifying.

A breeze ruffled the wall of beautiful flowers near her bed. In the fluttering sunlight and shadow, she saw something move near the edge of the jungle. Someone was watching her; she wasn't alone.

She froze.

With the utmost concentration, she forced her finger to trace the path of the snake on her leg. She wanted to appear to be totally absorbed in the drawing as she darted glances to the thick growth of trees. She saw the movement again, someone small and quick slipping along the edge of the jungle. She reached to push back her hair and felt a welter of flowers. Instinct made her hold back the cry of surprise. Her hands deftly searched through her hair, realizing that whoever had made her the canvas for his artwork had also woven flowers all through her long hair. Another flare of cold fear raced through her. Someone had been making preparations, but for what?

Before she could think about it, a second, more terrifying question shook her. What had been done to Mark?

Something about the painting and the flowers made her more afraid for him than for herself. From the back of her brain a piece of insane memory sprang forth. It was something Rebecca Tretorn had said, something about Barry

Undine. He'd told the Tretorns that he was involved with Celeste—romantically involved. Was it possible that Barry had completely flipped out and acted on some twisted fantasy? She knew he didn't care for her. If anything, he hated her. But Rebecca had also said something else very revealing—that hate was just another form of love. Who else in the vicinity of Chichén Itzá would want to hurt her? Who else could hate her so much?

As her mind accelerated, her eyes kept a furtive watch on the figure slipping in and out of the jungle. The person had stopped for the moment and was hunched down in the brush watching her.

She stood, moving to the edge of the shelter. If she could judge the sun, she'd say it was noon. On what day, she had no idea. She looked at the drawing on her arm. How long had it taken? A morning? A night? How long had she been completely at the mercy of her abductor? What else had been done to her?

She fought back the urge to examine the rest of her body. It didn't matter if she was painted from head to toe. What mattered was finding Mark and making certain that he wasn't hurt. But how? She was being watched, and even if she weren't she didn't know which direction to take. There wasn't a landmark she knew in sight.

She made a circuit of the shelter, pausing to touch a flower or to move a leaf. The whole time she watched for the movement in the jungle. She was afraid she'd lost the person. Maybe he or she had slipped back into the dense undergrowth. Maybe they'd left her.

She found a seat on a small stone pedestal and sank onto it. In a moment she would get up, choose a direction, and strike out through the jungle. Anything was better than sitting around waiting for the mad artist to return. She let her head drop forward onto her knees for just a moment's rest.

"Señorita Coolridge!"

She jerked up, searching the jungle near her. In a moment she saw the worried face of Wilfredo.

"Come, *señorita!*" he urged. "Come!"

She stumbled up, slipped through the curtain of flowers and entered the jungle only a few feet behind the rapidly moving Mayan.

"Wilfredo!" she called to him as she jogged behind him. "We have to find Mark."

"Hurry! We must get away before they return!" Wilfredo tossed back over his shoulder.

"Who?" She was panting, but she had to have some answers. The jungle closed tighter and tighter around them with each few yards. Now, instead of jogging, they were crawling over and under a tangle of vines and brush. All sense of direction was gone.

"I followed you," Wilfredo said. "The police officers have been looking for you and Señor Grayson. I waited until it was safe to help you."

"How long?" Celeste swallowed a gulp of panic.

"Two days. Señor de Solarno has been wild. He has hunted day and night. He found only your sandals and Señor Grayson's shirt in the observatory."

"Where is Mark?"

Wilfredo motioned for her to move faster. "We must hurry or they will cut us off and prevent us from getting to the camp."

"Who will cut us off? Is Mark okay?"

"No time for questions. Run instead."

"Wilfredo, is Mark okay?" The worry was almost paralyzing. "He is, isn't he?"

"I don't know."

"How far is the camp?" Celeste found she was struggling through the jungle with renewed energy. She had to get to camp.

"It will take us several hours of steady work. We must not use the paths."

Celeste was close enough to Wilfredo that she could catch his shirt. She tugged with a sharp downward movement.

"Who is after me?" she asked, clutching the shirt with all of her strength.

Wilfredo turned an impassive face to her. "I do not know, *señorita*." He looked at the snakes on her arm and leg. "We must keep moving."

THE CAMP WAS deserted when Celeste and Wilfredo entered. Wilfredo helped her to her hut and urged her to stay quietly inside.

"It is better if no one knows you have returned," he said, slipping out the door. He was back in a moment with some food and water for her before he slipped into the jungle.

Still uneasy from the drug, Celeste ate and then laid on the cot. Time seemed to stand still. An hour passed, then two. She filled the wash basin and began to scrub at the drawings. The only result was a reddening of the skin beneath the paint. The glistening snakes seemed indelible.

Disgusted, she threw the cloth into the basin. She couldn't wait any longer. Everyone was out looking for Mark, and she was going to hunt, too. She jerked open her suitcase and got the gun Roberto had loaned her days before.

Striking out toward the observatory, she picked up speed as she walked. The nausea left her, and she felt her limbs growing stronger. The food had helped, but finding Mark would be the cure.

She retraced the path to the observatory, thinking that only forty-eight hours had passed since they were there, together. It seemed like a lifetime ago.

Inside, she found the stub of a candle and the telescope still in place. She examined the telescope, wondering if there might be something significant in the setting. Without the night sky, it was impossible to even guess. As she tried to find some scrap of evidence that might lead to Mark's whereabouts, she clung to the fact that as long as there was not a body, Mark was alive.

When she was certain there was no clue, she left, scouting the ground for any signs. The hard-packed earth gave up few secrets, but her imagination was on full blast, and she thought she saw indentations where something large had been dragged.

She had to remind herself that she was no tracker. Wilfredo was, though, and he would have started at the observatory. If there was anything to find, he would already know it, she reassured herself.

Unable to think of a better plan, she moved to the Iglesia and the nunnery and searched. The old buildings contained centuries of secrets, but there was no trace of Mark.

Hoping that the others might have found more clues, she started back toward camp. The flying facade of the Red House caught her eye and she slowed. She hadn't searched it yet, but what was the point? She felt as if she'd been run over by a big truck. Her body ached in every joint and a sense of hopelessness had begun to seep through her. Mark had disappeared.

A second impulse, the high gear of responsibility told her otherwise. She'd given herself the task of searching the buildings in this section of the ruins. Even though it was probably futile, she needed to finish the task. Compulsive finisher. It was one of the best and worst of her character traits.

The building was set high atop a raised platform, and the flying facade and roof comb made it appear even taller. She'd heard Mark talk of the design and the late-classic period from which it dated. She could barely think of him without feeling the panic grow inside her. She had to find him. She had to at least look. She climbed the steep stairs and stepped into the shade of an open doorway.

She was so absorbed in her thoughts she failed to recognize the warning rustle of the rattles called buttons. The sound was soft, distant, but it penetrated her subconscious with an edge of fear. Celeste froze her body completely. Not a muscle twitched.

The rattling came again. This time closer, more distinct. It was a continuous sound that seemed to increase in volume. She couldn't be certain, but it sounded as if she'd walked into a roomful of rattlers.

As her eyes adjusted, she saw them. Five big snakes were coiled, two within striking range of her legs. Her mind jumped back to everything she'd ever read about snakes. They couldn't see well, but they had extraordinary hearing. They only attacked if provoked. Hah! Tell that one to Thomas. She'd also read that a person could grab them behind the head—one trick she wasn't going to try.

Very slowly she felt into the waistband of her shorts for the pistol. It was dangerous, shooting in the building. The bullet could ricochet and go anywhere. The thought crossed her mind, but it didn't deter her from cocking the hammer. She had to shoot the two closest snakes fast and with accuracy. This wasn't the time to mess up.

She eased her body into the correct shooting stance she'd been taught. She had to squeeze off her shots before the snakes decided to strike; she wasn't practiced enough to hit them while they were in motion.

She picked the one by her right leg as the first target, then the one to the left. Without taking time to think any further, she pulled the trigger, swung and shot again. Both snakes appeared fatally wounded, though they continued to move.

A feeling of revulsion made her clutch the gun again. The other snakes were far enough away that she didn't have to kill them. She could simply avoid them and cause them no harm. Quickly she stepped back, but a muffled sound came to her. The sound of the shots was still ringing in her ears and in the building, but she knew she heard something else. Something beyond the twitching bodies of the snakes. She moved past them, her eyes watching the remaining three. They continued to rattle, but they didn't move.

The ringing was dissipating in her head, and she distinctly heard the sound of a voice and something else . . . stone scratching? She kept her eyes on the floor for snakes, but she moved to the back part of the structure. She was confronted with a solid wall. Yet she heard that muffled voice even more clearly.

Her fingers searched the surface of the stone, hunting for a chink or a chasm. Mark was somewhere behind the wall. She knew it! She could feel him, sense him, alive and trying to get out! She worked her way down the building until her sensitive fingers found the stone that was slightly displaced. Her feet gritted in the shale of ground stone. She was certain, one stone was not flush! She pressed and pulled, feeling the stone budge slightly.

"Mark!" She put her mouth to the tiny opening and cried. "Mark!"

"I'm here," he answered.

He sounded weak but okay. She tugged and pulled at the stone, moving it another fraction. Should she go back to the camp for help? The memory of the snakes convinced her against it. There could be some in the room with Mark. She gripped until her fingers could get a better purchase and she pulled hard. She could feel the stone slide. With each inch, it became easier to move. She made another effort and was rewarded with a substantial gain. The block was thick, nearly a foot, but it was shifting out of the way.

"Now, one final time," Mark said, and she could hear him clearly. She put everything she had into the effort and the stone slid out, revealing a small, square opening.

"Celeste, are you okay?" Mark came through the opening and gathered her into his arms. "I've been worried sick about you."

"I got the better prison," she said when she could finally speak without crying. "Mine was flowers instead of stone."

"It doesn't matter," he said, holding her so tight he thought she would blend into his own flesh. "All that matters is that you're okay."

"And you," she answered. "Let's get out of here. Snakes."

"I'd given up until I heard those shots," he said. "I thought I'd die in there."

She took his hand and they walked into the sunshine, watchful for more snakes. When they were at last on the path, Mark cast a long sideways glance at Celeste. In the afternoon light, she was incredibly beautiful with the profusion of flowers entangled in her hair. He immediately noticed the snakes painted on her arm and leg, but he didn't say anything.

The journey back to camp was slow and tedious. Celeste's body ached, and she knew Mark felt worse, though he didn't say. His normal stride was shortened by half, and he paused to rest on occasion.

When they made it back to camp, the place was as empty as it had been when Celeste left. She looked around, hoping for Wilfredo or Roberto, but there was no one. She left Mark resting in her hut while she made something for him to eat.

She had the tray and was walking across the clearing when Rebecca walked up, cool and perfect in a red gauze shirt.

"We were afraid we'd lost you to some jungle tribe forever," she said.

"Where are Roberto and Wilfredo?"

Rebecca shrugged. "They've been scarce since you and Mark disappeared. By the way, we found Mark's shirt and your shoes. Was it some type of card game you were playing?"

Celeste was too tired to answer. She started past.

"Well, a tattoo is going to be hard to explain to the Wall Street mentality of a brokerage firm. Good luck, dear. Maybe you'd better start looking for a circus job. Or is it that you've decided to throw over your career and live barefoot and content in the Yucatán?"

"I'm not worried about it. I don't think it's a tattoo," Celeste said. She kept a careful grip on her temper. Rebecca had a way of really getting under her skin.

"We wondered what you were doing for two days and a night. Now we know. And Charles complains when I'm in the beauty shop for over three hours! At least I don't come home looking like one of those funny blue cartoon characters."

"If you talk with Roberto, please tell him I need to see him." She brushed past Rebecca.

"Wait a minute, Celeste. The captain had something for you. Now where did I put it?" She put her manicured fingertips to her mouth. "Yes, in my lizard handbag. I'll be right back." She turned away before Celeste could protest or even ask a question.

Celeste was forced to wait fifteen minutes, fuming, until Rebecca returned.

"Here it is." Rebecca put the telegram on the tray. "In all of the turmoil you caused by disappearing, I forgot about it. The captain said he'd opened it, but he didn't say what was in it, so I checked to make certain it wasn't a dire emergency." She smiled. "I think Captain Guirdion thought you'd skipped out, actually."

Celeste put the tray on the table, took the opened envelope and lifted out the single page. She scanned the brief message rapidly.

Undine has been charged and suspended. You've both been implicated. The scheme is exposed, but do not give up. I will continue to work to clear your name. No matter what you've done I will support you.

> Love, Uncle Alec

The white page trembled a moment before Celeste folded it and put it back into the envelope.

"You'd better call in the calvary, Celeste," Rebecca said. "I think the home defense forces have folded."

Chapter Thirteen

March 15. The sun scalds the land of the Maya. It is Akbal, a day of bad omens. There is danger in the air. The small serpents prepare.

The dusty patrol car pulled up in front of the ruins. Tired and gritty, Celeste got out. It had been a long morning, on the heels of a sleepless night. She'd shown the telegram to no one. She was sure Rebecca would spread the word fast enough. Her only concern had been getting to a telephone.

"Do not attempt to leave the ruins," Captain Guirdion noted from behind the steering wheel. Celeste slammed the door, raising a cloud of dust.

"I know," she said. She was too tired to put up much of a defense. The captain had taken her to a phone, as he'd promised. There had been no answer at her uncle's home, and the receptionist at Stuart McCarty had been reluctantly helpful. Celeste had learned that Alec Mason was not at work; had not been at work for several days, and had left the office in a terrible upheaval. Celeste had hung up as soon as the questions started. Apparently Uncle Alec had not revealed her whereabouts to anyone at the firm. At least not voluntarily. She shivered at the idea of Barry Undine.

"I'm sorry about your uncle, *señorita*." The captain did not bother to hide his scrutiny. "Perhaps they will find him soon."

"If anything has happened to Uncle Alec, it's my fault." She didn't mean to let the words escape, but she'd been thinking them all the way back to Chichén Itzá. Uncle Alec had left no messages, no instructions for his accounts. Stuart McCarty was in a panic. And to further complicate matters, formal criminal charges were in the works against Barry Undine—and her. Instead of clearing her name, Uncle Alec's investigation had turned up evidence linking her with Barry in a scheme to defraud their clients of millions. It was unbelievable.

"Your cooperation in the murder case is advisable," Guirdion said, "if you wish to return to the States in the near future."

"There is a chance that I will have to go back to Tampa, whether it is my choice or not," Celeste said carefully. "I'm sure you will be notified by U.S. authorities, if that becomes necessary." If she was indicted, she'd have to return home.

"With the proper notification, you *may* be allowed to leave Mexico. You are a suspect in a murder case here, Miss Coolridge. This is not a trivial charge. Surely you must know that."

"A suspect? You don't think I killed Timma?"

"Anything is possible." The captain smiled. "Anything." He looked at the blue snake that showed from beneath the long-sleeved shirt Celeste had been forced to borrow from Rebecca.

She tugged her sleeve down. She had worn long pants, socks, tennis shoes and Rebecca's shirt in an effort to hide the handiwork on her arm and leg. Now the captain had seen it. His eyes were like those of a watchful snake.

"If I have any messages at the hotel in Cancún, will you see that they're forwarded to me? I am worried about my uncle."

"Of course," he agreed.

"I know you're going to read them, but please don't leave them with the Tretorns again. I'm not interested in the entire camp knowing my personal business."

"Especially not business of that nature. I understand. *Adios señorita.*" He gunned the motor and drove off.

Celeste walked through the gate of the ruins, waving away the guides who rushed up to give her the tour. On second thought, she paused and turned around. Since she was covered from head to toe, now would be a good opportunity to visit Thomas. He was recovering from his snakebite. Juanita kept her informed of the boy's condition—and the fact that he'd been asking for Celeste repeatedly. She was eager to see him and make sure his progress was as rapid as reported.

The walk was only a couple of miles, but in the shirt and slacks, Celeste felt the hot sun every step of the way. The heat burned into her, but it was nothing compared to the recriminations she turned on herself. She'd tucked tail and run from Tampa. She'd let her uncle convince her to leave, and because she'd shirked her responsibilities, Uncle Alec was in danger. While she was down in Mexico playing at solving an ancient riddle, Uncle Alec had been pulling her slack. Now Uncle Alec was in danger, or worse. He'd disappeared.

Thomas's house came into view, and she was delighted to see the young boy lying in a hammock in the yard. Beside him was an empty chair.

"Señorita Coolridge," Thomas's voice was charged with happiness. "You are okay? I heard you were missing and that the men from the village were looking for you." He struggled to get out of the hammock, obviously favoring his left leg.

"I'm great. How about that leg of yours?" She took a seat on the edge of the chair where she could hold his hand and gently insist that he stay in the hammock.

"I'm fine. You and Señor Grayson saved my life." He looked at her with a strange new awareness. "You saved me."

"No, it was Mark. He knew the techniques. I only helped."

Thomas looked toward the house. "Mama will bring us something cool to drink. She knows you're here. Some of the other children saw you walking this way. It is too hot to walk, especially in those clothes." He looked at her with disapproval. "Where are your shorts?"

"I had to call my uncle. You haven't heard from him, have you?" It was a wild shot, but what did she have to lose?

"No, is he coming to Cancún, too?" Thomas's face held a little disappointment. "He will not want a guide who has been bitten by a snake."

Celeste couldn't help laughing at Thomas's woebegone expression. "You'll heal. The worst is over now. Soon you'll be back on your feet and ready to go."

"No." For a moment he looked much older than his twelve years. "Everyone knows about the snake…that I was bitten in my sleep."

"So?"

Thomas looked toward the house and lowered his voice. "I have displeased the gods. I have been marked. It was only you that saved me."

Celeste was stunned. Thomas was too smart to believe such foolishness. He was a bright kid who'd been exposed to a lot for someone his age. He had potential and dreams. He wasn't fodder for the cannon of superstition. "People get snakebite every day. This isn't punishment or some sign. It's not like that." Her voice rose a little louder. "Boys sleep under trees. Snakes bite. That's two rules of nature. When the boy sleeps near the snake, sometimes the snake bites him. That's another rule of nature. That's what happened to you. This has nothing to do with gods."

She had to make him understand that there was no magic or reason for what had happened to him. If he once started to believe that natural happenings were the signs of the gods, he might never get beyond the boundaries of his own small village.

"I heard the jaguar speak," he said slowly, glancing again to make sure his mother wasn't coming. "It said your name." His gaze never left her face. "It said you were to be obeyed. That you were chosen."

"Chosen for what?"

Thomas paused. "I am not certain. But you are special. You have the gift of life, *señorita*. You will see. Mama and Carlotta were talking about you. You have come to help the Maya people. When you disappeared, they were very upset. They were afraid someone had taken you away."

A flutter of panic raced around her heart as she remembered the strange indelible drawings and the flowers in her hair. "Well, that's all over now. I'm back and I wasn't hurt at all. Now we have to get you well so we can continue our vacation plans. We never intended to stay in Chichén Itzá so long. Where should we go from here?"

"You will leave?" A third voice asked the question in a soft but disapproving tone.

Celeste turned to find Maria standing behind her with a tray. Two tall glasses contained fruit juice.

"Eventually I will have to leave. I was hoping, if I didn't have to go back to the States right away, that maybe Thomas would be well enough to show me a little more of Cancún."

"My son may not wish to return to the beaches." She looked at Thomas. "He understands the ways of his village much better since he was bitten by the snake."

"Thomas?" Celeste looked at him. "What about James Bond?"

"My place is in my village," Thomas said, unable to meet her eyes. "I am no longer a boy. I cannot think of growing up to be a spy or a secret agent. I must accept the responsibilities of a man."

"There's a whole big world out there, Thomas, and you're a bright boy. I wouldn't give up too easily."

"My son has accepted his fate," Maria said slowly. "That is how the Maya people survive. We accept and endure."

"And if Thomas decides to struggle and work for more, is that wrong? If he wants to go to university and learn a profession so that he can help his people, is that a bad thing?"

Maria held the tray out to Celeste. "It is only bad if he does not do what he should for his village. Please have some juice."

The glass was cool, and Celeste took it out of politeness. As her fingers grasped it, her sleeve shifted back. The blue snake was partially revealed.

Maria's grip on the tray shifted, and she nearly dropped it. Celeste caught the edge and steadied it just before the second glass of juice spilled to the ground.

"Are you okay?" Thomas saw the shock on his mother's face.

"*Sí,*" she managed, in a halting voice. "It is good of you to visit Thomas," she said, backing away step by step. She turned and hurried back into the house.

Thomas looked at Celeste. "What frightened her?"

Celeste turned back the cuff of her sleeve. "This. What does it mean, Thomas? Do you know?"

"It is the symbol of Quetzalcoatl."

"So I've been told. What does it mean?"

"Blue is the color of the god." He looked at her, a coldness in his normally warm brown eyes. "Blue is the color of sacrifice."

The fear that had laced through her tightened. "Sacrifice?"

"*Sí.* In the old days, when someone was being prepared for sacrifice, they were painted blue from head to toe. Blue is the color that best pleases the gods."

"And what does the symbol of the blue snake mean?" She could barely ask the question her heart was beating so.

"I don't know," Thomas admitted, "but I am frightened for you. The jaguar has spoken your name. You've been given the art of healing, *señorita*. You saved me. There is talk in the village that soon the Eye of the Jaguar will be returned, and Quetzalcoatl will walk in the shadows of Chichén Itzá once more."

"Did someone from the village destroy the stela?"

"I can't be certain, but I don't think so. Does Señor Grayson believe that it was one of the villagers?"

"I don't know," she said slowly. "I don't even know what I believe. Thomas, there is a man here. Barry Undine. Or at least he was here."

"The American?" Thomas grew excited. "Yes, your friend. He was asking for you."

"Where is he?"

"He went back. He said you would not leave, and he went back home."

"Are you certain?"

Thomas thought for a moment. "He hasn't been in the village for several days. Who is this man?" He looked at her. "You do not like him. He isn't your friend."

"No, he isn't a friend. He may have been the person who kidnapped me."

"I will tell Carlotta, and she will see that if he hasn't gone, he leaves immediately. He cannot stay here if he intends to harm you." He was very serious. He reached out and took Celeste's hand. "I will never be James Bond, but I would not let anything happen to you, *señorita*. You saved my life."

"I didn't!" She pressed his hand. "Mark saved you, Thomas, not me. Mark knew how to treat the snake bite and he had the antitoxin. I didn't do anything."

"Go to Carlotta and show her the snake on your arm. She will be able to tell you what it means. She will guide you."

"Carlotta sometimes frightens me," Celeste said in a moment of unguarded honesty. "She's so caught up in all of this ancient Maya lore, I don't know if she can tell reality from her own make-believe world. If I show her this drawing or tattoo, or whatever the damn thing is, she might really go off on a tangent."

"What other choice do you have?" Thomas asked softly.

For a moment, Celeste thought through her options. The boy was right. Where else could she turn for some coherent understanding of the events in her life? Maybe Carlotta was her best bet. "I'll think about it," she said. "And if you hear of Barry Undine in the area, please send me word. I have some things to discuss with him." She hesitated a moment. She didn't want to burden the boy, but it was fair that he should know. "Thomas, my uncle has disappeared. Someone may have injured him, or they may be holding him hostage."

"You believe it is the American, Undine."

"I think that's a strong possibility, but I don't have any proof. My life in Tampa is very complicated."

"Your life here is less complicated, isn't it? Perhaps you should stay here forever."

A real smile crept up Celeste's face. "You are very sly, Thomas." She bent and kissed his forehead. "And I thank you for wanting me to be here, in your home."

"You belong here, *señorita*. We have accepted you. Now you must accept us."

CELESTE PRESSED HER BODY against the pile of T-shirts that were stacked like a small mountain in the back of Carlotta Bopp's shop. She was sweating, the perspiration trickling down her back. She'd come, as Thomas suggested, to talk with Carlotta about the snakes. The trip had been impulsive, a momentary decision she'd made after leaving Thomas in his hammock. What she'd found had been a shock. Barry Undine was sitting at the same little table where she'd once sat with Carlotta. The Maya woman was talking to him in low, throaty tones that Celeste couldn't quite understand.

"Leave Chichén Itzá," Carlotta said in a louder voice.

"I will not!" Barry half rose. "She isn't going to do this and get away with it. I know she has something. There were millions!"

Celeste pressed herself into the pile of clothing, praying that nothing would topple down and suffocate her. She'd intended to call out to Carlotta, but she'd heard the voices, and natural curiosity had led her to her current predicament. Once she saw Barry was there, she'd had no qualms about trying to hear everything she could.

"Señor Grayson will not allow this," Carlotta hissed. "Leave now, before he finds you."

"Grayson isn't involved in this. This is between me and Celeste. But I'm warning you and everyone else. I'll do whatever I have to. I'm not going to take the blame and end up with nothing. One way or the other, I'm not leaving empty-handed. Rebecca has told me about the ruby. If I have to, I'll take that."

"You are a fool!" Carlotta rose and leaned toward Barry. "Are you blind, Señor Undine? Have you not seen the way Grayson looks at her? Leave now, before he hurts you. That is my last word with you—leave before you die!" She swirled away from the table, her multicolored skirt brushing across the floor.

Celeste pressed as far back as she could into the T-shirts, covering herself with several as Carlotta approached. She held her breath until the woman had swept by. The door to the shop swung shut, and she knew she was alone in the back quarter with Barry Undine. Her heart triple-paced.

After several moments with no movement from Barry, she leaned out to catch a glimpse of the table. It was empty. There was no sign of Barry, and no noise to indicate where he might have gone. He'd moved as stealthily as one of the Maya workers in the jungle.

Pushing the clothes aside, she moved into the aisle. The idea of being in the storage space alone with Barry was more than a little uncomfortable. She could feel again the hands at her shoulders and throat, the smell of the sweet drug being pushed into her face. Sweat broke out on her forehead, and she wiped at it with clammy hands.

She was totally unprepared for the avalanche of clothes that smashed down on her. When the first bundle struck her right shoulder, she staggered. The towering aisle of T-shirts was caving in on her. She held up her hands, fending off the first wall. The entire room seemed to be shifting and tumbling toward her. The weight, nearly a hundred pounds, knocked her to her knees just as another onslaught came.

"*Detenga!*" Carlotta's voice echoed through the building.

"Stop it, Señor Undine, or you will die an exquisitely painful death." All of the urgency was gone from Carlotta's voice. In its place was the icy promise of pain.

Celeste struggled to her feet as the landslide of clothing stopped. She was buried up to her waist, and her head was reeling from several blows the heavy bundles had given her.

She looked up to see Barry Undine jump lightly to another stack of clothes and then to the floor in front of her.

"You haven't gotten out of this yet," he said in a cutting whisper. "You and your uncle have framed me, and I'll get even one way or the other."

"Barry!" Celeste called after him. She struggled out of the clothes, but the heavy bundles held her down. "Barry, wait!" She had to ask him about her uncle.

She felt a restraining hand on her shoulder. "Let him go, Celeste. He is a dangerous man. Very dangerous. His temper will lead him to a deep pit and push him in. Then the jaguar will devour him."

"Stop him," Celeste pulled free of Carlotta's grip. "I have to talk with him. Stop him."

"It is too late," Carlotta said as she pulled several huge stacks of clothing away from Celeste so she could breathe. "It is too late."

"I have to catch him." Celeste floundered forward and felt herself fall. She was slightly stunned, and her balance was a little off. Carlotta's strong arms caught her and eased her down onto the bundles.

"Sit here, Celeste. Rest a moment. I will get you a cold drink." She hurried away, sweeping down the aisle in a rapid but majestic walk. She returned in only a few moments with an icy bottle of cola. "Drink this and relax. Señor Grayson is coming for you. I sent a message to him."

"I really don't think that's necessary." The first burning swallow of the drink helped clear her head. "I was just a little dizzy. One of those bundles hit me square on the head."

Carlotta's strong fingers probed through her hair. "*Sí*, here is the knot. You must lie down." She eased her back. "It is not serious, I don't think, but we should take care."

"I'm okay," Celeste insisted, feeling ridiculous in the mountain of clothing. "Let me finish the drink, and then I'll head back to the camp. I'm sure Captain Guirdion's watchdogs are eagerly looking for me by now."

"Señor Grayson will be here soon." Carlotta's voice was soft, soothing. "Why did you come here?"

"To see you." Celeste felt a moment of shame. "When I saw Barry was here, I couldn't help but listen. I've been looking for him. I thought he'd left the area."

"He will. I'll see to that. As I said, he is a dangerous man."

"I have to talk with him before he leaves," Celeste said. "I have some information he wants, and he may have some for me."

"Did you come for any other reason?"

"Like what?" Celeste was instantly suspicious.

"The snakes on your arm and leg."

The words took the breath from Celeste. "How did you know?"

"Wilfredo saw them, Celeste. Such a symbol cannot be kept quiet. It is a powerful sign, a mark."

"And what does it mean?" She propped herself on an elbow.

"The snake is the sign of Quetzalcoatl."

"I know that much. And blue is the color of sacrifice." She repeated the things Thomas had told her.

Celeste took her arm and pushed back the sleeve to her shoulder. The entire snake was revealed.

"See how it coils about your arm. That is a sign of possession. It is on the left side, the seat of creation. The open mouth of the snake is an invitation. You must decide."

"An invitation to what?" Celeste felt overwhelmed. "What should I decide? None of this makes a bit of sense." She was angry, at Carlotta and herself. She'd known better than to come to Carlotta for an interpretation. The woman was obsessed with ancient lore and superstitions.

Carlotta eased her to a reclining position. "You must rest. Señor Grayson..."

"Celeste!" Mark's voice boomed in the storage room. "Where are you?"

"Over here," Carlotta answered, standing up so that Mark could see her. "She is here, and she is not hurt. She has been frightened and a little damaged."

"Celeste!" Mark rushed forward, striding over the clothes until he was beside her. "What happened?"

"Barry Undine tried to smother me," she said. "Luckily, he didn't succeed. Carlotta stopped him."

"Barry Undine!" He spoke the name with anger. "Where is he?"

"He is gone," Carlotta said. "And he is not your concern. Celeste is. Get her back to camp and take care of her. You lost her once, was that not warning enough?"

She turned to Celeste. "Go back to camp and stay there. I must talk with Señor Grayson a moment alone."

Celeste felt the urge to protest, but she had no choice but to leave. She lingered at the doorway a moment, shamelessly trying to hear because she knew she was the topic.

"She is in danger, Señor Grayson, grave danger. You must choose between Celeste or the Jaguar's Eye. If you persist in trying to have both of them, you will lose both."

Chapter Fourteen

The pattern of the days continues unabated. There is no rain, but black clouds touch the sky and promise the anger of the gods.

The spiral of black smoke drew Celeste's attention and slowed her pace. She'd fled Carlotta's, unwilling to listen to Mark's answer. The idea that he was somehow being forced to choose between her and his dream was intolerable. Perhaps it would be the best for all if she left Chichén Itzá. The concern for her uncle was a constant gnawing.

She watched the spiral of smoke with more attention. Something big was burning. She knew without being told that if a brush fire scattered out of control in the dry Yucatán, many people would suffer. Another troubling factor was that the fire seemed to be coming from the direction of the camp. The only positive aspect was the straight upward spiral of the smoke. It appeared intense, but self-contained.

Concern made her move forward at a fast pace once again. The smoke was getting thicker and heavier, the black column climbing straight up the sky in the windless day. It looked as if the entire camp was burning. The smoke was so thick, it seemed to block the sun. She pressed forward, her fear mounting with each stride.

Before she had reached the camp clearing, she realized her worst thoughts were reality. The camp was on fire!

A wave of heat stopped her as she tried to break through the undergrowth. She dropped to ground level and crawled forward, determined to find out exactly what was on fire. As she inched along the ground, she could see that the hut Mark and Roberto shared was sprouting flames across the thatch roof. The cooking hut was also in flames.

The Tretorns' hut seemed to be intact, as did her own and the larger building that housed the graduate students. She crawled around the perimeter of the camp. A slight breeze had cleared the worst of the smoke away from her own accommodations, and she took a moment to rest. It was apparent that no one else was in camp. She hesitated at the clearing. If she ran for help, there would never be time to find anyone. The cooking hut was burning hot and fast, aided by the stores of grease. There was nothing she could save. A sudden flash of inspiration struck her, and she ran toward Mark's hut. The artifacts would be safe enough in the vault-like chest he had. It was the sketches she had to find.

Choking on the acrid fumes, she ripped down the cloth door and forced her burning eyes to peer into the dim room. Overhead she could hear the crackle of the thatch. At any moment it could all topple. If that happened, there would be no escape. She would burn under the weight of the roof. With a deep breath, she plunged inside. She flipped the cots, finding nothing. With one sweeping motion, she cleared Mark's desk, pushing everything into the top drawer. With a jerk she pulled the drawer free and threw it out of the room. The remaining three side drawers followed, along with the four suitcases she found stacked in a corner of the room.

The heat and smoke were becoming unbearable as she aimed at the door and leapt through. There was a warning crack as the center support of the roof finally snapped. The thatch crown tumbled into the center of the hut.

Celeste jerked her feet closer to her body and rolled away from the side of the building. A wall broke free and fell only a few yards from where she stopped. Breathlessly she crawled to the scattered drawers and rifled through them for the sketchpad. She had to find it and hide it before anyone saw her.

The pad was in the large, center drawer. She took it to her hut and stowed it beneath her own suitcases. Returning to the flaming building, she picked up the drawers and threw them back into the blaze. It would be better for everyone if the sketches were thought to be destroyed. Later she could tell Mark the truth. She looked at the suitcases. Should they go back into the flames, too? Maybe not. It was possible that she'd been able to save something. Suitcases would be the logical choice. Exhausted, she went to her hut and sank to the ground so she could lean against the building and watch the fire slowly begin to die.

Minutes passed. Celeste had no way of telling how many. She'd given up expecting to see Mark. Bone weary, she leaned against the supporting wall and waited. The smoke was much less dense. The burning huts were a total loss. The thatch roofs had gone up like tinder, in a matter of minutes.

Her skin prickled at the thought. If someone had set the fires, he or she might be nearby. They might be watching her even now from some safe, secluded spot. And not a single member of the dig anywhere in sight. Where had everyone gone? Surely they could see the smoke from any point in the ruins. Why hadn't they returned?

She rubbed her arms, aware of the goose bumps beneath the long-sleeved shirt. The idea that someone was watching her increased. "Charles! Rebecca!" The shoe-dynasty duo were seldom far from the camp. A mental image of the two of them, trussed and bound, sent her hurrying to the door. She shouted again.

When there was no answer, she pushed back the curtain. "Rebecca!" Stepping into the room, she instinctively moved along the wall. The hut, much like hers except larger with two cots and several enormous trunks and suitcases, was a wreck. Clothes and shoes were thrown about, draped over the cots and piled on the floor. She stepped over a white dress and recognized a designer label. It had cost plenty, and Rebecca had tossed it to the floor like a rag. For a split second she had a pang of sympathy for Charles. He was so easygoing, and so obviously enamored of his wife. Rebecca Tretorn would be a handful to tolerate.

Since the hut was empty, she knew she should leave, but something held her in place. As the fire burned itself out, reducing half the camp to embers, she was caught in the rich clutter that defined Rebecca. She quickly estimated there was easily close to fifteen thousand dollars' worth of clothes junked about the hut. It was appalling in a distant, unemotional way.

"Rebecca!" she called once more as she went back to the door. She had no right to invade the Tretorns' private room. It was more than time to leave.

Her foot crunched lightly on a small object, and she lifted the hem of a dress to find an opal earring. She picked it up, studying it for possible damage. The stone was firmly set, and the clasp in place. She sighed. Thank goodness she hadn't stepped down hard. Lifting the hem of the dress, she searched for the mate. She could at least put them on top of the bedside table. In all the disarray Rebecca would never notice.

A rectangle of paper floated from the dress and settled face up. Celeste saw at once that it was a color photograph. She picked it up, stifling a little cry of shock. It was a picture of her. She was sitting at her desk at Stuart McCarty, holding an enormous chocolate cake Uncle Alec had brought in to celebrate one of her birthdays. There were a dozen or so people gathered around her—the friends of her profession.

She stared at the picture, suddenly struck by the realization that it had come from Uncle Alec's office. He'd framed it and put it in an inconspicuous place among his bookshelves. Someone had taken it from his office. Maybe the same someone who had done something to detain him from going to work. Whatever in the world were the Tretorns doing with a photograph of her?

She heard the sound of wild exclamations outside the hut. Heart pounding and picture clutched in her hand, she picked out Roberto's cries of alarm and the answering tones of Charles Tretorn. Celeste froze. Escape from the front door was blocked, and she didn't want to be caught in the hut. With great caution, she slipped across the room to the window. As she climbed out, her foot caught the edge of a table. An avalanche of books and papers toppled, along with a camera and a flashlight. She didn't wait to assess the damage, she went through the window and slipped around the opposite side of the hut.

"Celeste!" Roberto caught sight of her. "What happened?"

"I came up and the camp was in flames. I was able to grab a couple of suitcases." She nodded toward the luggage. "Since there was no wind, there didn't seem much danger in the fire spreading to the other buildings." She shrugged, her heart still racing from nearly being caught in the Tretorns' hut. For the first time she noticed Charles and Rebecca. Sopping wet and nearly prone, Rebecca clutched her husband. She sobbed weakly against his chest. Charles held her tenderly as he watched the blaze in amazement.

"What happened to Rebecca?" Celeste asked Roberto. "And you?" He, too, was dripping wet.

"Someone tried to drown her at the cenote."

"She was swimming?" Celeste took another look at the expensive dress Rebecca was wearing. There was little doubt it was ruined.

"She was exploring. Someone came up behind her, pushed her in, then dove in after her and tried to hold her underwater." Roberto's face was grim. "It is time to end this dig. Before another one of us is killed."

"Where are the graduate students?" Celeste looked around.

"Mark sent them to Cancún. I doubt any of them will return. Timma's death is a serious business. In Mexico, it can take a long time to settle such a thing. If those students are smart, they'll leave while they can. I suggest the same to you, and the Tretorns. Daniel is here now. When he goes back to Cancún, perhaps he can convince the captain to let you accompany him."

"What about you and Mark?"

Roberto shook his head. "Mark will never leave. Not even after the sketches of the stela have been destroyed. He will stay here, determined to solve this riddle. He is obsessed."

"And you?' She started to tell him about saving the sketches, but Charles and Rebecca were too close.

"Much of the thrill for this project has gone for me. I am not like Mark. My life will continue at another dig, at a university, in some other capacity. I prefer another life," he waved his hands toward the dying flames, "to this."

"Roberto, what is going on here?" Daniel came down the path, slightly out of breath from the fast pace. "I saw the smoke. What's happened?"

"It isn't serious, Daniel. No one was injured." Roberto's voice lacked the necessary enthusiasm.

"Well, that might make Mark feel a little better, but I'm ready to pull out of this expedition. When I drove up, the smoke was so thick it blocked the sun. There was a cluster of villagers mumbling something about another sign. What is going on at this dig?" The last question was in a more impatient tone.

"If we knew that, Daniel, we would be much further along," Roberto said. "It is obvious someone is trying to burn us out. Most of our supplies have been destroyed."

"I have some brandy," Charles said, attempting to mediate the awkwardness. "Rebecca could use a small glass."

"What's happened to her?" Daniel's worried face belied his brusque tone. "Don't tell me someone tried to drown her."

"Something of the sort," Roberto answered, and for the first time his sardonic grin flashed briefly at Celeste. "Another stroke of bad luck."

Judging by the expression on his face, Celeste couldn't tell if the bad luck was the attempt or the failure. She turned to

Daniel. "I'm afraid that I need your help on a serious matter, Señor Ortiz."

"More serious than this?" He swept his hand toward the smoldering ruins of the huts.

"In a way, I think so. My uncle has disappeared from Tampa. I'm afraid someone may be detaining him."

"Celeste!" The word slipped from Roberto on a hiss of air. "What has happened?"

"No one knows."

"I know neither Roberto nor Mark will tell me what's happening here," Daniel said as he approached Celeste. "Let's find some seats for poor Mrs. Tretorn and her husband, break out that brandy and have a talk. I want some answers before Mark gets back here."

Celeste found enough spare cups to serve the brandy, but her answers were woefully inadequate.

"Where are the police officers who were stationed here?" Daniel looked around the camp. "Maybe they set the fire."

"Maybe," Celeste agreed. "Rebecca, wouldn't you rather go lie down?" She wanted to say as little as possible in front of the woman. She didn't trust her at all.

"No, I'm feeling better." She finished her brandy and held out her glass for more. "My clothes are ruined. The demon who attacked me had every intention of holding me under until I was dead." Tears sprang to her eyes. "It was horrible."

"Have you any idea who it might have been?" Celeste knew the question was loaded. Rebecca might say anything, with proof or not.

"It was one of those terrible Mayan women," she said. "I remember the arm. It was a woman's arm, without hair. And it was strong. It slipped around my throat…oh!" She shook her head and leaned into Charles's chest, sobbing.

"Why would one of the Mayan women want to hurt you?" Celeste was honestly puzzled. "That doesn't make any sense. Were you at the cenote alone?"

She saw Rebecca start, but she had no way of knowing why.

"I was exploring the observatory and the Red House," Charles said, his voice laden with guilt. "Rebecca was alone. I never should have left her, but it seemed safe enough. I had no idea that some of those savages would attack my wife." He kissed her forehead. "We're going home, Rebecca."

"I wish that were possible." Daniel got up and paced around the table. "Unfortunately, my last conversation with Captain Guirdion was anything but a success. He says you are all confined to the ruins until the murder of the Maya workman is settled. I'm afraid, Charles and Rebecca, you won't be able to leave now."

"Are you also held here?" Celeste asked.

Daniel shook his head. "No. Or at least I don't think so."

"You said you knew my uncle." She knew she sounded desperate but she was.

"Not in a personal way. Just casually. Why?"

It was Celeste's turn to pace. "If you can leave here, would it be possible for you to check on his whereabouts? Hire a private investigator if you have to. I'll pay you back as soon as I get to the States." She couldn't stop the catch in her voice. "I'm afraid he's been injured and no one is looking for him."

"I'll do what I can," Daniel promised. "As soon as I can get away from here, I'll start the process."

"THANK MARIA FOR US," Celeste told Juanita. "The food was delicious. We very much appreciate her help, and all the others', too." She looked at Mark for some response, but he was lost in his own thoughts. If his face was any clue, the thoughts were black and ugly.

She'd tried repeatedly to get him alone, to tell him that the sketches were safe. He'd avoided even looking at her. Carlotta had put a hard choice to him, and Celeste knew which he'd chosen. She'd never have asked him to make that decision, but now that she knew his answer, she couldn't forget. Roberto had warned her that the Jaguar's Eye was more important to him than anything. Now she had to accept that it was.

"Everyone in the village saw the smoke," Thomas said, breaching the awkward gap. He was perched on the back of the small cart Juanita had used to deliver the food. Since the cooking hut was destroyed, Maria and several other women had donated the evening meal. Thomas had insisted on accompanying them, especially since he could ride on the cart without putting a strain on his leg.

"Lucky the students are gone," Roberto said, leaning back in his chair. "This whole dig has become a nightmare. It's just as well they've gone home, and I suggest we do the same as soon as Captain Guirdion allows it."

"I'm not leaving."

Mark's voice was so strained and tense that it cut across the night like a clap of thunder. He looked up, shifting his gaze from one to the other. "The Jaguar's Eye is here, and we were getting very close. Someone is trying to stop us. That's what all of this is about. The fire, the kidnapping, the attempted drowning. Someone is desperate to run us away from here." He looked from one to the other, completely avoiding Celeste.

Roberto's voice was light, but all of the relaxed posture was gone from his body. "Mark, the stela is gone, your sketches are gone. There is no chance now. We should accept the inevitable and leave. The Jaguar's Eye will remain a mystery, but we will find other expeditions that involve us."

"Give up if you want to," Mark said angrily, "but I won't!"

"There comes a point when a wise man cuts his losses," Daniel agreed, agitation evident beneath his calm demeanor.

Mark stood. "Before you all quit, do me one favor. Think about who you've told about the jewel. Think hard. Someone is trying to deliberately halt this dig and I intend to find out why." He left the camp area without a backward glance. His tall silhouette disappeared on the path toward El Castillo.

"Should he be alone?" Daniel asked. "He's very tense, and bitterly disappointed, I suspect."

Celeste sat perfectly still. She wanted to tell Mark that the sketches were safe, but she didn't want to follow him.

"This has been rough for Mark," Roberto said. "His memory is good, but he's worried he'll forget some minor detail. And the damnable part of it is that he was getting very close to solving the glyphs. Very close."

"And you really believe this incredible jewel would have been found?" Daniel was more than a little skeptical.

"When it is returned to the Jaguar, then Quetzalcoatl will return to us," Thomas said. Celeste turned to him abruptly. For a moment she'd forgotten his presence he was so quiet.

"That's a myth, Thomas," she said more sharply than she intended. "It's a legend. Very much like the James Bond you used to admire so much."

Thomas shook his head. "I used to believe the same as you do," he said carefully, his gaze only on Celeste. It was as if the rest of the gathering had vanished. "Quetzalcoatl will return. You will see him for yourself. The ruins hold the secret of his resurrection. Deep beneath the stone and water, he will return."

"It is time for Thomas to go to bed," Juanita said hurriedly. "His mother will be worried. We must go." She was packing the cart as she spoke. "There is food for breakfast. Bread and cheese. Coffee." She picked up the shafts of the little cart. *"Buenos noches,"* she said, pushing Thomas off into the darkness.

"Buenos noches," Celeste called.

"Now that sounded sinister," Rebecca said, breaking her long silence of the evening. "Our Celeste will meet the god. The boy didn't include anyone else in that conference."

"I'm his friend," Celeste said easily. "He's a generous child."

"He's also simpleminded, if he believes some snake god is going to slither back to this hellhole," Rebecca said irritably. "I want to speak with the captain first thing tomorrow. I want everyone in the village questioned about their whereabouts this afternoon. Since no one else seems overly interested in finding out who tried to drown me, I'll do it myself."

"I'd drop the subject, if I were you." There was a warning in Roberto's careful words. "The less the captain knows about our business, the sooner he's going to let us go home. If we continue to have trouble, he will only detain us."

"Yes," Charles said softly, "let's forget this. You're safe now. For the remainder of the time we're here, you must never go anywhere without me."

"Don't be so tiresome!" Rebecca snapped.

Celeste rose. "I think I'm going to call it a day. Please excuse me, but I'm exhausted."

Roberto and Daniel stood. "A good idea," Roberto said, moving toward the students' old accommodations with Daniel. "Until the morning," he said, blowing a kiss toward Celeste, and then another at Rebecca.

Always the diplomat, she thought as she went into her hut. Roberto was certainly good at what he did.

From beneath her luggage she pulled the sketches. Though she didn't want to dog Mark's footsteps, she decided she must let him know the sketches were safe. He was consumed with the glyphs. It was time to tell him the news, and the Maya night would offer some privacy.

Checking the clearing, she found that everyone had left to go to bed. If she knew Mark, she'd find him at the top of El Castillo, brooding. He would be alone.

She slipped out the door and padded silently toward the ruins. She'd changed to shorts and a T-shirt, more than glad to rid herself of the long-sleeved pants and shirt. The drawings of the snake were barely visible in the darkness.

She found Mark, as she expected, perched at the top of the pyramid. He was watching her as she made the arduous climb.

"I have some good news for you," she said as she caught her breath. "I saved your sketches. They're in my hut. I wanted to tell you, because if I get a chance to leave in the morning I'm going to."

Instead of the reaction she expected, he simply sat. "You're a remarkable woman," he said at last. "I've been sitting here thinking about it. You're definitely remarkable."

She turned away from him to survey the darkness. "I think we've been here before, and this time I want to pass."

"I don't blame you."

His reply was totally unexpected, and she swung back to face him. "We're a lot alike," he said softly.

"I know." Her fists were clenched so tightly her nails were cutting into her palms. This wasn't the conversation she'd intended to have.

"We're so much alike that it unsettles me," Mark continued.

Celeste took a deep breath. "That's true. But I have to say that the characteristics I see in you are the ones I dislike the most in me. All of my life I've been completely wrapped up in myself. I fought for an education. I scrapped my way into one of the best jobs in the stock market. I've pushed and clawed and climbed my way to the top." She took a deep breath. "And it took coming here to make me realize I don't like what I've become. It's sad to say, Mark, but you're just like me, or at least the person I was. I wish you well in finding the jewel."

"Everything you've said is true. I won't try to deny it. But it isn't as simple as you see it."

This was the explanation she'd hoped to hear. Now she didn't know if she could endure it. Her impulse was to run away, not to listen. She'd dropped her defenses once for him. It wasn't wise to listen too long.

Sensing her reluctance, he closed the distance between them. He picked up her hand and held it. "I don't think I've ever made the effort to explain myself to anyone. Please give me a chance."

He was so close, so terribly close. She shifted slightly away, but she left her hand in his. "Okay."

Instead of answering, Mark folded her against his chest. "I couldn't leave, Celeste." He kissed her hand.

A pebble skittered across the top of the pyramid. Celeste and Mark turned toward the sound in time to see a heavy shadow emerge.

"How touching," Barry Undine said. The moonlight glinted off a revolver. "So, Uncle Alec's little princess has some female qualities. I was beginning to think her only talent was in making money."

Mark started forward, and Barry aimed the gun at his heart. "Don't try it Señor Grayson," Barry said sarcastically. "Celeste Coolridge isn't worth dying for. Take my word for it."

Chapter Fifteen

When the gods are crossed, there are no innocents.

"There's no need for a gun," Mark said softly. He eased several inches away from Celeste.

"He's totally irrational," Celeste whispered to him. "He'll kill us both."

"That's right," Barry said, a grin shifting across his restless face. "I will. I've made up my mind that I'm not going to take the blame for your actions, Celeste. I may go to prison, but you won't be larking around scot-free."

"Barry, I didn't do anything wrong." Celeste kept her voice low and unemotional. "I swear to you, I never did anything illegal. You know that. I don't want to see you punished, I just want to be left alone."

"Sure!" he sneered. "That's why you went to such trouble to frame me. How about that little trade in Branden Olsen's account you did—and forged my initials to it. If the people in Stuart McCarty weren't so stupid, they'd see what an amateur frame it was! Like I'd initial a trade in one of your accounts!"

"What are you talking about?" She looked at Mark and shook her head. "I never traded anything for Branden before I left. His account never changes. He's blue-chip and nothing else."

"So why did he have seventy-five thousand shares of Donmak Computer Software?"

"Barry, I've never heard of that company." Celeste was puzzled enough to overcome her terror. "How could I sell something I didn't know existed?"

"Liar!" Barry lifted the revolver and pointed it at her chest. "Donmak is my cousin's company. He was supposed to get a government contract that would put him in competition with the big boys. I was the only one who knew this, and I wasn't selling the stocks until the company went public. But you found out, and you executed the trade so you could frame me."

Celeste was stunned. "I never did such a thing. I promise you. Even if I hated you, I'd never risk Mr. Olsen's investments for revenge." Her voice softened. "What happened?" She was almost afraid to ask. No wonder she was under suspicion. It did look as if she and Barry were in collusion.

"Donmak went bust. MissileWare got the contract. It seems there was a family connection in the Pentagon. Too bad for your client."

For some strange reason, Celeste didn't doubt anything Barry was telling her. She was less certain of the role he'd played in it. There was always the chance that he'd been playing in her accounts, was caught, and now had decided to drag her down with him.

"Is this the information Uncle Alec uncovered?" She had to get around to asking him about her uncle.

"Part of it. I must say the old man was properly shocked." He laughed. "He never showed it publicly, I'll give him that. He staunchly supported you, denied that it was possible. Stood on his dignity. But it was his investigator who found that particularly nasty piece of evidence."

"And you, of course, let everyone think we were working together." She saw Mark's signal to keep her cool, and she knew she had to clamp down on her temper.

Barry nodded. "What did I have to lose? I knew I'd been set up, and I figured if you were manipulating your accounts to blame me, I wasn't going to let you get away with it. That's when I decided to come down here and have it out with you. That job is my life. I've worked hard for it, and I want it back. If I lose my broker's license, I don't have a future."

"The same applies to me, Barry," Celeste said softly.

"No, that's not true. You'll figure how to get out of this. You have your uncle to help you. You have connections. People like you always come out on top."

"What is it you want?" Mark asked. He'd shifted several steps away from Celeste so that they didn't make such an easy target.

"I want a statement saying she rigged that Donmak sell, and the others."

"The others?" Celeste felt her heart drop.

"There are more. A lot of them in your uncle's accounts."

"Barry, where is Uncle Alec?"

He looked at her. "What are you getting at?" The muzzle of the gun inched over to Mark.

"I called the office and he wasn't there. He hasn't been at work for several days." Celeste saw Mark sizing up the possibility of making a dive for Barry so she kept talking. "I'm worried sick about him. Do you know where he might have gone?"

"He's probably making personal visits on some of those accounts. Some of his friends dropped millions."

"This is incredible." Celeste walked away to sit on the stone steps. "Was anyone else involved?" The damage at Stuart McCarty was in the millions, she didn't have to feign dismay.

"It was pretty much company-wide. The trades were insidious. A few here and there, until just before you left. Then there was a rash of big money transferred. What did you do with it all?" he asked. "I tore your home apart. There weren't any records there. That's why I came here. To get a confession, and to find out where you've put the money you made. If I have to start a new life, I intend to do it in style."

"There is no money."

"I'm not an idiot," Barry said. He shifted the gun from one to the other, alert once again. "I'll use this if I have to. Judging by the intimate scene I witnessed, you two care for each other. I'll hurt him, Celeste, if you don't give me what I want."

"If I had it, Barry, it would be yours. This is all news to me."

"Barry, who else at the brokerage firm would have access to all of the files?" Mark tossed the question in as he moved even farther from Celeste.

"Don't try to shift the blame. Celeste is the only one smart enough to have figured out how to get into the computer programs. Believe me, it was an ingenious plan. She must have millions stashed away somewhere."

"No wonder Uncle Alec sent the telegram saying indictments were going to be handed down," Celeste said softly, almost to herself. "When I left, it was a simple case of a few trades. There was no clear evidence of insider information, like the Donmak case. It was mostly speculation. Now, though, it's a major scandal. Maybe Uncle Alec disappeared voluntarily. Maybe he's so ashamed he couldn't go back to work."

Mark saw a possible opening. He had to get Barry to lower his guard, even if only for a moment. "If Celeste didn't do this, and Barry, you didn't, maybe you two should join forces instead of warring with each other. Someone sure as hell is guilty of illegal acts. Who could it be?" It was an old tactic, but there was a chance that it would work. He had to get Barry's gun.

"She's got you eating out of the palm of her hand, too," Barry said with disgust. "Well, I know her. I've watched her work for the past six years. All sweetness and professionalism on the surface, working her uncle and Vic as hard as she could behind our backs." Instead of relaxing, Barry swiveled the gun back and forth, more angry than ever.

Celeste rose. She could sense what Mark was trying to do, and she might be able to distract Barry. "That's untrue, Barry. I can't prove that I'm innocent of the other things.

God knows, I'm shocked by the depth of the charges. But I never used my uncle. I never once allowed him to intercede on my behalf. Never! You've been choking on that suspicion since I walked into that office. If you'd ever taken the time to look, you'd see that I've done well because I worked hard. The plain facts are that I worked harder than you."

"Yeah, harder at what?" he sneered.

"This isn't going to solve the problem," Mark said calmly, scrapping his plan to lunge for the gun. Barry was too antsy. "Put aside your suspicions and think. Who else could have figured out the scheme? Who would want to hurt the two of you?"

"No one." Celeste said dully. "Barry is the only one at the office who really hates me. There's no one else but him."

"A lot of people dislike me," Barry said. "None of them is as smart as Celeste. Not a single one of them could have figured out how to do this. And none of them had access to the office." He glared at Celeste. "Victor gave you access to his private computers, didn't he? So you could work your trades late, or early, and have all of the files whenever you needed the tiniest little thing."

"He gave other people access, too. That was for a special occasion, Barry, when that double bond trade was building. I haven't been near those computers for months."

"Wait a minute," Mark said, holding up his hand. "Wait one little minute. Who is this Victor?"

"Victor Rosen," Celeste said. "The head of Stuart McCarty."

"He had access, if he was able to give it to Celeste." Mark made the point slowly.

"Victor has total access," Barry agreed.

"Maybe you two should think about Victor. I've listened to you both hurl accusations back and forth, and I know Celeste isn't guilty. I've come to think maybe you've been framed, too, Barry."

"Victor?" Barry spoke the word with doubt. "He's a company man down to the laces of his shoes."

"And if he could pull off a scam where he gets all the money and puts the blame on two innocents, he wouldn't lose his company standing," Celeste said, her voice rising in excitement.

"They'd fire him for mismanagement." Barry was doubtful.

"Not if Alec Mason had to take the blame. Not if Alec Mason's beloved niece were the guilty party." Celeste jumped to her feet. "That's it!"

"Damn!" Barry said, lowering the gun to waist level. "You may be right. I've been down here chasing you around when I should've been in Tampa trying to track good old Vic's bank records."

The sense of relief Celeste should have felt was missing. She was too stunned. "No wonder Vic was so ruthless when he told me to leave. And he left you there for the next sacrifice."

"Your uncle seemed to age ten years the week after you left," Barry said. "At the time, I took a lot of delight in it."

"He was okay, wasn't he?" At the mention of Alec's health, Celeste felt the panic build again. "Where could he be?"

"I don't want to upset you any further, but Victor can be a calculating man, Celeste," Barry warned. "If he's guilty of what we think he's guilty of, then your uncle could be in danger."

She turned to Mark. "I have to get back to Tampa. I have to go now."

"As much as I wish I could give you that, I have to remind you that Captain Guirdion will not let you leave." Mark put his arm around her. "We can talk with him. We can try. Until we discover who murdered Timma, though, I don't think he'll allow you to leave."

Celeste looked at Barry. "You may be able to help find him. You can leave here freely. You've done plenty of damage, burning huts, kidnapping people and trying to drown others."

"Wait a minute!" Barry resisted. "You can't push all that on me. You haven't got a shred of proof."

"Did you mean to frighten Rebecca when you tried to drown her?" Celeste asked. "She almost had a heart attack."

Barry grinned. "Rebecca's heart is plenty strong, it just isn't very pure. She has her own agenda here, and I have to admit that I volunteered to scratch her back if she scratched mine. But I wasn't near the cenote when she gave her performance."

"She was pretending!" Celeste's weariness burned away in a flare of anger. "She is a stupid person. Really stupid."

"I told I'd help her find some jewel. She's certain it's around here somewhere," Barry said.

"Yeah, I'll bet." Celeste nodded to Mark. "Captain Guirdion or not, that woman has to go."

"I agree," he said softly, "as soon as humanly possible." He started toward Barry, but the rising gun barrel stopped him. Barry Undine wasn't a careless man. "You didn't kidnap Celeste?"

Barry wagged the gun. "Take it easy, Grayson. I didn't have to kidnap Celeste. You have your own set of problems here in Chichén Itzá." A smile touched his lips again. "I think it's time for me to go. I have a rendezvous with Victor. He doesn't know it yet, though."

"Barry you can't leave without promising that you won't endanger my uncle." Celeste started after him, but Mark's hand restrained her as Barry cocked the gun.

"Don't push me, Celeste. I could kill you both right now."

"Whatever you do to Victor, please don't jeopardize my uncle."

"I intend to find out where Victor Rosen has hidden his accounts, if he's actually the guilty party. If he's stashed away millions, I'll find them. Anyone who gets in my way is going to get hurt, and that includes your uncle." He raised the gun higher and motioned them back. "Don't try to stop me. Since I know all of you are being held here at Chichén

Itzá, I'll have a few days without interruption. Time is all I need..."

The sound of a shot came simultaneously with the expression of amazement and then doubt that crossed Barry's face. With a murmur, he fell backward, disappearing from the edge of the pyramid.

Mark instinctively knocked Celeste to the ground and rolled on top of her. He searched the darkness, looking for the killer, but he could see no one. Beneath him, Celeste was rigid with fear.

"Señor Grayson."

Mark couldn't believe what he heard. "Wilfredo? Is that you?"

The small man came quietly from near the center of the pyramid. "He was going to hurt you. I saw the gun pointed."

Celeste remained frozen, unable to say or do anything. She felt Mark move away from her and then pull her to her feet.

"Are you okay?" he asked, his hands moving over her arms and shoulders.

She nodded. "Barry," she whispered, her gaze fixed on the edge where he'd disappeared.

"I did not mean to kill him," Wilfredo said. Panic was in his voice and he came forward slowly. "He had a gun. He said he would hurt you. I meant to wound him."

"Maybe he isn't dead," Mark said, but there was little hope in his voice. "I'll have a look. Wilfredo, you take care of Celeste. Keep her up here," he added gently. He slipped over the edge of the pyramid, disappearing from sight.

"He was going to hurt you, wasn't he?" Wilfredo asked. "I had to protect you. Carlotta said he would try to hurt you."

Celeste responded at last to the frightened note in Wilfredo's voice. "He might have," she said. "I believe that it looked as if he might hurt us." She tried to sound reassuring.

"He was a mean man," Wilfredo insisted. "Carlotta said that he was dangerous, that he hated you."

"I suppose he did." She swallowed. "He was desperate. That can make a man say and do stupid things. The important thing is that you were protecting me and Mark. The authorities will understand that."

Wilfredo shook his head miserably. "I have killed a man, an American. The police already think I killed Timma. It will not matter to them what my reasons were."

"Maybe he isn't dead," Celeste said, but she knew that if the bullet didn't kill him, the fall surely had. If he were alive, Mark would have called for assistance.

"You must go back to camp," Wilfredo said. "The police will be here soon. They will have heard the shot. I must hide." He moved away from her. "I didn't mean to kill him," he said again, the panic growing in his voice.

"Go to the jungle, Wilfredo." Celeste tried to think, but her thoughts were jumbled. "Stay in the jungle until Mark and I have a chance to explain this."

"I tried to protect you." Wilfredo stepped closer. "The ring was meant to help you, but the dangers were too great, too powerful. Now I must go. If I do not see you again, remember that it was an honor to be chosen to protect you." He held the gun out to her. "Take this, please."

"What should I do with it?"

"Return it to Señor Ortiz. He gave it to me. It will only make more trouble if I have the gun. If I am armed, they will shoot me before I have a chance to speak."

Before she could resist, Wilfredo pressed the pistol into her hand.

"Be careful, *señorita,* the jaguar walks. Even though the others will try to protect you, it will become more and more difficult until the day of the season's change."

The sound of voices floated on the clear night air. Someone from the camp was headed toward the pyramid. The sound of the shot had alerted everyone.

"Go hide," she whispered. "Now, before it's too late."

Wilfredo vanished into the shadows on top of the pyramid. There was the clatter of a stone as he went down the far side, then silence. Much against her will, Celeste walked to the edge where Barry had disappeared. She could see the darker shadows of Barry, prone on the steps, with Mark beside him. Flashlights were approaching from the camp. She negotiated the steep steps as if she were in a dream, finally stopping beside Mark.

"He's dead," Mark said, standing up so that he blocked her view of the body. "We'd better report this as quickly as possible."

"Wilfredo's gone. He gave me the gun. He said they'd kill him for certain if he was armed. What are we going to do?"

"I don't know," Mark answered, looking at the gun in her hand. "If Wilfredo is accused of Barry's murder, it will have international implications. I'm afraid he wouldn't have much chance of a fair trial, not on top of Timma's murder."

"Then he can't be suspected," Celeste said in a voice she barely recognized as her own. Her fingers tightened around the gun. At last she had a plan to help Wilfredo.

CAPTAIN GUIRDION, DANIEL Ortiz, Mark, Roberto and Celeste were gathered in the center of the camp. The light from several lanterns cast deep shadows on their faces.

"He attacked us," Celeste said, looking at her hands on the arms of her chair. "It was an accident."

"How accidental is it that a tourist is carrying a weapon in my country?" Captain Guirdion said carefully. "Especially one who is already under suspicion."

"The gun is mine," Daniel Ortiz said, standing up. "And Celeste is my guest here. I gave her the gun for protection. She said Mr. Undine's death was an accident, and we should believe her." He patted her shoulder reassuringly. "Your uncle will have my hide if anything bad happens to you," he said.

Celeste gave him a grateful look. She'd given the men no choice but to play along with her when she'd assumed the responsibility for Barry's death. She could sense Mark's cold anger, but once she'd declared to the captain that it was her hand that pulled the trigger, Mark had to back her up.

"Miss Coolridge, why were you carrying the gun to the pyramid?" The captain watched her with disbelieving black eyes.

"I know you don't believe there's a jaguar running wild in this jungle, but I saw it. I carried the gun for protection."

"And you killed a man instead of a jaguar. A slight miscalculation, I'd say." He nodded his head once, as if he were considering the facts.

"The man had a gun pointed at both of us." Mark's words were crisp and cold.

"Why don't you tell me exactly what happened," the captain said, turning his attention from Celeste to Mark.

"It happened the way Celeste said it did. Undine was threatening us and when he charged, Celeste fired. That's all there is to it. I think it's time we ended this discussion."

"The man is dead," Roberto said with his Latin shrug. "Talk will not bring him back. It was an unfortunate accident."

"This exploration of the tombs has suffered from a number of unfortunate accidents," the captain said. He put his hat on and stood. "I will not press charges tonight. Tomorrow, we shall see."

"Thank you, Captain." Daniel Ortiz offered his hand, but the officer ignored it.

"Where are the other Americans?" Captain Guirdion asked, looking around the gathering.

"The students have gone home, since they weren't required to stay. The Tretorns are in their quarters. Mrs. Tretorn was a friend of Mr. Undine's. She's disturbed and upset," Roberto said smoothly. "It is very traumatic for her."

The captain nodded and motioned his men to follow him to their cars.

As they left, Mark let the air escape his lungs. He swung round on Celeste. "That was stupid and foolish. He could have taken you with him to jail. I told you once before, that's not a place you want to be."

"And Wilfredo would fare any better?" she shot back. She was shaken by the events. By declaring herself the murderer of Barry Undine, she'd put herself in the direct glare of the police captain's suspicions. He was smart enough to know that the story she'd concocted was not the truth. But the other alternative was to sentence Wilfredo to death.

Mark knew her point was well taken, but his own fears were running wild. "He can come back here at any time and simply take you, Celeste. None of us could stop him."

"Let's don't court the devil unless we have no other choice," Daniel said. "He left, and for the moment that's all we can ask. Now tell me what actually happened."

Mark and Celeste recounted the story. "The worst part is that Barry might have been able to locate Uncle Alec," Celeste said at the end. "What am I going to do now? The captain will never let me leave."

"I can check on Alec tomorrow," Daniel assured her. "In fact, I'll go to Tampa myself. I don't know your uncle well, but I feel a small degree of responsibility here. I did tell him about the Jaguar's Eye. If I hadn't been such a convincing salesman, he would never have thought to send you here. Mr. Undine wouldn't have followed." He shook his head. "This is a terrible tragedy."

"You'll find him?" Celeste was ready to beg. "I feel that I've put you in a terrible position, having to assume my responsibilities for me. Do whatever it takes."

"I'll see that your uncle is safe and sound," Daniel promised her, patting her hand. "Just leave this to me. Now, what are we going to do about this shooting?"

"Protect Wilfredo," Celeste said.

"That may not be possible," Roberto said, speaking for the first time in a long while. "Wilfredo took the law into his own hands; perhaps we cannot protect him."

The words shocked Celeste. She turned on Roberto, her green eyes like shards of glass. "Wilfredo isn't expendable," she said. "I'm surprised that you would think he was."

"You feel some guilt, since he was protecting you," Roberto said, completely unruffled by her attack. "Unfortunately, he committed a crime."

"Roberto is right," Mark said reluctantly. "You did a very brave thing trying to protect him, but the captain did not believe you. If he decides to press the point by trying to arrest you, I will have to tell him the truth."

Celeste pushed her hair from her overheated face. "You both know that I stand a better chance than Wilfredo. Why are you doing this?"

"Because it's your fault, Celeste." Rebecca Tretorn had entered the clearing. She had obviously been drinking, and her face was pinched with anger.

Rebecca's true emotions were suddenly clear to Celeste. Rebecca had developed feelings for Barry. Bored with her husband, bored with her life, she'd found excitement in helping Barry with his schemes. She'd believed that he was actually interested in her.

"It isn't anyone's fault," Mark answered, signaling to Daniel to shift to Rebecca's side. He gently grabbed an arm while Daniel took the other. "I think you should lie down, Rebecca. You look over-excited."

"Where is Charles?" Roberto asked pleasantly.

"He's finishing a roll of film. He says he's going to get proof that the stupid jaguar is out in the jungle."

"What?" Daniel swung round to face her. "What jaguar?"

Rebecca smiled, then laughed. "Oh, he's seen the cat all along. He came across it not an hour after Celeste saw it. Since then he's seen it several times near the village. He's set some stupid trap for it, so he can photograph it. He'll be back by dawn, he said." She shook her head angrily. "But I don't care. I hope he doesn't come back. I had plans..."

Her voice broke into sobs. She ran from the clearing and Mark followed to make sure she reached her hut safely.

"That particular cat is more likely to be found in the bottom of a bottle of Scotch. In case you haven't noticed, the Tretorns are liberal drinkers," Roberto said softly. "They would have left long ago had they not been so greedy. They had hoped to find the Jaguar's Eye, all for themselves."

"How much is the ruby worth, Roberto?" Celeste asked. "I've never bothered to ask."

"If it is indeed the stone that Mark thinks it is, it would be worth millions."

"But Mark intends to turn it over to the authorities, to create funding to preserve Chichén Itzá."

"Yes, those are his intentions," Roberto agreed.

"And yours are different?"

Roberto's answer was obliterated by a sharp, piercing scream. The sound came from the jungle.

"That's Charles Tretorn," Celeste said.

"You're right!" Roberto grabbed a flashlight from the table. "Get Mark," he said tersely. "It sounds like it was coming from the south. I'll go to the wall of skulls. Tell Mark to head for the observatory."

"Right," she agreed.

Another wild cry of anguish shattered the still night.

Chapter Sixteen

The messengers of the true god roam the jungle. Creatures of the Maya await his word.

Mark took the lead and Celeste followed in his footsteps. They crashed through the jungle, pausing only when another cry of terror rang through the night. Celeste wanted to cover her ears and hide, but she knew she had to keep pushing forward. Charles Tretorn was in horrible pain. They had to find him fast. They had to find him before someone, or something, else did.

The thought of meeting the large jaguar on the dark jungle path almost tangled her feet. She felt Mark's hand of assistance and recovered her balance without ever breaking stride.

"Thanks," she managed, between gasps for breath.

Mark kept moving forward, like a relentless machine. "Everything's going to be okay," he said, and Celeste knew that he spoke for her benefit. He could sense her fear. She could only wonder if he knew she was thinking about the jaguar. The villagers believed the cat was a prophet. It was certainly a mythic creature. No matter where she turned, the image or shadow or mark of the jaguar was confronting her.

Wilfredo had given her another warning only a few hours before. Something about how he'd tried to protect her, but the jaguar was walking the night. She fingered the ring he'd sent her for saving his life. Did she wear the image of the animal as a totem against harm? Was that the reason some-one had painted her with the sign of Quetzalcoatl? A chill raced along her limbs and she pushed harder to keep up with Mark.

Once again, the anguished cries of Charles Tretorn floated through the darkness. Celeste felt the responding surge of adrenaline.

"He's more south," Mark said under his breath. He cut off the trail and directly into the undergrowth. Slashing with a machete and trying to hold the light, he struggled for-ward. Their reward was the sound of another scream, this one much closer than the last.

Celeste started to yell out, but Mark whirled around, warning her to remain silent. "We can't be certain who has Charles."

"Who?" Celeste had never considered the possibility that someone might be hurting Charles. The jaguar was the only creature that had occurred to her. Who would be hurting Charles? The only real suspect was Rebecca, she thought with grim honesty, and she was back at camp.

Mark gave Celeste the extinguished flashlight and the machete and took her elbow. His hand on her arm was gentle but firm. Celeste had no time to probe her own re-action. It was enough that his touch was comforting.

In the darkness they were almost completely silent. After a few yards, Mark reached into his waistband and with-drew a pistol.

An attack of apprehension made her shiver and she stumbled slightly. A twig snapped beneath her foot.

"Shush!" he froze her with a light pressure on her fin-gers.

A short distance away she heard a terrible thrashing sound, as if something large rolled in agony in the under-growth.

"The cat," she whispered softly. "Maybe Charles wounded it."

"Maybe," Mark agreed, inching forward. "If you see it, drop flat on your stomach. If it's wounded, it could come at us. One shot may not be enough."

With Mark's fingers guiding her against his side, they eased forward. "The light," he hissed.

She flicked on the button and swung the beam around in a circle. The intense beam picked out a man's feet. They flopped feebly against the hard-packed earth, as if the person was in the throes of some seizure. She played the light up the legs, her hand shaking as she realized what the small darting shadows moving over the twitching body were. Charles Tretorn was covered in lizards. Small, medium and large, the reptiles ran over him. A large green one had perched on his chin. Charles shuddered once more and then was still.

"I've never seen anything like this," Mark said as he rushed to Charles's side. At his approach, most of the lizards scurried away, then turned and circled back. They seemed to watch Mark and Celeste.

"Is Charles hurt?" Celeste knelt beside Mark. She knew the lizards were basically harmless, but she'd never been able to overcome a certain fear of them.

Mark swept his hands at the lizards, scattering them into the brush. Still a few seemed reluctant to leave. "Their behavior is abnormal," he said, his hands moving over Charles's body. "This reminds me of those ants. I haven't gotten a response from the experts I called, but you can bet I'm going to check this out, too."

"There are a lot of strange incidents. That jaguar, for instance. It could have killed me, and it didn't. And Thomas, bitten by a snake while he slept. You said pit vipers normally didn't go out of their way to attack."

"You're right, on both counts. Can you help me sit him up? I don't think he's hurt."

Together they pulled Charles into a sitting position. "Charles!" Mark patted his face. "Charles!"

Charles moaned and slumped against Celeste. The smell of alcohol was strong.

"Is he . . . ?"

"I think he's been drinking heavily and has passed out," Mark said. "Help me get him to his feet. We can't leave him here."

Celeste held the light in the crook of her arm and grabbed Charles's hand. There were tiny red marks on his flesh. "They bit him!" she exclaimed. "Lizards don't bite, do they?"

Mark looked at Charles's hand. The marks were hard to distinguish, but they could easily be bites. "Let's get him back to camp." He didn't want to pursue his own thoughts about what might have happened to Charles Tretorn. At least not while he was virtually unprotected in the jungle.

"The jaguar," Charles mumbled as they hoisted him to his feet. "Beware the jaguar."

Celeste looked around, the darkness thick and dangerous. "Do you think he saw the cat?' she asked Mark.

"I doubt it, unless it was an alcohol vision."

"That's what Roberto said." She staggered slightly beneath Charles's weight. "But I'm not convinced. The cat is real. I saw it." She pulled Charles's right arm over her shoulder. Mark took the dazed man's left arm. Together they stumbled down the narrow path to camp.

"Beware the jaguar," Charles mumbled.

"Keep moving," Mark said, hefting more of Charles's weight on his shoulders. "Let's get this guy to camp and see if we can find out what's really ailing him. A few lizards shouldn't have put him in such a state."

"Not normal lizards," Celeste said, thinking of the red blotches on Charles's hands and face.

"Some species do bite," Mark said as if he read her mind. "I'm wondering why they all congregated on Charles. The more I think about this, the more it seems to me that someone is deliberately creating these incidents. Those ants had to have been brought to El Castillo and left. They weren't there, and then they were. Wilfredo said it was some sort of sign that the god was coming. Now these lizards. It's as if the scene was deliberately set to give the impression that the reptiles were attacking Charles. The question is why?''

"It's bizarre, and creepy," Celeste said, her voice choppy from the effort of supporting Charles.

Dragging Charles between them, they slowly made it back to camp. Celeste felt as if her spine would snap with the pressure of Charles's body. She could also smell the alcohol on his breath, but she felt a twinge of sympathy for him. They made it into the clearing and were moving toward the Tretorns' hut when she heard Rebecca's voice.

"Charles! What have they done to you?" Rebecca rushed to her husband. She tried to push Celeste away. "What have you done to him?" she demanded.

"Take it easy," Roberto said. He grabbed Rebecca's shoulders with no pretense at gentleness and pushed her away. "Let me have him," he said to Celeste. "I'll help Mark get him inside."

With Rebecca's accusations and cries following, they carried the incoherent man into his hut and placed him on one of the cots. To Celeste's amazement, the hut was immaculate. The clutter of expensive dresses and jewelry that she had found on her last visit was nowhere in evidence. Rebecca's packed suitcases were in a corner.

With the light cast by several lamps, Mark was able to examine the small red marks on Charles's hands and face. Mark made no comment, but Celeste saw his mouth tighten.

"There's a knot on his head. He probably hit his head when he fell down," Mark said, his attention still focused on Charles. "Otherwise, he seems to be okay. His color is good; his breathing normal."

Charles moaned slightly and began to thrash. "The jaguar! The legend!" he cried and struck out with his hands, catching Mark unexpectedly in the chest.

Mark grabbed his hands and restrained them. "Easy, Charles. You're safe now. Take it easy. What happened?"

Very slowly Charles seemed to return to the present. His eyes focused on Mark, then darted around the room to lock on Rebecca. "The jaguar came at me," he said softly. He blinked several times and looked at Mark. "It was enormous, and it came out of nowhere." He must have recognized the expression on Mark's face as disbelief. He rose on his elbows. "It was the cat. I'd seen it before, but I didn't say anything. It came straight out of the bush toward me, leaping and growling. I ran and then I tripped." His hands tightened on the blanket and his fists began to clench and unclench. "My head." He touched the bump with a grimace.

"Did someone hit you?" Celeste asked.

Charles paused, his gaze going once again to his wife who was uncharacteristically silent. "I tripped and fell onto my hands and knees. I remember I crawled forward. I was terrified the jaguar was going to attack me. There was a low chuckle, not exactly a laugh but a sound like someone was enjoying watching me. Then I saw a pair of leather shoes about three feet from my hands. I remember thinking they were very expensive shoes. Almost new. I started to look up, and something crashed into my head." He looked at Mark. "But I saw the jaguar. He didn't attack me."

"Who did?" Celeste asked, unconsciously stepping closer to the cot.

"I don't know. But I do know I need a drink." Charles motioned to his wife, who silently stood beside Daniel Ortiz. "You said it wouldn't be dangerous. You sent me out there to be killed, didn't you?" He waved at the suitcases neatly lined up by one of the cots. "You were all packed to leave, weren't you?" His color mounted to red, and he tried to throw himself at his wife. Only Mark's strong grip detained him.

"Don't be a fool," Rebecca hissed at him. "I didn't send you out there. You went on your own. You were determined to get a picture of the cat. By the way, where is the camera?" She addressed the question to Mark.

"I didn't see one. Maybe it's in the brush somewhere." He stood up. "It would seem you'd be more interested in your husband's health than in a camera."

"That camera was going to make her fortune," Charles said bitterly. He picked the pillow from behind his head. "And where are the pictures, Rebecca? Don't you think I know you gave the film to Barry Undine? Where are they? Those were to be our ticket to wealth, remember? The only photographs of the stela so we would have plenty of time to find the ruby." He threw the pillow at her with enough impact to knock her against the wall.

"Shut up!" she warned him.

"You think I'm so obtuse that I didn't see the way you were hanging all over Undine? And look what it got you. He took the film and never brought the pictures back, did he? He ran off with your ticket to the fortune. Now what are you going to do?"

"I'm warning you, Charles," Rebecca said, advancing toward him with hatred on her face. "Shut up now!"

"I've shut up for too long. That's the trouble."

"Charles, Barry Undine is dead," Roberto said in a low voice. "He was accidentally shot tonight."

"Too bad," Charles said, falling back onto the cot, exhausted. "I was hoping he'd take my wife off my hands." He darted a look at Celeste. "You'd better get out of here! Now! Leave while you're still alive!"

"What are you talking about?" Mark demanded, his tone harsh and grating. "Is there a threat to Celeste?"

"You are a fool," Charles said, weariness replacing the anger in his faded eyes. "How many tragedies does it take for you? First Timma, now Undine. You seem to think all of these things are unrelated."

"Shut your mouth." Rebecca advanced toward him slowly. When she was only a few feet away, she jumped forward with the pillow and pushed it against his face. "Shut up, you idiot!"

Mark pulled her back, handing her off to Roberto like a sack of potatoes.

"What are you saying?" Mark said, grabbing Charles's shoulders until he flinched. "It's obvious you destroyed the stela. Don't compound your troubles by lying."

Charles didn't bother to deny it. "I'm telling you to get out of here. This place is dangerous for Celeste. No stone is worth the price you've paid, is it? Just leave and forget the Jaguar's Eye. Take Celeste and save her."

"Save me from what?" Celeste felt the chill of danger brush across her skin.

The look Charles gave her was filled with scorn and pity. "Look at yourself, and then pretend to be so innocent. You didn't happen here—you were selected. Get out or die!" He turned toward the corner and was silent.

"I'm going to kill him," Rebecca raged. "No man should be so incompetent and so stupid. All of his life he's talked when he should have kept his mouth shut!"

"Calm yourself," Roberto soothed, pulling her toward the door. "You must calm yourself." Daniel assisted Roberto in forcing Rebecca out of the hut.

Her fury thwarted, Rebecca gave in to her tears. She collapsed like a rag between the two men and offered no resistance.

"What a scene," Mark said under his breath. He could see the tension on Celeste's face. "Why don't you take a breather outside."

"We need to talk," she whispered. "Listen, Mark, maybe we should leave for a while. It seems that everyone here is losing control. Maybe this place is cursed. Charles has been drinking, but I believe he saw the jaguar."

"And shoes?" Mark's humor was grim. "What else would a shoe magnate see but shoes? I don't think the villagers have a stash of leather shoes around here."

Celeste refused to yield. "Don't discount what he says. Someone hit him. I believe that."

"Let me try to talk with Charles. Alone. If he knows something, maybe I can pull it out of him," Mark said.

"Yeah," she agreed. She was disgusted with Rebecca and Charles. She wanted to be outside in the clear night air, away from the greed and anger and cruelty she'd witnessed. She slipped out of the room undetected. In the glow of the lantern, Roberto and Daniel were fussing over Rebecca at the dining table. She had fallen on her arms on the table and was sobbing violently.

The idea of a chat with Thomas suddenly had tremendous appeal. It might be her last opportunity to see him. Life was moving far too fast in Chichén Itzá.

It was a long, dark walk to the village, but she didn't mind, not since she'd taken the foresight to tuck Roberto's pistol into her shorts. There were plenty of things to think about.

She couldn't shake the memory of Charles, lizards crawling over his body. If she were a superstitious woman, she'd almost believe that the natural order had been turned upside down. That some god was sending messages about something. The clincher was the jaguar. Drinking or not, Charles had seen the cat. She believed him. That meant that twice, when the wild creature had been easily within striking distance of a human, both times it had stopped.

There was something else about Charles's story that troubled her. The shoes. She didn't believe he was too dazed to know reality from fantasy. Expensive leather shoes. That could mean only one thing! The man who attacked Charles was not a native. Barry was dead. The only other man who had been to the ruins in expensive shoes was Daniel Ortiz.

The San Diego businessman knew the area well enough to slip around in the dark. He also knew enough about the Jaguar's Eye to know what events might be interpreted by the villagers as signs from the gods.

The delicious warmth of the night was all around her, but she failed to notice as she increased her steps toward Thomas's home. Of all the people she knew, Thomas might be the one who could help her the most. She had to pry some information from him about the legends. If Ortiz was up to no good, then it meant that Mark was actually very close to finding the valuable stone. Her blood rushed with excitement as she started to jog.

She was almost at the village when she saw the jaguar. He was standing in the middle of the road, a darker shadow among so many others. She paused, amazingly calm. In her heart, she knew she'd expected to find him. His tail twitched as if he sensed her intent. She made no effort to speak or soothe him. They simply stared at each other.

At last the animal took three small steps forward, allowing her to see the magnificence of his body in motion. She felt her fear swell, rising into her throat like wet wool. Still she made no effort to run. Again, the cat stopped, his intense green gaze leveled directly at her.

Her ears registered the rustle of vegetation, but her mind didn't attach any significance to it. Her entire concentration was on the jaguar. She was completely unprepared for the harsh arm that circled her waist or the hand that grasped her mouth. But her body recognized what was going to happen and she drew her leg forward and kicked back with all of her might.

She was rewarded with a cry of pain, which echoed in her own body when she felt the slap against her ear. The ringing noise almost undid her, but she tore free of the man and spun away. Her hands were at her shorts, pulling the gun out as she found her attacker in the dark. The lower half of his face was covered with a kerchief, but the erect body was familiar.

"Put the gun down," Captain Guirdion said in a voice he tried to disguise. "The jaguar will kill if you don't."

She pivoted her gaze from the man to the cat. The jaguar stood in the road, watching only her.

"You should have stayed put," the captain said. There was a hint of ruthlessness in the tone. "You make life so much harder for all of us."

"Stay back or I'll kill you," she warned, cocking the gun.

A paralyzing pain shot from her shoulder up her neck. She tried to turn, but she was in the grip of someone very strong. The gun fell helplessly from her fingers. Captain Guirdion's laugh was triumphant, and it was the last thing she heard before something stuck her on the side of the head.

MORE DISTURBED THAN he'd been in a long time, Mark finally left the Tretorn's hut. The sequence of action, as described by Charles, was clear. Charles had seen the jaguar and then stumbled back. The cat had come at him, but instead of attacking, it had simply jumped over him and disappeared into the jungle. Someone hiding nearby had hit Charles on the head.

Mark still felt a sense of unreality. Jaguars leaping over victims and lizards crawling and biting—it didn't make sense. As much as he wanted to discount the story, though, there were the tiny red bite marks on Charles's flesh.

In his private conversation with Charles, he'd discovered that the Tretorns were heavily in debt. Rebecca's spending habits and several bad business decisions had combined to create a situation that made Charles desperate. So desperate that he'd agreed to Rebecca's plan to destroy the stela. Charles had taken photographs of the stela before he smashed it with the sledgehammer. The Tretorns had planned to solve the riddle themselves and cash in the jewel. Without Charles's permission, Rebecca had given the film to Barry. It was a complicated web of deceit and betrayal, and it sickened Mark. He'd failed in his effort to get Charles to say any more about Celeste, and he doubted that Charles actually knew anything concrete.

The cool night breeze touched his hot face, and he decided to talk with Celeste. Charles's story about the jaguar and the lizards troubled him greatly. It was all related to Celeste. She'd seen the jaguar. Her skin was painted with the symbol of the snake. And Charles had said something about her being "selected." Mark had always believed that Barry Undine was behind Celeste's kidnapping. But now Barry was dead, and Mark wasn't so certain of the broker's guilt. The Tretorns had destroyed the stela, but who had killed Timma? There was an undercurrent of danger at Chichén Itzá, and he felt that it stemmed from Carlotta Bopp and her ancient stories.

Celeste, in all innocence, had stepped into the middle of something, but he couldn't pin it down exactly yet. He tried to juxtapose the snakes which had been painted on her limbs with the lizards. He could not find the logical link. Whatever it was, he wanted her away from the ruins. In the shadows of Chichén Itzá, something threatened her safety. If nothing else, Charles had convinced him of that. Celeste had to go back to Cancún, or better yet, the States. He would accompany her, if he had to. It was a big decision, but one that was far less painful than he thought it would be. Whatever it took, he wanted to protect her.

He also wanted to see her. To hold her and kiss her. He moved toward her unlighted hut. If she was asleep, how would she react when she felt his lips on hers? Anticipation turned up the corners of his mouth.

"Celeste," he whispered at her door. He didn't want to scare her. She'd had enough bad moments in the past few days. "Celeste?"

He slipped into the hut. The night was illuminated by the moon and stars, but the interior of the hut was like a cave. Inching forward to the bed, he gently felt for her. The bed was empty.

Slipping back beneath the cloth, he stepped into the night once again. On a hunch he moved toward the ruins. She found a similar type of peace in them that he did. Perhaps she'd gone there to think.

He searched for over an hour before he admitted she wasn't there. Celeste had probably gone to the village to visit Thomas.

He set a brisk pace toward Thomas Ibba's thatch hut. His heart demanded that he run faster, but he kept his pace steady. Let her be safe; let her be safe; let her be safe. The words echoed again and again with each stride. He hated to admit it, but his talk with Charles had unsettled him about Celeste's safety. Charles had warned him to get her out of the ruins. Now her absence had taken on an ominous overtone.

Around him the jungle was unnaturally silent. The whir of the ever-present insects was missing, as was the sound of the birds, another constant. He felt his fear grow, and he tried to label it irrational. Celeste was safe. She was having a cool drink with Thomas, laughing with the little boy. He created the mental image, forcing himself to see her, glass in hand as she bent to whisper something into Thomas's ear. He saw the way her hair fell forward, creating a curtain of beautiful reddish gold. She was laughing, happy with the conversation with Thomas. Waiting for him to come and find her.

The image dissolved, and he was left with the harsh reality that she was missing again. How had he let her out of his sight. His pace increased to an all-out run.

Celeste was in danger. He knew it in the same way that he'd known about the stela and the glyphs. It was a certainty in his mind that made his body rush forward at a reckless speed.

A dozen yards ahead, the glint of moonlight against something metallic caught his eye. He slowed his pace, curious and yet also apprehensive. As he came upon the shiny object at the side of the road, he saw what he'd dreaded. Celeste's necklace lay in the sand of the road. Beside it was the perfect print of an enormous jaguar.

THE VILLAGE was unnaturally silent as Mark approached. The laughter of children playing in the cool night, conversations, the tinny sound of a radio, all were missing.

Mark found Thomas swinging gently in the hammock outside his house. The boy was alone, and Mark moved forward and called his name.

"Yes, Señor Grayson. I thought you would come here."

"Will you help me find Celeste?" Running through the night with Celeste's necklace in his hand, Mark had come to a few conclusions. The sand beside the necklace had shown him that Celeste had been taken against her will. Charles had warned him that she was in danger. The footprint of the jaguar was his only clue. And Thomas Ibba was his best hope. The young boy knew the villagers inside and out. If someone from the village was involved, Thomas would know.

"I cannot help you. My mother will not allow it." There was a full flatness in the boy's tone, as if he were reciting a lesson he neither liked nor wanted to repeat.

"Why not? I know she likes Celeste."

"I cannot," Thomas said, never looking at Mark. "It is Celeste, or my people. I have made a choice."

Mark felt the revelation like a kick in his head. In one simple sentence, Thomas had summed everything up—the necklace, the strange behavior of the jungle creatures. "Celeste plays a role in the reincarnation, doesn't she?"

"Juanita told Carlotta about Mr. Tretorn and the lizards as soon as she could get here. It was the final sign." Thomas's voice shook. "It is the will of the gods." Tears moved down his face. "No one will harm her. She will be loved and cherished forever."

Mark grabbed the boy by the shoulders. "You have to help her, Thomas. Where is she? Where have they taken her? What are they going to do to her?"

He had a terrible image of the ancient rituals. In some, the human sacrifice was tied while a priest cut the heart out with an obsidian knife. In others, the sacrifice victim was thrown into the cenote with his or her hands tied. The drop alone was usually fatal. The survival rate of such a fall was virtually nil. That's why survivors were elevated to the stature of prophets.

"They will not hurt her," Thomas assured him. "She was sent to us to bring our god back. It is an honor. The Mayas will step forward in time, with the help of Celeste. She will blend the blood of the ancients with that of the future."

"And if she refuses?" Mark asked. "Have you thought what will happen to her?"

"She cannot refuse. It is the will of the gods," he repeated, but there was a shadow of doubt in is voice.

"Thomas, Celeste doesn't believe in your gods. She has no reason to obey them. What if Quetzalcoatl doesn't appear? Will that be interpreted as a rejection of Celeste? Will it seem that he has found her in disfavor? Think about it!"

He gripped the boy's shoulders a little tighter. "What will they do to her then?"

"That will not happen. She is beautiful, perfect for the god. He would never reject her." Thomas made no effort to release himself from Mark's grip. He stared into the gaze of the archaeologist, seeing the real fear in Mark's eyes.

"When will all of this take place? At least tell me that." Mark felt his desperation growing. How much time did he have? The Mayan calendar ruled the practice of rituals, but there were so many factors, so many gods. "Please, Thomas."

"When the day and night are of equal value," Thomas whispered.

"The equinox!" It was the equation in the glyphs from the stela that he'd been trying to work out. "Where?" He had three days at the most. He had to find where Celeste was being held and then get her out.

"I don't know," Thomas said. His gaze did not falter from Mark's. "They wouldn't tell me where. They were afraid I would not be loyal. That's why I'm here alone."

Mark forced his voice to remain steady. "Thomas, her life is in danger. If the god doesn't come, they will throw her into the cenote. It is the rule of the Maya, Thomas. You know that in your heart."

"They would not!"

"Are you willing to risk Celeste's life?"

Thomas looked away, his gaze dropping to the hard-packed earth. "She saved my life. She is chosen. Nothing will go wrong."

"She may well be chosen to die, unless you help me. This whole Quetzalcoatl business is a myth. There is no truth to it, no matter how much you want to believe it. If the Maya people want to have power in the future, they must learn the ways of the outside world. No god can come and help them. They must help themselves."

"I do not know where she is, *señor*. They would not tell me. That is the truth."

"Who knows?" Mark rubbed the boy's shoulders where his fingers had held him.

"Carlotta. Maybe a few others." He bit his bottom lip. "Wilfredo," he whispered.

"Wilfredo, too?"

"*Sí*. They have been preparing for days. I think even before she came they knew she would arrive soon. They expected her, but I did not know."

Mark remembered Celeste's first evening at the camp. Wilfredo's reaction to her had been odd. Now he understood why. She had walked into Chichén Itzá like a character from a legend. The woman in the necklace. The goddess on the glyph.

"Can you tell me where to find Wilfredo?"

"He must see that no harm befalls Celeste before the ceremony. It is his duty."

Mark stood slowly. His back was aching and his eyes felt dry and gritty. So that was why Wilfredo had killed Barry Undine. Wilfredo had been guarding Celeste. When he'd come upon the scene at the top of the pyramid, he'd shot before he thought. Charged with the responsibility of protecting the goddess, he'd become overexcited.

"What are you going to do?" Thomas asked.

"I'm going to find Celeste. Chances are good that they're holding her somewhere nearby. The ritual will be performed at Chichén Itzá somewhere in the ruins."

"Do not interfere," Thomas said, his face a mask of fear. "Once the ritual has started, if you interfere, they will kill you."

"That's right, if I don't get Celeste back, they'll have to kill me."

Journey with Harlequin into the past and discover stories of cowboys and captains, pirates and princes in the romantic tradition of Harlequin.

Printed in Canada

Chapter Seventeen

March 18. It is the day of Cimi. The time shall come when the clamor of drums will be heard. The bud of the flower will sprout, a time of changes.

Gentle chanting floated above Celeste's head as her body registered the chill of the hard surface on which she lay. She tried to move, but her body refused to obey. Even her eyes were weighted against her command to open. It was far too tempting to sink back into sleep as the soothing chants seemed to demand. A pungent odor, not unpleasant but sharp, teased her. Too much effort was required to identify it.

She thought she heard her name being called, but she couldn't be certain. Using all of her strength, she forced her eyes to open to slits. A feathered creature seemed to move and shift around her, dancing to the rhythm of the chanting. She tried to focus, but it was impossible. The brilliant shades of blue and green confused her. A second figure shifted into her line of vision. Although she could see it was a human, it was covered in the skin of the jaguar. The cat's head completely covered the dancing figure's face. It was like a movie, something seen long ago and almost forgotten. She drifted back into the darker world of sleep.

Celeste couldn't be certain how much time had passed when she finally opened her eyes. She remembered her earlier sensations, but thought they'd come from some strange dream. Now her body ached from the hardness of her bed, from the cold of the stone. She slid her palms along the surface where she lay. The smooth stone felt like one of the ancient Mayan altars.

The chanting, if it had ever existed, was gone. A trace of the pungent odor lingered, but it was not nearly as over-powering as she remembered. At last she forced her eyes open, no longer able to postpone the moment she dreaded. Stone walls surrounded her. Forcing her elbows under her, she searched the smooth stone interior for an opening. There was none.

Two flares stuck in the wall burned brightly, and Celeste held onto the certainty that someone had brought her to this place and left the flares. If there was a way in, then there had to be a way out. She only had to get up, move to the wall and begin to search. When Mark was imprisoned in the stone room of the Red House, there had been an exit.

As she swung her legs off the smooth stone platform, she almost gave in to a massive clutch of fear. Her own clothes were gone. In their place she was dressed in a gown with a brightly colored drape over her shoulder. It was belted at her waist with a bright blue sash. The gown exposed her left arm and leg, giving full view to the pattern of the snake.

The floor was cool to her bare feet. Since the stones were smooth, they didn't hurt, but she cast a quick look about for her clothing. In a corner she saw the flowers. They were ranked in lines and rows in a formal design. She stepped to-ward them, a chill spreading across her skin. In the center of the bouquets was a small altar with burning candles. She moved toward it slowly, hardly daring to breathe. In small earthen saucers the remains of some type of incense had turned to ash. She picked up one of the saucers and took it to the flare for a closer inspection. Etched in the bottom was the image of the snake. The god Quetzalcoatl. Looking at her gown once again, she saw that the material was pale blue, blended with darker shades. The drape had threads of gold and red, but the predominant color was blue. Thom-as's words came back to her. Blue is the color of sacrifice.

She knew then why the flowers had disturbed her so. Was it a wedding or a funeral?

The dancing figures were not part of her dreams. They had been there, weaving and chanting about her prone body. The painted snakes had been no joke.

She was marked for some sort of sacrificial rite.

Among the flowers she saw a brightly painted figure. She recognized the stone figure of the woman. Beside it was a metal figure of the god Quetzalcoatl, disrobed of his serpent plumes and in the guise of a man. The two figures stood side by side in the midst of the flowers and candles.

A sigh of understanding slipped from Celeste. She was too afraid to make any other noise. At last she knew what purpose she would serve.

FROM THE EDGE of the jungle, Mark watched the police officers play cards at the dining table of the camp. There were at least a dozen officials at the campsite, and three other teams were in the jungle looking for him.

He'd spent the past twenty-four hours circling the camp again and again, hoping for a chance to talk with Roberto. It seemed that Captain Guirdion was holding the members of the excavation crew under house arrest.

Mark shifted his weight, trying to relieve a cramp in his left leg. When he looked up, Roberto was standing at the door of Celeste's hut, the roll of drawings in his hand. Roberto gave the drawings to one of the officers, then signaled him down the path to the ruins. The police officer moved away, taking the direction that Roberto had indicated.

Mark didn't wait to analyze what he'd seen. He slipped through the jungle, moving faster and more silently than the police official. He was in place when the officer passed by. Mark struck him cleanly from behind, dropping him in the dirt. The roll of drawings fell to the ground, and Mark retrieved them before heading back into the undergrowth.

Instead of going toward the camp, he took the direction of the vendors' stalls. Why had Roberto given away the drawings? He had to answer that question before he could ask his friend for help in saving Celeste. If he could not count on Roberto, then he would have to find Wilfredo on his own.

Tired, hungry and fighting anxiety about Celeste, he slipped through the thick foliage.

He took a position where he could watch the vendors and the police cars. It was only half an hour before Captain Guirdion arrived with the Tretorns in tow. He allowed them to pack their belongings into the rental car, but he made it clear that the charge of destroying the stela was severe. Mark could hear him lecturing the two Americans, warning them that an escape attempt could result in death. Mark felt a pang of sympathy for Charles, who looked completely beaten. Rebecca was making every attempt to ignore the situation. She waited at the car door for the officer to open it as if he were her chauffeur.

Mark had little time to speculate upon the Tretorns' possible punishment. As soon as the car with the Tretorns had disappeared, Daniel Ortiz walked, unescorted, out of the jungle. He went directly to Captain Guirdion. The two men spoke briefly before Daniel removed his billfold. The police captain took the money and opened the passenger door of a car for Daniel. In only a few moments the San Diego businessman was gone.

Mark had never suspected the debonaire Californian. Now he did. Daniel had been the agent who sent Celeste to Chichén Itzá. Daniel had convinced her uncle that the dig would be good for her. Now he was leaving, driven away in a police vehicle. Was it possible that Daniel Ortiz had been in on a scheme to get Celeste to Chichén Itzá?

He wiped the sweat from his brow. How deeply was Roberto involved? It wasn't possible that his old friend had betrayed him, but he'd seen Roberto give up the drawings. There was no one he could trust. He had to concentrate on staying free and finding Celeste.

His legs cramped from the squatting position he'd held for so long. He was about to stand when he saw a movement across from Captain Guirdion. He froze, concentrating on the sway of a small frond. The vegetation shifted again, and there was a glimpse of a man spying. Mark didn't wait for positive identification. He circled back behind his hiding place and made a wide arc toward the man hiding in the bushes.

Using the most extreme caution, Mark eased up on the man who watched Captain Guirdion with total interest. "Don't move," Mark said as he pressed the point of the machete into the man's neck.

The Indian did not make a sound.

"Where's Wilfredo?" Mark asked.

"No," the man answered.

He turned his head slightly, and Mark realized he had never seen him before. He pressed a little harder with the machete. "Have you seen a woman with long red hair?"

The man shook his head, indicating he did not understand.

Mark pressed hard enough that a tiny trickle of blood oozed from the nick in the man's skin.

"I don't believe you. Tell Wilfredo I must see him. Tell him to meet me at the base of El Castillo. Tonight, at eight. *Wilfredo, El Castillo, ocho.*" Mark repeated the three key words in Spanish. He lifted the machete and the man sprinted away into the jungle.

Checking his watch, Mark found that he had three hours to prepare for the meeting with Wilfredo. He'd hoped for Roberto's assistance, but he would do it alone rather than risk betrayal. He felt his precious time slipping from his fingers. He had to find Celeste, and fast, before they could harm her.

The jungle closed around him as he withdrew, hunting for a secluded place where he could study the drawings of the glyphs. He had a hunch that the drawings might help him find Celeste, but he didn't have time to study them closely. They were a riddle, designed to thwart the efforts of those who attempted to find the Jaguar's Eye. Only the god was supposed to decipher the symbols.

As Mark looked at the different scenes, he felt a sense of hopelessness about being able to actually determine what the figures meant and how they could be pieced together. Symbols had to be researched. Dates had to be established. It would take hours and hours of work. There was no time.

With a sigh of exasperation, he picked up the drawings and began a circuitous route to El Castillo. He wanted to pick his location, where he could watch for Wilfredo and not fall for a trick. He felt certain the Mayan would come. He had spared a man's life with only a request for a meeting. Wilfredo would understand the gesture and feel obligated to appear. At least that was what Mark was counting on.

He took a position in a cluster of small shrubs to the right of the pyramid. Thirty minutes after he arrived, a patrol of police officials went past. Mark had a moment of grim humor as he wondered if he was their primary target, or Wilfredo. They were both being hunted by the police.

Sitting cross-legged, he leaned back against a tree and waited. Darkness crept across the ruins, casting El Castillo in darker shadows. Mark watched and waited. When he saw movements at the base of the pyramid, he made sure it was Wilfredo before he left his hiding place.

"I cannot help you," Wilfredo said before Mark had a chance to ask anything. "She is beyond your help."

Wilfredo's words created a strange anger. "What have you done to her?" Mark demanded.

"She is safe. Her life will be comfortable. I can promise you that." He stepped back. "You have been good to me. The *señorita* saved my life. I will not let anything bad happen to her."

"What are they going to do to her?"

"She will become the bride of the god. She will be honored by all the Maya."

"And if the god doesn't come, if he rejects her, she will die." Mark lifted one hand to Wilfredo. "You can save her. You did once before, didn't you? When she was taken the first time. You saved her then because you knew what they were doing was wrong."

"I was afraid for her," Wilfredo admitted. "It was too soon. I wasn't certain she was the one. Not even the necklace convinced me. Now the signs are complete. The ants have invaded the holy altar. I saw them with my own eyes, even though you killed them. The small serpents have begun to crawl and bite." He looked directly into Mark's eyes. "The jaguar has spoken her name. Thomas heard it."

"Wilfredo, this isn't about your people or your past or your gods. There's more here. Someone is using you and the Mayans to find the ruby. Can't you see that so much of what's happened here isn't actually possible? Those ants were put on the altar. The night Charles was attacked, someone had gathered those lizards and put them on him after he was knocked on the head."

"And the jaguar?" Wilfredo asked. "How do you explain that away?"

"I don't have the answers, but I do know that you're being tricked."

Wilfredo shook his head. "It is no trick. Quetzalcoatl will come. A new time will begin for the Mayas."

"You can't believe that, Wilfredo."

"Go to the jungle. Go due west five kilometers from the campsite. You will recognize the place, and you will be safe. I have left food and water there for you. Rest for the night. Tomorrow I will come to you, after I have thought about what you said."

"I won't wait long, Wilfredo. Time is running out for Celeste."

"For us all," Wilfredo said. "Until tomorrow." He turned and walked into the darkness.

A SEGMENT OF the wall opened, and Celeste sprang toward it like a gazelle. Escape was the only thing on her mind.

"Calm yourself," a voice ordered.

The unexpectedness of the order was enough to stop Celeste in her headlong pursuit of freedom. A feathered figure emerged from the crevice. It took a moment for Celeste to regain her composure. The winged creature was imposing.

"You have been chosen for a great honor."

Celeste immediately recognized Carlotta's voice. "I want to leave," Celeste said, realizing her voice was sounding weak. "Show me the way out." She put more power into that statement and was glad to hear that she sounded more in control.

"The gods have spoken, Celeste," Carlotta said simply. "You have no choice in this matter. There is no leaving for you now."

The skin along Celeste's neck tightened. Beneath the feathered headdress, she couldn't get a good look at Carlotta's eyes. Had the woman's obsession with the ancient ways driven her over the edge?

"Carlotta, I realize that you believe very strongly in the old ways, and I respect many of those beliefs. I don't believe them, though, and I have certain responsibilities. How long have I been here?"

"The moon has come and gone three times."

"Three days?" Celeste was astounded. "I've been a prisoner here for three days?"

"You have been fasting and purifying your body in preparation for the coming of Quetzalcoatl."

"How have I been purifying my body?"

Carlotta's hand touched her ear gently. "You have given blood."

Celeste's hand rose instinctively to her ear. She withdrew it at the first tingle of pain. There was a cut in her earlobe. She'd been bled in some bizarre ritual.

"Carlotta, you're a sensible woman. You have to let me go."

Carlotta smiled, motioning for Celeste to return to the stone altar. "Long ago I knew my destiny. Now I have come to show you yours. My people have waited hundreds of years. We have kept faith with the gods, eager yet willing to wait. Now it is time." She held aloft a rolled cylinder.

As Carlotta began to open the scroll, Celeste could see that it was cracked with age. She couldn't tell if it was made of paper or some other substance, but she knew that it was very old.

"This is the story of Quetzalcoatl," Carlotta said. "This is the time of rebirth, the moment when the Jaguar's Eye will be returned. The moment when the one true god will appear to claim his bride."

Celeste allowed Carlotta to lead her back to the altar without any resistance. Her only hope was to learn what Carlotta had in mind. Armed with that knowledge, she might be able to plan her escape.

At Carlotta's motion, Celeste took a seat on the altar. Carlotta stood in front of her, carefully unrolling the scroll. Celeste tried to fill her mind with as much detail as possible. Anything might give her a clue to escape. It might also keep her from giving in to her feelings of despair and hopelessness.

"On a day in time when the world is once again ready for the rule of the Mayas, the great god Quetzalcoatl will return. On that day, when night and day are equal, he will take a flame-haired bride. The blood of two races will mix and a new breed of human will be created."

Celeste was too stunned to speak. Her mind registered the words, but not the full meaning.

Carlotta looked at Celeste. "You are the chosen bride."

"Of course I'm not," she snapped, ready to fight. "I'm an American. I have a life in the United States. You can't force me into marriage and then keep me here like a prisoner." But the panic around her heart told her that such a thing might happen. After all, if she could believe Carlotta, she'd been a prisoner for days and no one had done anything.

"Accept the inevitable." There was a dark warning in Carlotta's voice. "Captain Guirdion can report you dead. For all the world, you would be so."

"I'm a suspect in two murders and accused of SEC violations in the United States. My government will send the marines down here to bring me to justice." There was a small degree of comfort in the knowledge that someone official would look for her.

"Your past has vanished," Carlotta said. "Do not speak of it again."

A lance of fear as sharp as a knife pierced her chest. "It doesn't matter if Guirdion says I'm dead or not. You can't erase my past, Carlotta. This is crazy. Mark will be hunting for me."

Carlotta shook her head. "He has already gone. The dig is abandoned. He cannot return."

The door opened and a young girl appeared with a tray of food and a glass of water. Carlotta signaled the child to put the tray on the altar and leave. "Escape is impossible. Guards remain outside the door." She motioned to the tray. "We have been feeding you and caring for you. Now you must do it for yourself. Eat and be strong. Tomorrow is a big ceremony."

"I won't do this," Celeste said with total conviction. "You can't make me participate in this ridiculous ritual."

"Destiny can never be stopped," Carlotta said, not disturbed in the least. "You are a bright woman. Use your intelligence. The wife of Quetzalcoatl will be honored and loved. Is that such a terrible fate?"

A sudden inspiration came to Celeste. "What if this god won't have me? What if he wants another bride?"

"Do not think you will displease him," Carlotta said. "Banish that thought from your mind, Celeste. If he rejects you, if he does not appear when the ruby is returned, then you will be taken to the cenote for sacrifice. If not a bride, then perhaps a prophet." Her dark eyes showed no ability for compassion.

Chapter Eighteen

March 20. The day of Lamat. It is the tenth in the Maya count, long awaited. The earth and sky are balanced. The sun is hot; the fields warm for planting.

Armed with a machete, a gun and the glyphs from the stela, Mark forged a path through the jungle. The jungle had been too thick, and too dark for him to travel during the night. But he was up at first light, intent on making the rendezvous with Wilfredo. He spent the night searching every building in the ruins. His fingers were raw from touching the stone walls, hoping against hope that he would find a secret passage. Wilfredo was his last hope.

He was upon the open hut before he realized it. It was just as Celeste had described it. Or at least it had once been. There was little left of the building. The flowers had been ripped and torn from the trellises. Even portions of the thatch roof had been destroyed.

Mark moved closer, taking care that no one was around to see him. He was amazed at the wreckage, as if someone had come in and torn the place apart in a fit of anger. It was wanton. It took several moments for him to notice the cage, hidden beneath a fallen section of the roof.

It was a large cage. Large enough for a jaguar.

The door was open, and the straw on the floor looked old, unused. Was it possible that someone had been insane enough to turn a live jaguar loose in the jungle?

For the first time, Mark had the feeling that the force he was up against was more formidable than he'd ever anticipated. To the Maya, the jaguar was a prophet. It was also an effective weapon of fear. He thought of Timma and his brutal death, deliberately designed to imitate the way a jaguar would kill. Who would do such a thing?

He could immediately discount Carlotta and her band of followers. To them the jaguar was a sacred animal. Who then? After he'd made certain that the building was completely abandoned, Mark looked for water. He found several jugs, and what had once looked like a small supply of goods. The food had been destroyed, but the water was drinkable. He sat beside a vine of bright pink flowers and tried to puzzle out the answers he sought.

No matter how he twisted the questions, the answer always seemed to turn back to Daniel Ortiz. Over and over again, Mark returned to the fact of Celeste's arrival. She'd come to Chichén Itzá on a whim—just at the equinox. It was more than coincidence. And it was Daniel who'd set the trap for her to come. Daniel was the one person he knew who could manage to ship in a live jaguar, with a little help from his police friends.

It had to be Daniel who was using the Maya's belief in legends for some reason, and the ruby was the only thing Mark could think of valuable enough to motivate a man of Ortiz's wealth. Daniel and the police captain. They were using the Mayas to get the jewel.

Mark checked his watch. It was mid-morning. There was no sign of Wilfredo, or anyone else. He took another long drink of water and wished for a canteen.

Now Carlotta was his only hope. Celeste was somewhere in those ruins, and he was going to find her. No matter what he had to do.

CELESTE ATE the food despite her determination not to do so. She was ravenous. She'd refused to eat the first day, and as a result she'd been left completely in isolation. Without a watch she had no way of telling how much time had passed, and she felt as if she would go mad.

Her first hours were spent trying to force the heavy door open, but she'd met with total failure. She'd slept fitfully, on and off, awakening to study the figures of the god and the woman. She knew that somehow she'd been selected to act out the part of Quetzalcoatl's bride. Charles had actually said it—selected. But how? She didn't have any answers.

She was tormented by thoughts of what had happened to Mark and the others. Carlotta had assured her that they had left the premises under armed guard, to be transported back to the States. She wasn't so certain that it wouldn't be simpler for Captain Guirdion to dispose of Mark. The archaeologist could be as tenacious as a water rat. Somehow, Captain Guirdion didn't impress her as a man with a lot of patience.

Along with worries about Mark's safety was concern for her Uncle Alec. If Barry's accusations had been correct, Victor Rosen was a very dangerous man. Her heart pounded with the possibilities.

The door opened, and Carlotta entered the room again, bringing a fresh tray with a pitcher and bowl. "The night has passed. It is time to prepare," she said, putting the tray on the altar. Behind Carlotta the young girl reappeared, this time bearing a tray of fruit. "The papaya is a delicacy. A special treat for the bride of a god."

"Who is the child?" Celeste asked when the girl had gone.

"Thomas's youngest sister, Angela," Carlotta said. "She will serve you once you are wed to Quetzalcoatl."

"And if there is no wedding?"

"She will join you in your journey to the sacred well," Carlotta said. "She has volunteered. I think Thomas must have convinced her."

"He wouldn't do that. Thomas has seen the outside world. He won't let his little sister die."

"I, too, have seen the outside world," Carlotta said with a hint of amusement. "That is how we judge the truth. Now wash and prepare yourself. I will come back for you very soon. The moment of Quetzalcoatl's return is fast approaching. You must be ready."

Celeste ate the fruit. She was thirstier than she'd ever remembered, and the papaya was delicious. She took the cloth from the warm water in the bowl and scrubbed at the image of the snake on her arm. It was useless. The paint could not be rubbed away.

"We are ready for you," Carlotta said, silently entering. She was wearing a gown of yellow woven with black.

Celeste stood, and for the first time, she realized she was unsteady. A wave of dizziness made her giddy. She leaned against the wall, trying to steady her legs.

"The fruit?" she whispered, finding that even her voice was not her own any more.

"A sedative to relax you," Carlotta said. "We will make this as easy as possible for you. Now come."

From out of the shadows two men who Celeste did not know took her arms and assisted her out of the room. She found that she was in a tunnel, a long passageway lit with burning torches stuck into the wall.

"Where are we going?" Her question dragged on the still air, taking forever to leave her mouth.

"To the observatory," Carlotta said softly. "You will be prepared to await the pleasure of Quetzalcoatl. It will not be long."

Celeste wanted to ask more questions, but her mouth refused to work properly. She was surprised when they stepped from the building into the sun. It was very bright, and she turned her head to block her eyes. In that flash of a moment, she thought she saw someone standing on the comb roof of the Red House. It was a small figure, a young boy. Thomas! She knew it was him, but she didn't know if he'd come to watch or to help her, and she couldn't find the strength to make a sound.

THOMAS CLUTCHED the knife in his hand as he hid behind the facade of the Red House. He could see that Celeste had been drugged in some manner. They had lied to him. She wasn't a willing participant as they'd claimed. To his horror, he saw someone else carrying his youngest sister, Angela. The child was completely unconscious.

He watched as the procession, strangely silent in the bright glare of the day, entered the observatory. He knew now what he had to do. Mark Grayson was the only person who could save Celeste. He had to find Mark and get him back here before the ritual went any further. He jumped to the ground in a series of three long jumps and hurried toward the jungle. He wasn't a great tracker, but Mark Grayson had not bothered to cover his path.

He rounded a corner, ducking beneath the low-hanging fronds of a plant. When he stood, he saw the jaguar only fifteen feet away. The cat stood in the center of the marginally marked trail, as if it had been waiting for him.

"Attack!"

He swiveled to the right to see the tall, blond man who spoke.

Out of the corner of his eye, he saw the jaguar crouch and begin to snarl. The cat eyed him, growling in a low, throaty tone that promised action. For a single second their gazes locked.

Thomas sensed the jaguar shift its weight onto its powerful hindquarter in preparation for the spring. The cat could clear the distance to him in one leap. He fell back a half step, trying to command his legs to run, but he knew it was futile.

"Attack! Ganor commands you—attack!" The snaking lash of a whip rode out through the green vegetation, snapping off several branches a few inches from the jaguar's rump.

The jaguar roared its anger, lifting a paw to strike at the shredded bush.

"You will obey!" The man insisted, sending the whip through the air again, this time catching the cat on the hip. "For the money you cost, you will obey."

The cat screamed in anger and turned to confront the man with the whip.

Thomas tore out through the jungle, his feet hardly knowing where they stepped. Behind him he heard the loud laughter of the man.

"Run, little rabbit," the man called after him. "Beware of the jaguar!" He laughed again.

Thomas ran on instinct instead of thought, crisscrossing the path to the cenote and to the stela. He went toward the campsite. Mark had to be there.

"Señor Grayson!" He cried when he made it to the clearing. "I have news. Señor Grayson!"

Mark watched the young boy, making certain that he was alone. When he was sure Thomas had not brought anyone with him, he stood up from behind the thick foliage where he'd stopped to eat some bread and cheese he'd found.

"Celeste is at the observatory. The ritual has begun. There is a man in the jungle with the jaguar. He is whipping the cat and trying to make him attack."

"What man?" Mark was instantly alert.

"I don't know him. He speaks with a foreign accent. It is the same voice I heard on the night I was bitten by the snake. I thought it was the god."

"Let's go," Mark said, checking his waist to be sure the gun was there. The pistol was loaded, and he had one more full clip. And the machete.

"We must hurry," Thomas said. "There are underground tunnels beneath the observatory where we must go.

It is very dangerous. There are places where the stones fall down and people have been crushed to death."

"We'll find her," Mark promised.

"They have my sister, Angela, too," Thomas said, his twelve-year-old voice cracking in an attempt not to cry. "They will kill her, also."

Mark took up a jog and motioned Thomas to follow. It was broad daylight and he took no pains to conceal his movement. Time was too short. He didn't slacken his pace until he was at the entrance to the observatory with Thomas at his side.

"Inside," the boy whispered. "I will show you, as far as I know."

At the back wall, Thomas maneuvered the stone that blocked the passage to the tunnel.

"Last January we searched this observatory high and low," Mark said. "How did we miss this tunnel?"

"Wilfredo was in charge of the search," Thomas said over his shoulder. "He could not allow you to find this. We must be very quiet. Sound carries here."

"Indeed." Mark could already hear the rhythmic drumbeats, the flutter of a flute. Several torches had been left in the passageway, and he followed them with Thomas at his side.

The passage dissolved into darkness, and the air was much cooler. Mark had the sensation that they'd been traveling down, as if the tunnel slanted toward the inner core of the earth. He halted Thomas with a hand on his shoulder. "Wait here."

"No, I must come," Thomas said.

"I think both of you should relax and remain silent."

The voice came out of the darkness at the same time that Mark felt the bore of a pistol in his back.

"Grab the boy," the voice said again.

Mark felt Thomas struggle, but there was nothing he could do. "Who are you?" he asked. The voice had sounded educated, cultured, American. And it was not Daniel Ortiz.

"Alec Mason, Celeste's uncle."

"She's been worried about you," Mark said. "She'll be relieved to know that you're okay." He started to turn around but the muzzle of a gun stopped him. "I'm Mark Grayson. Celeste is in trouble. We have to help her."

"The only thing we have to do is wait until Carlotta Bopp produces the ruby. Then I'm afraid you're going to have to die. Tie the boy and get the cat, Ganor."

Mark was aware of a struggling Thomas being taken away, but in the darkness he couldn't see where.

"You were very kind to lead us here," Alec Mason continued in a conversational tone. "We knew the boy would never bring us on his own. It was simply a matter of waiting. I must admit, though, that it has taken far longer than I ever anticipated."

There was no need to second-guess Alec Mason's intentions. He'd made himself perfectly clear. What Mark didn't understand were his motives. "Why are you doing this? Celeste worships you."

"The jewel," Alec said, his voice mellow and reasonable in the darkness. "I'm afraid I made some mistakes in my accounts. I borrowed rather heavily from some of my friends and clients. Unfortunately several of them are trying to kill me."

"So you decided to set up Celeste and Barry Undine for the fall?" He knew it was true, but he still couldn't believe it.

"Barry is dead. Not that I planned it, of course, but in the long run it's just as well."

"And Celeste?" Mark turned to confront the man. "What about Celeste? Can you sacrifice her, too?"

"If Celeste doesn't like being a goddess, she can start over somewhere else. She'll weather all of this. She's young."

"For God's sake, man, she's your flesh and blood." Mark was incredulous.

"You could have avoided all of this by finding the jewel. I've given you months. I've listened patiently to Daniel Ortiz talk about his expeditions. At any rate, I will have the jewel and a new life. Celeste might as well stay here, with the natives. From what I've seen, she might actually be happy here. She's finished as a broker. She has no reputation left in Tampa. It's amazing how eager people are to see the total destruction of another. Now turn around and keep walking."

Mark tensed his back, hoping for an opportunity. He felt the nose of the gun press deeper into his flesh.

"Don't try anything rash," Alec said. "Now let's step forward and watch the ritual. I'm certain Carlotta will produce the ruby at any moment."

"You solved the riddle?"

"Oh, no. Carlotta interpreted it for me. You see, I've been assisting Carlotta in keeping my niece here. Ganor and I had her securely tucked away in that little hamlet, but Wilfredo helped her escape. He lost his faith in the legend, and he was afraid Celeste would get hurt. But a few ants and lizards brought him back to the flock. At least I found that Ganor was good for something. He hasn't been able to make that jaguar do much in the way of frightening people."

"How do you know Carlotta has the ruby?" Mark asked. "I only found the stela a few weeks ago. We couldn't move it."

"Carlotta has known the legend all along. The stela wasn't the only guide the old Mayas left behind. There was a scroll, which has been in Carlotta's keeping since she was a young woman. She's been waiting for the day when Quetzalcoatl would return."

"When did . . ."

"I knew Carlotta when she was in Europe," Alec interrupted. "She was a charmingly naive young girl, desperate to talk about her home. She was married to an old friend of mine, a man I'd done many investments for. When Carlotta left him, he was devastated. I learned that she'd gone back to her home. All of these years, I've been waiting."

"And Celeste! You deliberately sent her here. You know they will kill her when the god doesn't appear."

"Ganor and I have something arranged with the jaguar. I'm hoping it will preclude the necessity to kill Celeste."

"And if it doesn't work?" Mark asked.

"It will work. Like the talking jaguar, the swarms of ants, the biting lizards, the snakes." He prodded Mark forward with the gun. "The superstitious are easy to manipulate. Now move."

They stepped into the darkness. Mark was suddenly aware that the tall blond man called Ganor and the cat were also beside them. He could hear the soft clink of the cat's collar and chain.

As they closed the distance to the semicircle of lighted torches, Mark could hear the incantations. He saw Celeste, seemingly asleep on a flat stone altar. At her feet was a child, a girl he guessed to be Angela.

A band of twenty-five or thirty Mayas was gathered around the altar while Carlotta chanted, passing feathers over Celeste's prone figure. He couldn't understand the words, but he knew the ceremony was at its peak. The god would have to appear, or Celeste would be killed. He started to move, but the barrel of the gun pressed deep into his back.

"Just watch, Mark. As an archaeologist, you should find this fascinating. Are you ready, Ganor? Remember, frighten them, but don't let the cat maul anyone. Just enough to get Celeste and get out."

"Of course," Ganor replied, giving the cat's chain a vicious jerk. "This animal is too docile, but I will do my best."

"Another moment," Alec said, holding up his hand. "I want to see the ruby before you do anything."

As they watched, Carlotta drew forth an enormous stone. She held it aloft as two feathered men brought in a three-foot carving of a crouched jaguar. The men struggled beneath the weight of the carving, at last placing it beside the altar.

Mark recognized the carving immediately. The jaguar had been caught in the act of pouncing on some unknown prey. The work was alive with power and force.

"Ah, the ruby," Alec said as Carlotta fitted the jewel into the eye socket of the statue.

Mark knew this was the moment the god should appear. This was the moment that would seal Celeste's death, unless he did something.

There was a wild cry from the opposite side of the room. In a poof of smoke a feathered figure leapt onto the altar above Celeste, dancing in a wild, erratic fashion.

"It is the god," Carlotta said, falling to her knees.

"Who is that?" Alec said, obviously amazed.

Mark ducked forward, then dropped to the floor. With a quick motion, he flipped his body backward so that he struck Alec's feet. The older man toppled. With a startled rattle, Ganor dropped the heavy chain leash. Sensing its freedom, the jaguar leapt away into the circle of dancers.

Mark found his footing and jumped up, dashing toward Celeste. The feathered creature towered above her, arms spread in a gesture of possession. Mark was at Celeste's side before he recognized the figure as Wilfredo.

"Take her!" Wilfredo said. "I will stop the others. Go there!" He pointed toward the far side of the carvernous room.

"Grayson, put her back or you're a dead man!" He heard Alec call out. Mark ignored the command, scooping Celeste into his arms as he made for the tiny crevice Wilfredo had indicated.

There was the sound of a gunshot that echoed throughout the chamber. High overhead the sound of rock splitting was followed by a sickening roar.

Mark looked across the room in time to see a huge hunk of rock smash Ganor to the ground. A fragment of rock struck Celeste's uncle on the shoulder, knocking him to his knees.

As rocks and dirt continued to fall from the ceiling, the jaguar walked into the middle of the dancers, chain dangling.

Celeste moaned softly into his shoulder, and Mark turned away from the destruction.

"Here!" Roberto's voice called to Mark. "This way!"

"Roberto," Mark answered. "Where have you been? I went to the camp..."

"The police had me under guard, but Daniel paid them off. Late last night they loaded me up to take me to Cancún headquarters, but the drivers let me out about twenty miles down the road. I've been looking everywhere for you and Celeste. Daniel has a car outside, along with Captain Guirdion tied and bound in the back seat."

"Get the girl. Get Angela," Mark said as he hurried past his old friend with Celeste in his arms.

"I'd rather take Celeste," Roberto said, the old devilment back in his voice. "I think it's my turn—for a change. After all, I did find the smoke for Wilfredo's grand entrance."

"HAPPY?" Mark asked as he handed her a tequila sunrise. Below them the Pacific surf crashed against the rocks. "Acapulco is a little more civilized than Chichén Itzá."

"Yes, it is." Celeste watched the moon on the water. "At least in some ways." It had been a week since Mark had rescued her from the underground. A week of slow readjustment on her part, and great tenderness on his. After the interminable two days with the authorities, Mark had whisked her away across the continent to a quiet, exclusive resort.

A small sigh escaped her as she watched the crescents of light on the rolling water. "I spoke with Victor today and he said my old job was waiting for me. Everything with Uncle Alec is settled, at least at Stuart McCarty. Uncle Alec's trial date is set for late summer. Who knows when the Mexican authorities will bring their case? At least he's in prison in the States."

"Are you going back?" Mark restrained himself from kissing the portion of her slender neck exposed by the wind. Her long hair was furling out behind her. He wanted to touch her, to offer the support of physical reassurance, but he also didn't want to intrude. She had to make the decision for herself.

"No," she said. "At least not for a long, long time. Maybe never. That part of my life is over. I'm not certain what will come next, but I know I'll never go back to selling stocks." She sipped her drink. "What will become of Carlotta?"

"You know she was never divorced. Daniel managed to get in touch with her husband and he's in Chichén Itzá with her now. I think he's still very much in love with her. He'll help her work through whatever charges face her."

"She didn't realize what she did was so wrong. It's different, what she did and what Uncle Alec did." Her gaze dropped involuntarily down to her left arm.

He lifted her arm and kissed the place where the snake had once been. "Thank goodness she had the herbs we needed to make the salve that removed the drawings." He kissed her arm once again. "The artwork was excellent, you have to give Carlotta credit for talent. But I prefer you unadorned." He tried to lighten her mood.

"My own uncle had me kidnapped so he could make sure I was available for sacrifice. He left you walled up to die." She drowned her bitterness in another swallow of her drink. She suddenly had to focus on the water to keep back the tears. "He did say Timma's death was an accident. Ganor wasn't supposed to kill him. Uncle Alec said that when Ganor tried to frighten Timma with the jaguar, Timma unexpectedly turned and fought. Uncle Alec thought up the idea of pinning the murder on the jaguar."

"Celeste, he didn't mean for anything bad to happen to you. He intended to make sure you were safe." All trace of humor had left Mark's voice.

"Yes, and Timma is dead. And Ganor. Barry Undine is dead. What about them? They all got caught up in my uncle's plot to save his own skin, and they paid with their lives. And what about the villagers? They believed that a miracle was going to happen. All they got was a con," she added with a twist of bitterness.

Mark decided to turn the conversation from so much tragedy. "The ruby will go a long way toward bettering conditions for the Mayas. The Jaguar's Eye is now under study by top experts. The ruins will get more international attention." Mark took her empty glass and made a fresh drink. He brought it back to her, letting his hand hold hers a moment as he gave her the glass.

"Why wouldn't Thomas leave with us?" She had regained her composure, but her voice still held pain.

Mark put his drink aside and rubbed her shoulders. "Give him time, Celeste. He's only a child, and his life has been torn apart by all of this. His mother realizes she almost lost both of her children, and she needs him now more than you do. Ask him next fall about school in the States. I'll bet you get another answer then."

"Maybe a letter from Señor Bond would do the trick," Celeste said, the tiniest fragment of a smile in her voice. "He was going to rescue me with a pocket knife. Wisdom prevailed and he went for you."

"It was Thomas who finally caught the jaguar and saw that no one injured it. After Ganor was killed, Thomas was the only one who wasn't afraid to catch the chain. Lucky for all of us the cat was remarkably docile. Thomas said it wanted to be caught. He said that when they were in the jungle together, they looked at each other."

"He's a remarkable boy." Celeste could clearly see his mischievious smile, the brown eyes that showed his laughter. "Maybe he will reconsider my offer to go to school in the States." She felt a return to her native optimism.

"Give him time," Mark said. He kissed her neck. "It's all behind you now, except for the healing. The bad times are over." His hands slipped down her shoulders to stroke her back and arms.

"We're across the entire country from Chichén Itzá, and I can't forget," Celeste said, leaning back against his shoulder. "When I think what almost happened to me..."

"I know it's a letdown, almost becoming the bride of a reincarnated god, but I have an alternate proposal." He turned her around to face him and looked into her green-eyed gaze. "How about becoming the bride of Mark Grayson?"

For a moment the pain was stilled. There was only the intense happiness she felt at being asked to share Mark's life. "Do I get special privileges? I mean as the bride of Quetzalcoatl, I was going to be worshiped and revered for the rest of my days." The sadness would take time to overcome, but she knew that Mark was offering her a new chance, a different life, and one that she wanted. She loved him. It was as simple as that. As bad as the past few weeks had been, there was the promise of a happy future. She had to take the chance and reach for it.

"How about kissed every night and worshiped on Saturdays?"

"Will this be a mythic relationship?" Her happiness was growing with each moment.

"I'll have to consult some ancient scribblings before I can answer that one."

"Will we live forever in a hut in a steamy jungle?"

"Well, I was sort of thinking that maybe we could, until you got tired of it. Then I suppose I could teach and write and you could figure out how to invest all the money we're going to make."

"That doesn't exactly sound like godhood to me," Celeste said.

He kissed her, gently at first and then with growing passion. "You're right," he agreed, his lips almost touching hers. "That sounds more like heaven."

**Don't miss one exciting moment of you next vacation
with Harlequin's**

FREE
FIRST CLASS TRAVEL ALARM CLOCK

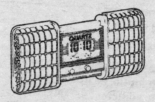

Actual Size
3¼″ × 1¼″h

By reading FIRST CLASS—Harlequin Romance's armchair travel plan for the incurably romantic—you'll not only visit a different dreamy destination every month, but you'll also receive a FREE TRAVEL ALARM CLOCK!

All you have to do is collect 2 proofs-of-purchase from FIRST CLASS Harlequin Romance books. FIRST CLASS is a one title per month series, available from January to December 1991.

For further details, see FIRST CLASS premium ads in FIRST CLASS Harlequin Romance books. Look for these books with the special FIRST CLASS cover flash!

JTLOOK

Take 4 bestselling love stories FREE

Plus get a FREE surprise gift!

REBECCA YORK

Labeled a "true master of intrigue" by *Rave Reviews*, best-selling author Rebecca York makes her Harlequin Intrigue debut with an exciting suspenseful new series.

It looks like a charming old building near the renovated Baltimore waterfront, but inside 43 Light Street lurks danger . . . and romance.

Let Rebecca York introduce you to:

> *Abby Franklin*—a psychologist who risks everything to save a tough adventurer determined to find the truth about his sister's death. . . .
>
> *Jo O'Malley*—a private detective who finds herself matching wits with a serial killer who makes her his next target. . . .
>
> *Laura Roswell*—a lawyer whose inherited share in a development deal lands her in the middle of a murder. And she's the chief suspect. . . .

These are just a few of the occupants of 43 Light Street you'll meet in Harlequin Intrigue's new ongoing series. Don't miss any of the 43 LIGHT STREET books, beginning with #143 LIFE LINE.

And watch for future LIGHT STREET titles, including
#155 SHATTERED VOWS (February 1991) and
#167 WHISPERS IN THE NIGHT (August 1991).

HI-143-1

Harlequin Intrigue®

A SPAULDING & DARIEN MYSTERY

Meet an engaging pair of amateur sleuths—
Jenny Spaulding and Peter Darien.

Harlequin Intrigue introduces this daring pair in
#147 BUTTON, BUTTON this month (October 1990).
And once you meet them, you won't want to say
goodbye to Jenny and Peter. They will be returning
in further spine-chilling romantic adventures in
future books. In April 1991, look for #159 DOUBLE
DARE in which they solve their next puzzling
mystery, the disappearance of the star of a popular
TV sitcom.

Join Jenny and Peter for danger and romance....
Look for the identifying series flash—A SPAULDING
AND DARIEN MYSTERY ... for Romance, Suspense
and Adventure ... At Its Best.

IBB-1

Harlequin romances are now available in stores at these convenient times each month.

Harlequin Presents	These series will be in
Harlequin American Romance	stores on the 4th of
Harlequin Historical	every month.
Harlequin Intrigue	

Harlequin Romance	New titles for these
Harlequin Temptation	series will be in stores
Harlequin Superromance	on the 16th of every
Harlequin Regency Romance	month.

We hope this new schedule is convenient for you. With only two trips each month to your local bookseller, you will always be sure not to miss any of your favorite authors!

Happy reading!

Please note there may be slight variations in on-sale dates in your area due to differences in shipping and handling.

HDATES